A Young Woman's Guide To Carrying On

by
Jilly Wosskow

'An entertaining read!

'Thoroughly enjoyable'

'This was a fantastic book. Well written, fantastic characters and the author did a fantastic job of carrying you through all the emotions of the characters and didn't let them do the 'right thing'. Nothing in real life is straight forward and we often go down a path that we regret later.'

'Fantastic book! I will definitely recommend it to my family and friends.'

'Made me laugh out loud – reminded me of my own family in many ways.'

Book group readers comments

Hookline Books
Bookline & Thinker Ltd

About the author

Jilly Wosskow was born in Sheffield in the mid-fifties and has been carousing there ever since. She enjoys reading, writing and entertaining. She favours extreme outdoor pursuits such as teetering from bar to bar in six-inch heels and sunbathing with just a smattering of factor two for protection.

When she isn't partying in Sheffield she can be found stalking her children in London and Thailand.

A Young Woman's Guide to Carrying On

by

Jilly Wosskow

For John

best wishes

Hookline Books
Bookline & Thinker Ltd

Jilly W

Published by Hookline Books 2010
Bookline & Thinker Ltd
#231, 405 King's Road
London SW10 0BB
Tel: 0845 116 1476
www.booklinethinker.com

The right of Jilly Wosskow to be identified as the author of this work has
been asserted in accordance with the Copyright, Designs and Patents Act
1988.

A CIP catalogue for this book is available from the British Library.

This book is a work of fiction. Names, characters, places and incidents are
either a product of the author's imagination or are used fictitiously.
ISBN: 9780955563096

Cover design by Donald McColl
Printed and bound by Lightning Source UK

Dedication

TO MICHAEL WOSSKOW

How to cut the umbilical cord

Playing Mummy's little angel wasn't the ideal way to spend my formative years. In fact, it was hell, which is why November 1973 found the 17-year-old me downing my halo, ditching my schoolbooks and slamming the front door with mother's words of encouragement reverberating in my head.

"If you leave now, our Kathryn, you needn't bother coming back," she screeched as I crossed the kitchen floor. "And don't think I'm going to give up my retirement to look after your illegitimate babies, either."

This was baffling for two reasons: first, mother had never gone out to work in her entire life so God alone knew what she would to retire from – thawing TV dinners or spying on the neighbours perhaps. Secondly, I wondered where she thought the illegitimate babies would come from. To the best of her knowledge, I was still little Miss Innocent, the preservation of my virginity having been mother's *raison d'être* since I hit puberty. "You mark my words," – a phrase that seemed to prefix every piece of advice she offered – "if you give them what they want, they won't respect you in the morning. And then what will you be? Damaged goods, is what – and no fella wants damaged goods, do they?"

I don't think she believed I'd leave home and, to be honest, neither did I. It wasn't as if I'd been planning my escape. I'd just got fed up living at home. Well, living with mother to be precise. Before she drove daddy away, family life was perfect. It just came to a head when she told me I'd have to leave school and get a job. This was a big deal. I was much cleverer than my big brother, Rees, and she'd practically begged him to go to Sheffield Poly, so I couldn't see why I couldn't go to university. Though I shouldn't, perhaps, have been surprised.

The main problem with mother was the fact that she had this imaginary daughter; who was prettier, more talented, and more devoted than I could ever be. The older I got, the harder it was for me to fit into this paragon's flawless skin.

Looking back, I should have realized that I would never meet mother's exacting standards. When I was about three years old – and this is my very first memory as I think I blocked out the earlier years – I was sitting on her knee. We were dressed identically in revolting *Broderie Anglais* frocks that mother had made herself. My determinedly straight, blonde hair had, in a complicated process involving mother's twirling finger and lots of spit, been fashioned into a semblance of curls. My aunties had been invited around for mother's latest pretension to being middle-class – afternoon tea.

Mother adhered to her own very strict rules. She never drank, well only the odd small sherry or Snowball – a revolting mixture of Advocaat and lemonade – at Christmas. Although she rarely went out, she was always fully made-up and dressed as if ready to receive passing royalty. She loved her magazines and sewing machine, and she was an amazingly frugal housekeeper. Mother's idea of a nutritious lunch was a small tin of Heinz tomato soup diluted with a can of water or, on the odd heady day, milk.

But on this occasion she'd set out a doilied plate of tiny triangular sandwiches filled with tinned salmon, Dairylea cheese and sandwich spread. Each offering was garnished with a sprinkling of mustard and cress. Battenberg – or window cake as my little brother Darren called it – was stacked high on an elaborate, tiered, chrome stand. There was even a platter of scones and jam.

Mother hated pop singers, but with two fairly predictable exceptions: Anthony Newley and Shirley Bassey. She would often sit at our shabby upright piano, wearing her best-martyred expression, enthusiastically bashing out an alarming rendition of Nancy's song from *Oliver*. "As long as he" – *plonk* – "needs" – *plonk* – "me, I know where I" – *plink* – "will" – *plink* – "be . . ."

Mother also despised the Labour Party, Catholics, miniskirts, and my father. The jury was still out on me, with this day being something of a decider. The two of us had spent a large part of my young life rehearsing mother's favourite Anthony Newley number, and she was manically keen to show it – and me – off to her sisters-in-law. All I had to do was sing, *"Why?"* at the appropriate time. Mother smiled down at her little prodigy. Naively, the little prodigy smiled back. Mother took a deep breath and began.

"I'll never let you go . . ."

Only the sharp pain of a nipped arm told me I'd missed my cue.

But that was then.

Today, the reign of terror is to end, I told myself as I stamped down the path trying to ignore Darren as he whimpered. "Please don't go, Kay-Kay. Mum didn't mean it."

The moment I banged the gate shut, it began to rain – great, big, ploppy drops that ran down my face and diluted the tears. But there was no way I was going back for my mac – not now, not ever.

I walked down the street. Nothing much had changed around our way since we moved in the Christmas before Darren was born. Still the same straggly hedges, unswept paths, and the smell of stale fat and bubble-and-squeak pervading the air. The occasional pebble-dashed house had been enhanced with stone cladding – a sure sign that the occupiers had bought from the council. Mrs. Youle at number 18 owned hers, which led to much nudging and conjecture as to where she'd got the money. Looking through her window and into the front room I saw her, head full of big, spongy curlers. She was drinking tea and dragging furiously on a cigarette. She waved at me, scattering ash all over the table. Guiltily, I waved back. Mother didn't allow us to mix with the likes of Mrs. Youle; it had something to do with her selling her babies into white slavery, I think. Or was it entertaining men after dark? Either way, she was no better than she should be and must be ignored.

Further down the street, huddled in the doorway of The Plaice to Be, I saw girls from school. They were doing their usual – bitching for England while consuming huge quantities of chips in curry sauce. I hoped they hadn't noticed me. No chance.

"Eh, look, it's Saint Kathryn."

"Where's your Bible?"

"Sing us an 'ymn."

Red faced, I hurried by, ignoring their friendly overtures.

"How come she believes in God? I mean, with a face like hers!"

I wouldn't mind, but I'm an atheist. Mother's fault again – after a childhood of enforced elocution lessons she only sent me to the crappiest school in the north. Obviously, everybody hated me, except the English master. I was his unchallenged favourite. I won the first-year English prize on the grounds that I was the only person in the entire school who could speak it – including most of the teachers. My reward was a navy blue dictionary, all leather-bound and gold-embossed. It looked for all the world like a Bible. Thrilled with my gift, I resolved to learn a new word every day, and to look up words I didn't understand. This resolution lasted all of nine days. Just long enough for the whole school to have me down as a born-again Christian freak.

To say I didn't fit in is a major understatement. I guess being small, skinny, and totally un-coordinated in a school filled with athletic amazons was not the ideal recipe for social success. When sides were selected for rounders or netball, I would cower in the corner of the changing room, inevitably the last girl standing. Lonely and unchosen, a brave smile on my face, I hoped my demeanour would conceal my churning stomach and all feelings of self-loathing as I listened to my peers discuss my sporting prowess. "Miss, Miss, that's not fair, we had her last week, can't we play one short?"

No matter how hard I tried to fit in, I always failed; if there was a baton to be dropped, a catch to be missed, or an own goal to be scored you could depend on me. I wasn't even picked for country and western dancing. To dispel any suggestion that I might be paranoid, on Sports Days the housemistress insisted on forging sick notes for me. She clearly missed her true vocation as they were far more convincing than her attempts at teaching.

By the time I reached the bus stop, my sodden tie-dye T-shirt had bled crazy purple patterns onto my Wranglers. Being something of an Enid Blyton fan, I kept telling myself what a great adventure I was on, but really I was cold and scared.

I didn't go far. I caught the bus out of Sheffield and into Derbyshire, a journey of about 35 minutes (I know, Marco Polo eat your heart out). I got out at Hathersage, and then walked through water-logged fields to the little village where I hoped to get work. I was heading to Grimley Manor (everyone knows the streets of Grimley are paved in gold.) I'd worked there in the summer holidays, when mother thought I was on a school trip to France grape-picking and learning the language (*Je ne pense pas!*) I spent six wonderful weeks holed up with my then boyfriend, Jimmy. That's all over now;

he dumped me. But that summer was fantastic; I was paid for having the time of my life and condensing all the rites of passage into one glorious season. No wonder it was hard going back to live with mother.

I reached the Manor but, as it was Monday, the restaurant was closed. I squelched my way down to the staff door around the back. The door was locked, so I put my bags down and climbed onto the bin, reaching up for the spare key above the doorframe. I found it there. But any joy was short-lived as the bin toppled over, sending me clattering onto the muddy ground, and into the scattered kitchen waste. If I'd looked a sight beforehand, I looked twice as bad now, potato peelings and fish bones like macabre confetti around me. Just then the back door opened, and I squinted up into the light.

"Eeh! Look what the cat's dragged in."

Oh no. It was bloody Dee-Dee, looking as irritatingly sexy as ever with her long, long legs and spiky black hair.

"I didn't expect you to be here," I said.

"Clearly. Nice of you to dress up on my account," she said with a well-practiced pout.

Ignoring her sarcasm, I scrambled up, blood dripping from my hands, onto the dank ground. I picked up my stuff, but the bottom of the carrier bag stuck to the mud so everything spilled out. I hoped Dee-Dee didn't notice my padded bra, or the teddy bear pyjamas.

"You'd better get that seen to," she nodded at my hand, but made no effort to help with my things which were now lying in a muddy, slimy soup. She made an elaborate show of holding the door wide open and inviting me in. With a toss of my hair and my best condescending look, I gathered up what was left of my possessions and walked back into Grimley Manor. Once in the kitchen, I reached down to the cupboard under the sink and pulled out some disinfectant to slosh over my cuts. The sting was enough to bring tears to my eyes, but I willed myself not to cry in front of her.

I cleaned myself up, put on my driest clothes and went in search of Mr B. He was in his office pouring over the *Reader's Digest Cookery Yearbook*. When he looked up and saw me it erupted into a proper Mr B welcome as he effortlessly lifted me off my feet and swung me around while swearing his hello. He seemed pleased to see me.

"Nah then, what the fucks tha doin' 'ere? Thought yer were goin' away to be a brain surgeon or summat."

I could have told him about mother, and explained how, as she was culturally some years behind Emily Pankhurst's reactionary great grandmother, she considered university a male domain, but what was the point?

"I've left school. I just wondered, is there any chance of any work? Living in, if . . ."

"By 'eck. Does tha' want jam on it too?"

I admit it. I grovelled, cajoled, and begged for my job back. It paid off, but I'd known I was on pretty safe ground; they struggled to keep staff in that draughty old mausoleum.

"Go on then, tha's a good worker. Go and find Dee-Dee, she'll sort you out." He wagged a good-natured finger at me, "But early shift tomorrow, mind."

I could have kissed him but settled for a hybrid of a curtsy and a nod.

As the first person in the kitchen the next morning, it was my job to breathe life into the food machine. Remembering the routine from summer, I percolated an industrial-sized pot of coffee and busied myself setting out trays with little dishes of preserves and butter ready for the continental breakfasts we served in the guests' rooms.

Mr. B came back from market at around seven, and together we unpacked gleaming ripe fruit, earth-crusted vegetables, and trays of fish with wet glistening skin and bright, unfocused eyes. The meat was delivered twice a week from the nearby Chatsworth Estate – ribs of beef, lamb shanks, venison, sausages, and the farm-cured bacon I was about to fry into a mountain of sandwiches for the staff breakfast.

We sat round the big wooden table eating bacon butties and drinking thick, dark coffee. To be honest, I preferred the instant stuff we drank at home but I didn't say anything, not wanting to show myself up. Mr B was running through the day's specials when I caught sight of my reflection in the shiny oven door – a face pink with exertion and excitement. The obligatory white cook's hat perched on top of my head was as crooked as my little brother's teeth. I wondered if mother would make him wear braces.

Tears crept into my eyes at the thought of Darren. When he was born, my brother Rees and I had spent the day with Nana, our dad's mum. I was seven and hadn't really understood that mother was pregnant, even though we'd all gone swimming in the Cornish sea that summer, and I'd seen her pat her tummy and say to daddy, "Look, it's going to be a water baby." We were a happy family then; maybe she liked being pregnant. Although I was disappointed when I heard I had a baby brother. I already had a brother and all we ever did was fight.

Nana said that when we went home we wouldn't see mother or the baby because they were both tired. I couldn't actually see why but I didn't say anything. It was dark when we got back so we tiptoed into the house and upstairs to bed. As Daddy kissed me goodnight, I remember thinking I had to be very grown up now that I was a big sister. I was nearly asleep when Daddy came back; he gently plucked me out of bed and carried me into their room. Mother was drinking tea. I wanted some but they didn't have a spare mug so I had it in the pink Tupperware cup they used to clean their teeth. I sipped the tea, which tasted of plastic and toothpaste, and peered into the crib to look at my baby brother. He was beautiful, better than any girl, and I loved him more than anyone in the world, even my daddy. Later, I wasn't a bit surprised when the baby doctor told us that Darren was a special baby. It was obvious to me. The funny thing was that mother and daddy didn't seem a bit pleased about it.

I soon got back into the swing of things at Grimley Manor – waiting on tables, getting orders mixed up, half-heartedly servicing the bedrooms, then spraying them with furniture polish so they smelt like I'd done a proper job – Dee-Dee taught me that one. We got on better now, really well in fact, but I still felt a little mad at her for snogging Jimmy. I didn't bring that up though; she was such a laugh that I couldn't risk falling out with her again.

On Saturday nights, Mr B would leave as soon as the last cover was seated, leaving Mr Purvis in charge. Mr Purvis was headwaiter, sommelier, and night porter rolled into one. He always wore a white, starched, wing-collared shirt with a stringy black bow tie and shiny trousers that flapped a good couple of inches above his even shinier patent shoes. He was easy meat for Dee-Dee, and she made his life a misery. He once told me that as a younger man he'd had aspirations to work on the Queen Mary or as a butler to a fine gentleman. Regret clung to him like yesterday's cigar smoke. I liked him. He called us his young ladies, as in "Your bill, Sir? Certainly, I'll get one of my young ladies to deal with it" or "You look chilly, Madam, should I get one of my young ladies to fetch you a rug?"

Dee-Dee said I was weird, liking him. She claimed that he used to brush up against her tits, accidentally on purpose, and touch her bum. I didn't believe it, even when Dee-Dee imitated him in a silly posh voice.

"Oh I do believe I've got an erection. I'll get one of my young ladies to deal with it."

I looked away, trying not to laugh. "He's not like that."

"He is so," Dee-Dee interrupted. "He feels you up then spends the night playing with his wrinkly old willy. Pervy, pervy, Purvis."

The thing is, looking back, Mr Purvis couldn't have been much older than forty, and what Dee-Dee didn't realize was how kind he was.

Soon after arriving at Grimley Manor I wrote to give Dad my new address and suggested that we get together at last. Mother had always made things so difficult for him that he'd been forced to give up on his access visits. He wrote agreeing that, without mother's interference, we could make a new start. We arranged to meet in the little village teashop on my next afternoon off.

I was so thrilled at the prospect of seeing him that I set my hair with heated rollers and ditched my usual leisure look of jeans and denim jacket. Remembering that daddy used to like his little princess to wear pink, I got all dressed in a fluffy pink mini skirt and matching cardi. (I know, needy or what!) Dee-Dee said I looked like an over-excited poodle but I think she was just mad because I wouldn't let her come along.

Of course I got to the café early. I'd bought a magazine in case he was late but I was far too excited to read it, or even sip at my chocolate milkshake. Every time the doorbell chimed I looked up eagerly hoping to see him. I was glad that Dee-Dee wasn't there; she'd be sure to tell me I looked like one of those nodding dogs you see decorating the back windscreen of cars.

After what felt like a lifetime, he finally arrived. He looked as handsome as ever and I noticed the waitress flutter her eyelashes at him as he ordered a pot of tea and two toasted teacakes. We chatted for ages, well to be honest, I did most of the talking. I told him about my new job and friends and made him laugh about the antics of Dee-Dee. He said he'd like to meet her one day, so I suggested that he walk back to Grimley Manor with me.

He looked at his watch. "I'm not sure I've got time."

"Oh please, it's only about half a mile."

"I really should get off."

I finally persuaded him to make a quick visit but before we reached the Manor gates, he said, "Look, I'm sorry, Love, but I've got to get back."

Trying hard to hide my disappointment, I smiled brightly and gave a nonchalant shrug. "Well, how about meeting them next week . . ."

He shook his head.

So, just to prove I had absolutely no pride, I grabbed his arm and said, "Well, the week after then? Or we can do something else – whatever you want."

He disentangled himself and said, "The thing is, Kathryn, I've got another family now. And they're young and they depend on me. You're all grown up and I'm so proud of you, but you don't need me like they do. I'm sorry."

"But I do need you," I said. "I do and I thought you wanted to make a fresh start." I was clutching at straws but obviously not very effectively.

He turned and walked away.

"You'll be in touch?" I called after him, but he just kept on walking.

I sat down on a mossy tree stump too stunned even to cry. And that's how Mr Purvis found me, much later, when it was cold and dark.

"Miss Kathryn," he said, wrapping his coat around me. "Whatever's wrong?"

He sat down beside me, took my hand in his and I found myself telling him the whole sorry story. He listened, saying nothing, just occasionally nodding his head or squeezing my hand. When I got to the end, he put his arm around me in a gesture more fatherly than any I'd experienced that day and said, "Please don't take on so. Of course he loves you. But the man's clearly bonkers to treat you so shabbily. I'd give my right arm to have a daughter like you. We'd have afternoon tea twice a week with hot, buttered scones and strawberry jam."

"And clotted cream?"

"Lashings of it," he said, which made me smile.

"The thing is, some people just aren't very good at showing their love. And who knows, maybe he's under pressure from his new wife to leave the past behind." He helped me to my feet. "Now come with me into the scullery. We'll have a mug of Horlicks to help warm us up."

So I went with Mr Purvis, feeling better for our chat. Of course, it wasn't my dad's fault; if only he hadn't remarried.

However much Dee-Dee sneered at Mr Purvis, she wasn't against flirting with him if that's what it took to get her own way.

"Oh please, Mr Purvis, please be a darling." She pronounced it dah-ling as a joke. "Let us go now, we've nearly finished. We've been invited to a get-together at the church hall. I'm sure it will be very good for our souls."

Wearily, he nodded his consent. He couldn't resist her. Nobody could.

"Oh thank you, thank you," she said, kissing his cheek. "We'll say a prayer for you."

If he thought she was overdoing it, he said nothing as she whisked me upstairs to change. She fumbled under the bed and took out two big bags.

"Fancy dress – Abba, I'm the blonde one."

Typical, my hair was miles lighter and l hers, but of course she'd bought a big, blonde nothing. Together we scrambled into spangled cat suits and white platform boots.

I wasn't convinced about the clothes so, as she applied sparkly makeup to both of our faces, I spoke up. "You don't think, you know, it's a bit much for church?"

"Church? Are you mad? Come on, Pollyanna, grab your purse." She rolled her eyes. "Church!"

We spent that night, and the next million Saturday nights, hanging out in an old barn with colourful hippy types that mother would have called common. I hadn't seen mother since I'd left home nearly six weeks ago nor had we had any contact, although I rang Rees now and then to find out how Darren was getting along without me.

Then, one day in early December, Rees rang me. I was in the bridal suite with Dee-Dee. We were cleaning up after a couple of newlyweds who had thoroughly consummated their marriage. Well, to be accurate, I was cleaning and Dee-Dee was dancing around and spraying air freshener on the curtains to mask the smell of the cigarette she was smoking. She was belting *Stairway to Heaven* into the Hoover handle when the room phone rang. I answered and got a ticking off from Mr Purvis because we weren't allowed personal calls, but in the end he put me through to my big brother.

Rees wanted to know if I'd come home for Christmas. Of course I refused. Well, what I actually said was, "You're joking aren't you? Anyway I've got to work, but Christmas with Cruella Deville? I'd rather spend the festive season indulging in clitoral circumcision." You don't spend day and night with Dee-Dee and not pick up the odd choice phrase.

"Okay. We'll come to you," he said.

"What?"

"To the Manor!"

"No way," I said, horrified at the thought.

"Yes! It's a public place."

"Rees, no, I'll ring her and send presents, but please no, don't bring her here."

"Okay," he said, "you win – but what's clitoral circumcision?"

Finding your work ethic

"Glory be to God and, on Earth, peace and goodwill to all men."

Naturally, this did not extend to Grimley Manor. We had just endured a month of corporate bashes and office parties. It had been a tough four weeks. You know the sort of thing: too much to eat and loads of drink, then tears and recriminations followed by a night of vomiting out the bedroom window. God knows what the guests made of us. By the time Christmas Eve dawned, Dee-Dee and I needed some recovery time before the next group of revellers checked in at teatime.

Unfortunately, Mr Purvis had other ideas. "We've just got a few families coming until Boxing Day, so let's make it nice for the kiddies." He proposed going to the market to stock up on sprouts and chestnuts, while his young ladies went into the village to buy presents for the paying guests.

You won't be surprised to learn that Grimley village is hardly the Knightsbridge of the north. There is a pub called The Pheasant, Shortcuts (the hilariously named hairdressers), and a newsagents-come-general store, which stocked little more than knitting patterns and wool. Mr Purvis gave us a list of presents to buy for the guests.

"No problem, Mr Purvis," I said. I enjoyed shopping.

Dee-Dee glared at him.

It's about 850 yards from Grimley Manor to the village, and Dee-Dee had to be dragged every inch of the way. The bright sun sparkled into glitter on the frozen path, and the fields had been transformed into a giant white duvet. A little boy in a bright pom-pom hat was struggling to stay upright, clinging onto his daddy's arm with one yellow-gloved hand and wiping his nose on the back of the other. I thought about Darren and waved. His dad shouted "Merry Christmas," so I smiled and shouted the greeting back.

"Fucking loser!" growled Dee-Dee.

I turned round, surprised. "What's up with you?"

"What's up with you?" she parroted in a nasty sing-song voice. "Fucking Christmas, that's what's up with me, fucking bastard Christmas."

I looked down at the path, which had somehow lost its shine.

"My fucking feet are freezing. Why couldn't the lazy bastard get the stupid presents himself?"

We walked. Well, I walked and Dee-Dee stamped the rest of the way in silence. It wasn't until we reached the village that her mood lifted slightly and she insisted on going into The Pheasant for a hair of the dog. The pub was quiet except for a distant radio playing Christmas songs. "*So here it is, Merry Christmas everybody's having fun . . .*"

I took a sneaky look at Dee-Dee. She caught it, and we both burst out laughing. The cross-looking landlady adjusted her bra, wiped her coarse, red hands over her belly, and gave us a welcoming glare. "Are you two old enough to be in here?"

"Of course," replied Dee-Dee, rattling off our fake birth dates. "We'll have two brandy and Babychams, please."

I felt alarm, I'd wanted a pineapple juice.

"Don't worry, it's out of the money Purvy gave us for the presents," she whispered. I inwardly shrugged as I accepted the drink. I wanted to know why Dee-Dee hated Christmas so much and, after a couple of drinks, I was brave enough to enquire.

"Don't fucking ask, okay? Just don't fucking ask!"

I pressed her to tell me but she wouldn't. Two drinks later, we left the pub with its fake log fire and Formica tables and caught the bus to the bright lights of Sheffield.

The next morning we were late for the 11.30 shift, even though we were woken obscenely early by the joyous sounds of the devil's children in the next room celebrating the birth of their anti-hero.

"That's not fair! He's got more than me. Mummy, tell him to put my Tiny Tears down. Mummy, tell him."

"I hate you."

"Hate you more."

I stumbled out of bed and poured two mugs of water from the tap at the little sink in the corner. There was frost on the inside of the windows and miniature icicles were forming on my toothbrush. The lino was freezing so, hopping from foot to foot, I bent down to switch on the tiny radiator that separated our beds.

"Bastard kids," said Dee-Dee. "Soon as I can afford it, I'm getting sterilised. Do you know that once your biological clock starts ticking you go completely mad and have sex with practically anybody, just to get preggers? And when you've had it, you go all saggy and lose your tits – disgusting!"

Once Dee-Dee was on a rant there was no chance of sleep. We lay on our narrow beds, chomping on selection box chocolate and doing the quiz in the *Jackie Christmas Special*.

Of course, Dee-Dee was the quiz master. "Would you be more likely to marry someone for their: a) looks, b) money, or c) sense of humour?" She grimaced. "Not applicable, I'm never getting married. What about you?"

"Sense of humour."

"No you wouldn't, not if they were poor and ugly. You're just saying that." She licked her pencil. "I've put you down as (a). Next question, if you saw your best friend's boyfriend kissing someone else under the mistletoe would you: a) tell her, b) tell him, or c) kiss him yourself because you've always fancied him?"

I was torn between a) and b) but it didn't matter because Dee-Dee suddenly flung the magazine across the room.

"This is boring; it's (c) of course."

I stared at her. "You wouldn't."

"What?"

"Kiss my boyfriend – would you? Not again."

"You haven't got a boyfriend."

"I know but . . ."

"Well then, how could I kiss him, and anyway, who said anything about you being my best friend?"

I turned to the wall, pulled the covers over my head, and pretended to be asleep. I must have dozed off because the next thing I knew Dee-Dee was shaking me awake.

"Come on, we're on shift in ten minutes. Oh don't look at me like that. Of course I wouldn't kiss your stupid pretend boyfriend."

"And, I am your best friend?" Dee-Dee didn't answer. She was too busy pretending to be sick.

We quickly changed into our best uniforms and made up our faces: bright pink lipstick and false eyelashes as standard. Twenty minutes later, we made our way down to the great hall.

Everyone was gathered round the Christmas tree listening to the Grimley Church Choir singing *"Ding-Dong Merrily On High."* Mr Purvis looked anxiously around. When he saw us, he gave a disapproving nod and tapped his watch. He gestured that we should pass around the light refreshments. It was a delightful scene – fresh from a Christmas card.

"I want orange juice. Daddy, get me orange juice. Now, Daddy!"

"GLO-OO"

"An orange juice please, and have you any beer?"

". . .O-OOORIA."

"I'm sorry sir, the bar isn't open yet. Can I offer you a complimentary sherry and a mince pie?"

"I hate mince pies. Daddy I want sweeties."

"HOSANNAH . . ."

"Mummy, he just pulled my Six Million Dollar Man's head off. I hate you."

"I'll pull your head off in a minute."

". . .IN EXCELCIS."

Thankfully, the singing ended, and the guests were herded outside for a treasure hunt. Dee-Dee and I escaped to the cool quiet of the dining room. It was time to put the finishing touches to the tables with trails of holly, party poppers, gold-wrapped chocolate coins, and a fat red cracker on each side plate. I was busy folding the napkins into disabled swan shapes when the restaurant door opened and in walked Giles Havers, one of the local gentry. He was pulling at his tie in a very distracted sort of way as Dee-Dee stopped him.

"Good morning, Mr Giles. Can we help you?"

"Good morning, yes, I hope so. Look, I know it's all a bit last minute, but is there any chance of a table for two? Nanny, the housekeeper, has gone AWOL – some family disaster – and obviously Mother's too frail to cook."

I didn't dare look at Dee-Dee. Lady Havers, with her enormous boobs and jutting-out bottom was the least frail person we'd ever seen. I could hear Dee-Dee stifle a giggle as she spoke.

"Well, sir, we are fully booked. It's just like Christmas round here today . . ." Relieved to have an excuse for merriment, we both laughed heartily at her thin joke. "I'll go and ask Mr B if he can squeeze you in." The idea of Lady Havers being squeezed in anywhere set us off again, but he didn't seem to notice.

For the next few minutes, Mr Giles engaged me in polite conversation. It was fairly one-sided, so I had time to notice his bright blue eyes and warm smile. Although he wasn't conventionally handsome I could imagine women wanting to mother him. Dee-Dee reappeared and said that Mr B would be very happy for them to join us for lunch. Mr Giles asked to be put on one of my tables. Dee-Dee was seething so I concluded he must be a good tipper.

Mr B agreeing to find them a table was a mere formality. Around there, whatever the Havers wanted, the Havers got. The whole of the dining room was moved around for their benefit; other diners were shifted nearer to the toilets or kitchen in order to put one table, far too big for two, in pole position by the Christmas tree.

During pre-lunch drinks, a solemn-faced pianist played the guests a selection of Christmas songs while we served them Asti Spumanti in those wide, shallow champagne glasses. Each glass had a pink-sugared rim and was decorated with a glacé cherry and a slice of orange, pure class. It was all so very jolly that no one noticed Dee-Dee and me taking it in turns to duck behind the drinks table and down a goodly number of festive cocktails.

Our timing must have somehow got out of sync because soon we were sitting on the floor together, drinking fizz from the bottle. Dee-Dee started on me, as usual.

"You've got an admirer you have. He can't take his eyes off you."

I thought she was winding me up about Giles Havers, so I ignored her. She pulled me to my feet.

"Look, over there – he's gorgeous."

I looked around for him and – it wasn't an admirer at all. It was the family from Christmas Past! My big brother stood awkwardly between our over-dressed mother and our hyperactive little brother.

As soon as Darren saw me, he flung himself across the room and into my arms. I buried my face in his hair, kissed him and inhaled the familiar smell of apple shampoo and pear drops. He put his fat little hand in mine and dragged me over to mother and Rees. Mother, I noticed, had gone for an extreme Christmas perm of uncompromisingly tight yellow curls – maybe that's why she was wearing the mad pink hat. It didn't excuse the garden party gloves, though.

Mother gave me a frosty hello, and Rees hugged me awkwardly. Darren shook hands with the many strangers in the room and pointed to me as if I were a famous celebrity.

Dee-Dee, eyes and mouth wide open, had followed me over. "Are you really Kath's mother?" she said. "You don't look old enough. I'm Dee-Dee, Kathy's best friend. I love your outfit."

I rounded on Dee-Dee; only I was allowed to be sarcastic to mother, but amazingly there was no visible trace of irony. Mother smoothed her hands down the lapels of her suit. She sounded almost shy as she replied, "You mean our Kathryn? Yes, I'm her mum. I had her very young. Do you really like my suit? I made it myself."

Crippled with shame, I looked wildly around for an escape route. Mr Purvis walked across – an unlikely shining knight. "Good afternoon, Madam. I trust my young ladies are looking after you."

He called mother, 'Madam.' She must have thought she'd arrived in heaven. I was squirming with embarrassment but knew that, much though it pained me, I had to confess my ancestry. "Mr. Purvis, this is my mother and my brother Rees, and that's my little brother Darren trying to climb into the suit of armour. I'm sorry; I didn't know they were coming. I'll stop him."

I noticed Darren was muttering to himself. He often gave a running commentary on his life. Mr Purvis put a gentle hand on my arm. "He's doing no harm." He turned to mother and Rees. "What a delightful surprise. I'm charmed to make your acquaintance, Madam, and may I say what a splendid addition Miss Kathryn is to our establishment. Your loss, as they say, is our gain."

Mother went as pink as her frothy hat with the excitement of it all. The ice melted and she gave me a loving smile. She'd always known I was made for greatness. But where was Dee-Dee when I needed her? Ah, there she was, topping up Rees's glass. She was in a surprisingly good mood – nothing like seeing me embarrassed I expect.

Suddenly, the lights were dimmed and, white-bearded and dressed entirely in red, Mr B ho-ho'ed his way over to the fireplace. He banged on the big, brass gong – according to the guidebook, one of the hotel's finest treasures – and then, assuming a strange variation on a West Country pirate-style accent, announced that luncheon was served. He made the whole event sound so threatening that all the babies burst into tears while older children took refuge behind parents. There were several asthma attacks.

"'Tis the season to be jolly," Dee-Dee whispered as we herded the visitors into the dining room. There were oohs and aahs, and the occasional giggle, as everyone admired the festive scene. It had been our job, Dee-Dee's and mine, to decorate the room late last night after coming back from Sheffield. In our enthusiasm, no surface had remained unadorned. Everywhere you looked there were trinkets, tinsel, frills, and flounces. Reindeer rubbed shoulders with wise men, and Madonna and child rested serenely under a forest of mistletoe.

Soon everyone was seated. The starter was already out so people began to tuck in. Mr Purvis stood and said Grace. It was impressive to hear him battle on to the end of the prayer, apparently oblivious to his audience's indifference and to the homemade paper chains falling from the ceiling into his brown Windsor soup. He looked so brave and sad when he sat down that I was glad I'd bought him a special Christmas present – a framed picture of the Queen Mary.

When everyone had finished the soup and we'd cleared the bowls and plates, Mr B, looking more himself in chefs' whites, stood behind a long table sharpening his knives, and threatening to chop the hands off any badly behaved children. The guests formed a disorderly queue, waiting to be served. Each took a warm plate from the trough and piled it high with roast potatoes, soggy sprouts, and mashed up carrot. Mr B carved the turkey, asking every person individually, "Does tha want leg, breast, else both?"

When it was mother's turn, she pursed her lips tightly. "Just white meat for me."

You wouldn't catch her saying "breast".

Of course, Lady Havers and Giles didn't queue for their food; they were served by an agitated Mr Purvis who couldn't have fussed more if they'd arrived from the East bearing gifts. I noticed that Lady Havers never once bestowed so much as a smile on anyone, including her son. Poor Giles busied himself around her like an anxious lover, moving flowers, picking up her napkin and wrapping her horrid fur stole around her shoulders. I offered to hang it up for her but she just eyed me suspiciously and clung on to it with her fat fist. Did she really think I was going to run off with the mangy old thing? She spent the entire meal looking like an overheated grizzly bear. The only time her expression changed from superior disdain was when it moved to something much nastier, and that was because Dee-Dee sashayed up to the table with a huge sprig of mistletoe and held it over the head of the heir apparent.

Lady Havers' face fell to furious. "Remember your place, young lady. You are here to serve. How dare you be so familiar with your betters?"

"And a very Merry Christmas to you too," Dee-Dee replied. Then she turned to Giles and asked if she could do anything for him, anything at all.

Giles went bright red; I don't know who scared him most, Dee-Dee or his mother. I took pity on him and told Dee-Dee that Mr B needed help in the kitchen. When she left, I smoothed the old dragon's feathers with the promise of a complimentary gin and tonic, just the way she liked it, with two lumps of ice and a twist of lemon.

We spent the next few hours playing referee to the knackered guests and their over-excited children. After the last crumb of plum pudding was devoured, we led them into the TV room for coffee and mints. Maybe the Queen's speech would quieten them down. Sadly, Her Majesty did little to calm her subjects that day, but where she failed, Billy Smart and his circus succeeded – at least partially. The children seemed engrossed in the clowns' antics, but the grown-ups were getting restless. We switched to plan B, turned up the heat, and served them gallons of alcohol in hope that they might nod off.

I went to get emergency port supplies from the storeroom and saw Dee-Dee sitting on a bench out near the croquet lawn. She must have been freezing in her thin uniform and strappy sling backs. She seemed to be arguing with a strange little man dressed in a navy Crombie. He gestured wildly with his left hand, the other clamped to a cider bottle. Dee-Dee jerked her head at him, her breath coming out in angry, steamy spurts. Suddenly, she stood up and yelled something. The man staggered to his feet and lunged towards her.

I grabbed the first heavy object to hand and ran out shouting. "Let go of her. I'm armed!"

Dee-Dee looked at me in disbelief. I was wielding a big, white, church candle. "What are you going to do, Kathy, wax him to death?"

She didn't seem very scared so she must have known him. Well he couldn't have known her very well, because he was trying to hug her – Dee-Dee did not do hugging. She shoved him away and he sprawled onto the icy ground, still welded to his cider bottle. She stalked away, dragging me back into the warmth of the kitchen.

Dee-Dee was very quiet for the rest of the day. When we exchanged presents, she barely thanked me for the white hot pants.

"Dee-Dee, what's wrong?" I asked her at bedtime.

"Nothing."

"Yes there is. I can tell."

"Kathy, the great detective."

"Why are you acting like this when we're supposed to be friends?"

"Told you, I hate Christmas."

I tried a different tack. "You never tell me anything."

"That's rich coming from you. How come you never mentioned the Walton's were coming for Christmas?"

"I didn't know."

"And you never told me about your brother."

I was angry now. "What did you want me to say? I've got this little brother, and he looks a bit odd. Don't worry if he tries to snog you, he often goes around kissing strangers – oh and, by the way, he's got Down's Syndrome."

"Actually," she said, taking the wind out of my sails. "Actually, I was talking about Rees. He's dreamy." She got me there. Rees? Dreamy?

"And your mum," she continued, "is all pretty and sweet and all you do is snap at her."

She'd clearly lost it. Mother sweet?

"And if you must know, that funny little man is my dad. He usually appears around Christmas to reminisce. He was drunk when he crashed his bloody scooter and he's been drunk ever since." She said it nastily, as if daring me to sympathise.

I didn't know what to do or say. But Rees – dreamy?

Finding a social network

On 9 February 1974, the miners went on strike. A state of emergency was declared, and so began the three-day week. For the miners and their families, this spelt hardship and worry.

We certainly felt at the forefront of sacrifice, especially when putting makeup on by candlelight. Streaky, with too much blusher was not a good look.

And then there was Lady Havers. She took a fall in a blackout leaving Giles Havers an orphan.

The day following his mother's death, Giles Havers rang to say he wanted to hold the wake at Grimley Manor. "Nothing fancy, just a finger buffet."

I took the call and heard myself agreeing to do everything, even though I wasn't sure what a wake was. I looked it up.

DEF: WAKE: i) Cease to sleep ii) Cause to be alert iii) A vigil beside a corpse, before burial.

I felt slightly alarmed. Would the Public Health people allow a dead body, however aristocratic, in the restaurant? Thankfully, Mr Purvis explained that nowadays wakes were usually held after the burial of the dear departed.

A few days later, Giles Havers arrived at the Manor to organize things. He asked for my help – mine in particular. He said that his mother had liked me; apparently, I'd got all my buttons on. He also said that I had a way with her – overbearing mothers are clearly my specialty. He stayed for ages, long after we'd planned the sausage roll extravaganza.

He seemed to want to talk about his mother's death and wondered if he could believe Dr. Jenkins when he said she hadn't suffered. Somehow I managed to convince him it was true and that she wouldn't have known a thing at the end. Though God knows why a man of his age would take the word of a 17-year-old waitress. He was kind and seemed to like me. I was beginning to really enjoy spending time with him

But then I looked up and saw Jimmy hand-in-hand with a very expensive-looking blonde. It was the first time I'd seen him since that awful night last summer when I'd caught him in my bed with one of Dee-Dee's horrible friends. He'd totally humiliated me, but it hadn't stopped me thinking about him every single day since. He looked just as striking as ever, and all heads turned to look as the leather-clad bundle of hostility swaggered through the room. I managed to stammer out a hello, but he didn't answer. Perhaps he didn't hear.

Dee-Dee glared at me; it was Valentine's night and she was rushed off her feet. The restaurant had filled with fawning couples, including Jimmy and his new girlfriend. I couldn't believe the way he was looking into her eyes and smiling that smile; he was even feeding her strawberries with his fingers. I forced myself not to look.

I tried to concentrate on what Mr Havers was saying. Giles I mean – he told me to call him Giles. "You must call me Giles and, with your permission, I will call you Kate. For I don't see you as a Kathryn, it's far too plain a name, and Kathy's too commonplace for one such as you."

I loved his old-fashioned way of speaking. He sounded so much like a Byronic hero that, as we chatted, I half expected him to say, "*I knew you would do me good in some way, at some time; I saw it in your eyes when I first beheld you.*" I smiled at the thought, and he smiled back and that's when he took my hands in his. They were warm and strong and much softer than mine; I resolved to start using hand cream. It was then that I realized he was trembling a little bit. I thought he was probably still in shock over his mother's death. I was scared that he might start to cry in the restaurant, in front of everyone, so I gave a little laugh and said, "If anyone sees us holding hands, they'll think that you're my Valentine."

He too forced a laugh and said, "You are a lovely young woman, Kate; thank you for your extreme kindness." He stood up to go, and kissed me on the back of my hand – an oddly gallant gesture – then said goodbye. It was then that I noticed Jimmy again. He was leaning on the door and had obviously been watching us for some time.

"What're you doin' with that creep? Thought you could do better than a ginger geriatric."

"He's just a friend – not that it's anything to do with you. Anyway, hadn't you better get back to your fancy piece?"

"She's gone. Anyway you know me. I do what I want."

"Oh yes," I said. "I know you alright." And with that, I hurried into the staff toilets. I didn't expect him to follow me in and lock the main door behind us.

"What do you want?" I asked, trying to act cool, telling myself that there was no way he could know how much I'd missed him.

"You!" He put his arms around me and kissed me passionately. I returned his kiss of course, running my fingers through his long, shiny hair, the same colour as blackcurrant Spangles. It was as if he'd never left me. He undid the buttons on my blouse, leaving faint strawberry stains on the white cotton. Then he grabbed my breasts – my nipples were swollen and hard even before he touched them. Then he sucked and pinched them between his lips, saying, as he paused to take off his jeans, "What was that stupid old sod doing settling for kissing your hand when he's got all of this to go at?"

Then he lifted me onto the sink, shoved my knickers to one side and without any thought of foreplay entered me. It was hard. It was wonderful. It was the best three minutes I'd had since we were last together.

As he got dressed I told him how I'd missed him and that I still loved him. I was just getting to the part about how glad I was that we'd found each other again.

He looked at me as he zipped up his jeans. "Get a grip, Babe. I'm with Imogen now."

He unlocked the door and left, whistling. No kisses, no declarations of love. He didn't even wash his hands.

I didn't sleep very well that night. Partly because I was worried about poor Giles – he seemed so sad and lonely – but more because I was really angry with myself. How could I have gone with Jimmy? And more to the point, how could he have gone with me if he was so keen on Imogen? It looked like Dee-Dee had been right about him all the time. He was just a shallow bastard of a Casanova. Well, as far as I was concerned, he'd had his last chance with me. More importantly, I decided that I was going to find a man who truly deserved me.

As we got ready for work the next morning, I apologized to Dee-Dee for leaving her to it last night. I said Mr Havers had needed company because he was lonely.

"Lonely? You're kidding. He's got the hots for you."

"Don't be silly; he wouldn't fancy someone like me."

"Why wouldn't he? He's a man and you've got tits."

"He's far too posh for the likes of me."

"So what if he's a bit posh? You might as well give him a chance. It looks like Jimmy Quinn's been well and truly hooked by that stick-insect on heat."

I was too ashamed to say anything about going with Jimmy, so I just said, "Mr. Havers is very posh; he says lavatory not toilet or loo or . . ."

"So what? Me dad says lav and he's not posh. Kathy and Havers up a tree K.I.S.S.I.N.G."

"Don't be stupid." I blushed and turned away.

At midday, a beautiful bouquet of red roses arrived. For me! It was the first time anyone had sent me flowers. I read the card.

Sorry if I spoilt your Valentine's Day. My heart flipped knowing they had to be from Jimmy. I turned the card over. *Please do me the honour of joining me for dinner.* That didn't sound at all like Jimmy. Then I saw the small writing. *To Kate, from G.G.G.H.*

Dee-Dee snatched it from me. "God, you'll be married next."

"No," I said. "Of course I won't. He's just being friendly."

GILES

I was just settling down to watch a documentary about the First World War when the blasted electricity was cut off. Damning the striking miners for spoiling my evening's viewing, I set about lighting candles before sinking into mother's favourite armchair to read my evening paper. I must have dozed off for I was stirred abruptly by the sound of rapping on the front door. I ignored it at first, half expecting mother to deal with it and then, as I awoke from my slumber, it hit me afresh that she had departed this world.

Rubbing the sleep and candle smoke from my eyes, I walked through the hall as the knocking became more insistent. Glancing at the door I could just make out a pair of eyes peering in through the letter-box and a voice saying, "Will yer no let me in? It's real brass-monkey weather out here."

I quickly unbolted the door to see on old friend crouched down. "Bertie!"

"Of course it's me; who did you think it was? A wee Scottish dwarf?" He straightened himself as I ushered him in from the cold dark night and into the semi-darkness of my home.

"Bertie old chap, good of you to come. How's the law these days?"

He put an arm on my shoulder, took my right hand in his, and shook it vigorously. "Awfully sorry about your mater, Old Boy, wonderful woman, called a spade a spade – always knew where you were with her. Bearing up alright are you?"

"Indeed yes, sorry business but life must go on, as they say," and with that awkward moment out of the way, we repaired to my study where we toasted mother's passing with a rather fine claret. One bottle turned into two, so we were slightly squiffy by the time the house lights came back on and in need of something with which to soak up the alcohol. I went to the kitchen and returned with two plates, a lump of dry-looking cheddar and a tin of biscuits.

Bertie regarded the snack with a certain degree of distaste. As he scraped off the mould, he said, "You need to get yourself a wife. A chap can't be expected to fend for himself – following a suitable period of mourning obviously."

"I don't think so."

"Yes, course you must. When am I going to meet, what's her name, that wee lassie of yours? You've been keeping her under wraps for too long, but surely she'll be at the wake?"

"No she won't," I said ending the matter. "I assume you came here to talk about my mother's will."

"Nothing much to say old chap. She left it all to you. I talked her out of bequeathing the lot to a charity for unmarried mothers, *haw–haw–haw*. Death duties will be a bit minty, but we can deal with all that after the funeral."

"I might have to sell some portraits . . ."

Bertie suddenly clapped his hands. "Felicity, that's her name, I remember now. Who did you say her people are?"

"I didn't. Bertie listen . . ."

"Because if they've got a shilling or two, then Bob's your uncle – death duties solved."

I'd hoped the whole Felicity charade would go away but there was no chance, not now. Bertie had got his teeth into it. I took a deep breath.

"The thing is, Bertie, she doesn't exist."

"Don't be ridiculous, man. How can you be betrothed to her if she doesn't exist?"

"I made her up."

"I say you're a bit old for imaginary girlfriends, don't you think?"

"It was Lucinda's fault."

Bertie eyed me suspiciously. "What's it got to do with my wife? I know she can be a bit meddlesome at times but I'm sure I've never known her invent people."

I knew it would be a struggle to make him understand but I blustered on. "The thing is, every time I went to stay with you, Lucinda would produce yet another of her spinster friends – I've met enough over-eager Veronicas, Vanessas, and Victorias to last me a lifetime, so I told Lucinda I was engaged and my, er, little misrepresentation somehow snowballed."

Bertie began to chuckle and soon I was chortling along with him. I watched the tears of laughter stream down his chubby, red cheeks as he carried on. "So what are you going to do with poor old Felicity, kill her off?"

Good old Bertie. Maybe that was the answer, but no, he came up a better idea.

"Got it!" He shouted as I was imagining the various ways I could dispose of poor, departed Felicity "She should jilt you on the very day of your mater's funeral. I'll announce the news straight after the buffet. Everyone will have downed a couple of Sherries by then, and the girlies will feel so sorry for you that they'll be queuing up to give you comfort. We might even manage a sympathy shag out of it."

"Bertie!"

"Don't look at me like that. It's all right for you. You've always got women crawling all over – I've got to grab my extracurricular wherever and whenever I can!" I wasn't sure if he was joshing or not but I made him promise to make no such announcement.

I cleared the plates and glasses into the kitchen sink to do in the morning, but then, imagining mother shuddering at my laziness, I changed my mind and washed up. Then I poured a couple of brandies and took them through to Bertie. The alcohol must have loosened my inhibitions because I found myself telling him a little of the events surrounding my recent loss.

"It's been a hellish week. I arrived home from a shoot on the Tuesday night to find mother motionless at the bottom of the stairs. The electricity was switched off, so I shone my torch at her dear face and to my horror, she seemed lifeless."

"Ghastly for you, Old Boy."

"Immediately, I covered her with my Barbour and telephoned old Jenkins who came straight round. He confirmed what I already knew in my heart – that mother had departed this world. He assured me that her death was instantaneous, and that she would not have suffered beyond the fall itself."

"Something to be said for a quick end, Lucinda's Ma lingered on for years – thought she was going to outlive the bloody lot of us!"

"I hate the thought of mother reaching such an undignified end."

"She'd know nothing about it, Giles. Now let's cheer up and have another snifter before we hit the hay."

Bertie went to bed before me, and as I plumped up the sofa cushions I could hear him in the guest room above me banging around, dropping things, and bumping into furniture. There was no way he could have driven home, as I explained to Lucinda when she phoned. She sounded most put out and said, rather fiercely I thought, that he'd better be back first thing in the morning. It was not, perhaps, the most compelling advertisement for matrimony and I was far from convinced of its dubious benefits.

Before I went to bed, out of habit, I opened the curtains. Mother always liked to come downstairs to the morning sunlight. Then I checked the locks on the doors and windows and used the candlesnuffer to make sure there was no danger of fire. It seemed strange ending the day without sharing a pot of cocoa with mother, just another of our little rituals. She never remarried after Father died and my few friends were scattered rather thinly throughout Blighty, so consequently we largely depended on each other for companionship. Occasionally, we would be invited to dine out but, ever conscious of her delicate constitution, mother would usually decline the invitation for both of us.

I was tired after the wine and brandy but sleep eluded me. So in the early hours, I found myself at my bedroom table writing mother's eulogy. Of course, I kept it purposely short and factual; mother abhorred sentimental outpourings of any sort.

When I eventually went back to bed, Bertie had stopped crashing around and the house was ghostly quiet. In sleep I dreamed not of mother's funeral or of the spirit world, but happy dreams of dear, sweet Kate.

How to bag a bloke (preferably a lord)

I didn't have sex with Giles until our fourth date. No particular reason, it was just customary to make them wait in those days. Somehow Giles had got it into his head that this was my first time, and he seemed so thrilled that it felt cruel to disillusion him. To be honest, I fancied him about as much as my deranged old granddad but, faced with his extreme ardour, it seemed rude to refuse.

I'll never forget seeing his baronial bedroom for the first time. It was bigger than mother's entire house, including her fancy new porch. The room was cold and dark, despite the blazing fire. Giles pushed a switch to light up the huge, glass chandelier that was hanging down from the highest ceiling I'd ever seen outside a cathedral. I wondered who was in charge of cleaning it – and how they managed to reach so high. Giles closed the heavy brocade curtains – he called them drapes. They were so old and faded I half expected them to disintegrate before my eyes. Mother wouldn't have given them houseroom.

The whole place was more portrait gallery than bachelor seduction pad. Wherever I looked a long-dead member of the Havers' clan glared down at me. It occurred to me that one day Giles would be up there frowning down on future generations. The thought made me shiver.

"It's much warmer in bed. Shall we get in?" Giles asked.

I gave a half-nod, half-shrug, which Giles mistook for enthusiasm. For an inherently slow man he wasted no time and whipped off his clothes without an ounce of embarrassment (I put this down to a lifetime of communal showers and streaking round the quad). In the face of his naked passion, I reluctantly began to undress.

From the moment Giles had shown interest in me, Dee-Dee had been preparing me for this moment. She'd even given me a book called *Bagging Your Bloke*. I tried to remember what it said in the sub-section, *Sensual Stripping:*

RULE ONE: Take your gloves off with your mouth, finger by finger. Don't forget to pout and maintain eye contact at all times . . .

Not applicable I'm afraid; the worst of the winter weather was over so I'd recklessly left my sheepskin mittens behind.

RULE TWO: As you remove your black fish-net stockings, keep your feet pointed, seductively, at your man, then do a playful little dance, maybe stretch the stockings above your head, and lick your lips invitingly.

I briefly considered this but doubted my American tan tights would have the desired effect, so I settled for a bit of pouting as I rolled them into a ball and stuffed them in my skirt pocket.

RULE THREE: Remember, you are a sensual creature – a creature like no other. Enjoy the touch of your hands on your body as you take off your clothes. Feel empowered as you sexily toss them aside.

I took off my shirt, stepped out of my skirt, and folded them into a neat little pile on the ottoman. Then I sat down feeling ridiculous in the frothy red bra that Dee-Dee had insisted I wear. I tried a smouldering look at Giles as he bounced around the room like an animated matchstick lighting candles, and pouring champagne into antique crystal flutes. Eventually he jumped into bed and held his arms out for me to follow.

And so it was on that Saturday afternoon, Giles, all pink and eager, and me, born-again virgin, got down to basics. In the same old four-poster that was home to Giles's very first breath all those years ago, I experienced my first ever orgasm, as well as my second and third. The man was insatiable. At last, I learned what all the fuss was about as he licked and bit and sucked me into a whole new ecstatic world. Then he turned me over and did it from behind. What stamina! I remembered to moan a lot (rule 12) but to my credit, I drew the line at rule 16. There were no shouts of *"Come on big boy, harder, harder, I'm nearly there."* Dee-Dee said I'd probably have to amend that one according to the size of what the book called his manhood (incidentally Dee-Dee couldn't have been more wrong). After hours of sticky, sweaty pleasure we drifted off to sleep, bound together like two exhausted castaways.

I woke to the sound of Giles singing softly to himself as he shaved in the adjoining bathroom.

"Kate-ee, Kate-ee, give me your answer do. I'm half-crazy all for the love of you. It won't be a stylish marriage. I can't afford a carriage. But you'll look sweet, upon the seat of a bicycle made for two."

He caught me looking at him through the mirror and blushed. "Marry me, Kate," he sang.

"Only if you can afford a carriage; I've never learnt to ride a bike." (It was a joke, I swear, a joke.)

"I'll buy you a thousand carriages." He strode over and gave me a long, soapy kiss. "I love you, Kate. I'll always look after you."

And that was that. The next thing I knew we were drinking champagne in Grimley Manor and naming the day. Even as we toasted our future life together, I wasn't sure what I felt about marrying Giles. Obviously he was a good catch and fantastic in bed but, more importantly, I knew he must truly love me. Otherwise why would he consider marrying so far beneath his class? My problem was I couldn't honestly say that I loved him – but I did like him. Maybe love would follow from that. And so what if it didn't? Loving Jimmy hadn't got me very far.

When I told mother that I was getting married she automatically assumed I was pregnant and began hyperventilating. When she eventually calmed down, I dropped the second bombshell. It wouldn't be held in our local church. She turned to me in horror.

"He's not . . . CATHOLIC?"

I smiled serenely. "No Mother, it's just that he's got a chapel in his garden." I said it all casually, as though it was a greenhouse or something. You should have seen her face turn triumphant. Her daughter had only gone and got herself a lord, a lord for goodness' sake. Although, to be honest, mother had always fancied the idea of Prince Charles for a son-in-law, provided that he agreed to have his ears pinned back for the photos.

From the moment I announced my wedding plans, mother and Darren all but moved in to Grimley Manor. Mother spent hours with Dee-Dee, who took her role as chief bridesmaid very seriously, poring over bridal magazines, planning colour schemes, checking flower arrangements and choosing hymns. It was like a military campaign and, if they were the commandos, I was clearly army surplus. I once timidly suggested that I'd like an ivory wedding dress. You'd think I'd expressed a desire to go naked.

Mother's voice was a faint screech. "What – and have them all think you're not pure?"

Dee-Dee looked at me and we sniggered, almost like old times. "Everyone knows cream is for trollops!" She said.

So, white it was, but I insisted (well, begged) that they should keep it simple. Simple? No chance. They chose a design in *Brides* magazine; all lace medallions and net swirls. Mother copied it in painstaking detail, right down to sewing tiny sequins all over the veil.

Then there was the great debate: What should the bridesmaids carry? Parasols? Hymn books? Flower baskets? And if flowers, should they be purple to match the dresses or pink to tone? It was nearly aired on Parky.

Getting through testing times

I hadn't had a period since the end of January. Ten weeks and three days to be precise. I'd been ignoring the fact; put it down to the stress of the forthcoming wedding. But for three days running I'd been violently sick. I knew in my heart of hearts that I must be pregnant. Worse still was the awful knowledge that Giles probably wasn't responsible.

I was with Dee-Dee in Fantasy Corner, Grimley Manor's answer to Disneyland. The only element of fantasy about the place was its name. There was a dejected-looking rocking horse, a roundabout with few spinning days left, and a couple of rusty old swings that squeaked backward and forward.

Mr B was expecting a visit from some big-wigs so we'd been sent to clear up the broken cider bottles, fag ends, and used johnnies kindly donated by next door's All Saints Youth Club. We were eating boiled sweets and betting on who could make them last the longest. I held the current record of nine minutes and eighteen seconds, but I was under pressure as Dee-Dee wasn't sucking hers. It was wedged between her back teeth. She called it clever new tactics; I called it cheating, but comforted myself with the thought of her teeth turning black and painfully rotting away.

"Anyway, what's up with you?" she asked.

"Nothing!"

"There is so."

I broke. "I just can't do it."

"Spit it out then. I'm winning anyway, look!" She opened her mouth to reveal a virtually unsucked sherbet lemon and two rows of perfect white teeth. Sometimes I hated her.

"I mean I can't get married."

"Kathy, you've got to. I've never been a bridesmaid before."

"I don't love him."

"Please, Kathy. Just think of you and me going down the aisle together; we'd be like sisters. Anyway, you said you really like him."

"Of course I like him, he's lovely . . ."

"And mega-rich."

"Yes, but I don't care about any of that . . ."

"And you'll live in that big house with lots of servants and you'll be able to buy all the shoes you want."

Ouch, that hit the spot. She was good.

"You marry him then," I said.

"I would if I could. Mmm, Lady Dee-Dee Havers."

It was obvious from the way it slipped off her tongue that she'd been practising.

"You're terrible. You'd nick my husband?"

"You just said you didn't want him. Anyway, I've no chance; he's scared of me," she said proudly.

"Aren't we all?" I muttered.

"And he's crazy about you; says you're his pocket Venus."

"But I can't eat or sleep."

"You'd be mad to let him go."

"I'm so worried. I was sick this morning." There, I'd said it. Dee-Dee turned to me, shocked.

"You're not preggers?"

"Of course not, Mother would go mad."

"Are you late?"

I nodded, feeling like a scared child, which is more or less what I was. "It's been ten weeks since I was last on. . . " The cold, hard pebble of worry that I'd been trying to ignore for the last couple of weeks had grown into a bubbling volcano of fear. It erupted and a lava of hot tears gushed down my face.

"Bloody hell, Kathy! Didn't you use owt?" Ironically, it was there in a children's playground surrounded by at least a dozen used-condoms that I had to confess my stupidity.

"He said he'd be careful."

"Yeah right, careful you wouldn't get away."

"He wouldn't do it on purpose," I sobbed. "Giles would never do anything to hurt me." But everything suddenly seemed unbearably inevitable.

"Oh bugger," said Dee-Dee.

For a moment, I was touched by her concern.

"I've finished me sweet," she said. "I owe you 50 pee."

I couldn't face the local chemist for a test, and I was scared of bumping into mother in Sheffield, so Dee-Dee decided we should go to Manchester. She insisted that she'd never had a scare but she seemed to know exactly what to do.

So on Monday morning we did the early shift with our going-out clothes hidden beneath our uniforms. I had a small jam-jar of wee in my apron pocket. I kept touching it as if it were a talisman.

The kitchen was boiling hot, and the smell of kippers made me want to throw up. I was sipping a glass of water when the kitchen door burst open. It was Mr Purvis.

"Ladies, ladies, I do hope everything is in order here. Mr B is giving a tour of Grimley Manor. They will be here very soon."

We didn't know who *they* were, maybe Health and Safety, but there were rumours that Grimley Manor was for sale. Great! I could be a jobless single mother by the end of the year.

I had no time to puke as we scurried round the kitchen, cleaning this and hiding that. Mr Purvis didn't seem too worried as we always kept what he called a "tight ship" in the food areas.

It was 45 minutes before anyone arrived so the kitchen was spotless. The two official-looking men barely noticed us as they poked down the sinks and prodded under the ovens. They took samples of food from the fridges and freezer, popping them into little sterile bags. It's a good job they didn't go in for body searches; if they'd found my sample, Grimley Manor would have been closed down for sure.

We should have finished our shift at twelve o'clock, but the food police made us late so we had to dash to Hathersage in our uniforms and get changed on the train. We only just made it. I was mute with terror for most of the journey, but Dee-Dee had a great time reading the birth columns in an abandoned newspaper.

"How about Guy for a boy? Or Ben? No he'd get called Benny like in *Crossroads*. Do you like Oliver or Tom?" I ignored her. I was too busy plea-bargaining.

Please God don't let me be pregnant. I promise I'll go to church and help the poor and never ever have sex again as long as I live.

Dee-Dee interrupted my silent prayer. "Or Lucy for a girl. No, Emma, Emma Dee-Dee Havers – you've got to call her after her godmother."

I didn't point out that Giles would never choose anyone less than a minor royal to oversee his child's religious development. Frankly, I was too concerned doing deals with fate to burst that particular bubble. *If the train arrives bang on time,* I told myself, *then I'm just late, not pregnant.*

The train juddered to a halt.

"*This is an announcement to all passengers travelling to Manchester Piccadilly. There will be a delay of approximately fifteen minutes. We apologize for any inconvenience."*

Inconvenience!

We eventually got off the train and made our way to the big Boots in central Manchester. We joined a massive queue at the pharmacy counter. There was just one person on duty – a middle-aged man with dyed black hair. He looked like he should be on a cruise ship dancing with rich old ladies for money. Instead, he was asking the walking wounded a battery of questions.

"Have you used this before?"

"Are you on any other medication?"

"You do know that this is for short-term use?"

Dee-Dee passed the time eyeing up the customers and making her own diagnosis. I pretended I wasn't there, that I didn't know Dee-Dee and I'd never had sex. Never ever!

Another ten minutes snailed by.

"God," said Dee-Dee. "You won't need the test. By the time we get served you'll be showing. See him?" She pointed to a skinny youth who was wiping his nose on his sleeve. "Ringworm."

I nudged her to shut up, and then it was my turn to be cross-examined. "I . . .erm . . . think I need a pregnancy test," I squeaked.

"Sorry, I didn't catch that. Speak up."

I took a deep breath. "I think I'm pregnant." It came out much louder than I'd intended, although maybe one or two people in the next building may not have heard. I could feel the line of people behind me stare at my head.

He took out a bright yellow form and peered at is as if it were the Magna Carta. "Are you on the pill?"

I shook my head; my audience tutted.

"How many times have you had unprotected sex and how late are you?" He was virtually salivating. I was seriously considering taking the jam-jar and treating his greasy, dandruff-speckled hair to an extra special golden rinse when Dee-Dee snatched the paper from his fat, sweaty hand.

"I'll do it for her." She quickly finished the questions and slammed it down on the counter beside the sample. "Now go somewhere else for your cheap thrills."

As we turned to go, an old lady – the one Dee-Dee said had piles – squeezed my arm and said, "Good luck, Lovey. I hope it turns out for the best."

That set me off again. Funny how kindness can make you cry. I blubbed all the way to the fancy hotel Dee-Dee had chosen for cocktails. I must have looked bad, because as anxious as she was to have a drink, she wouldn't go in before performing emergency repair work on my face.

We walked into the hotel and took the lift up to the top floor bar where we padded across the thick, black carpet to the sound of Diana Ross singing *"Wasn't it yesterday we used to laugh at the wind behind us?"*

I felt incredibly sorry for myself and couldn't imagine ever laughing again, unless of course, it turned out that I wasn't pregnant. Holding back even more tears, I looked at the bartender. He juggled bottles of vodka, Bacardi, and gin. He threw them high above his head, watched them fall nearly to the floor, caught them with a smug flourish and sent them spinning high again. Dee-Dee blew him a kiss as she sauntered towards the bar. He lost his timing for a split second and the bottles crashed to the floor. Mission accomplished. Dee-Dee perched herself on the edge of one of the high, chrome stools and asked the pink-faced juggler for a cocktail list.

"Hi, my name's Jason and I'm your drinks waiter today. We don't carry a list but I can shake any tail you care to name." Jason, who had clearly seen too many bad American films, counted off the repertoire of cocktails on his fingers. "Hairy Buffalo, Tropical Storm, Golden Cadillac,

Fuzzy Navel, Scarlet O'Hara, Bloody Mary. Oh, and I can make anything virgin."

"Have we got a challenge for you," giggled Dee-Dee, nodding towards my stomach. Jason looked alarmed. "She's pregnant?"

"Don't worry; it's not yours," Dee-Dee said.

"Not much chance of that, Sweetie; I bat for the other team." He turned to me. "Should you be drinking, you know, in your condition?"

Bloody hell! It'd started already, and I didn't even know for sure. But I did soon enough. After two cocktails (predictably, Sex On The Beach and a Slippery Nipple) Dee-Dee went off to get my results. I was grateful not to have to go back there and thanked her. She shrugged it off. "Well, if you're going to start roarin' again, at least it's dark in here."

She was right. The bar was a moody subculture of suited middle-aged men drinking with women that mother would have called vulgar.

While I waited for Dee-Dee to come back with the results, I sipped on my Malibu and lemonade – with extra lemonade to take the taste of alcohol away. I pretended I was enjoying it but my stomach was begging me to stop.

Jason looked at me sympathetically. "Will he stand by you like?"

"I expect so. We're supposed to be getting married next month, but I'm not sure I want to."

"Why not? Seems best thing to do if you are – you know . . ."

"It's just that we're worlds apart. Me, a skivvy in a hotel, and him, Lord of the Manor."

"Well if you ask me, you should grab him with both hands, don't tell him about the kid 'till after, then you can always get a divorce and take half his money."

"It won't work. We never have anything to talk about."

"Sweetie, husbands aren't for talking to." He went to serve another beer to a shady-looking man skulking in the corner and, at that moment, Dee-Dee returned. She handed me the yellow paper, but I didn't need to read it. Her face said it all.

I was pregnant! Thank you, God, and thank you bloody British Rail with your shoddy bloody timekeeping.

"When did you say you were last on?" Dee-Dee asked. "Only, according to the dates you told Mr Slime, you are over two months gone, but you didn't do it with Giles till last month which means. . ."

"Yes, I know what it means thank you, so just shut up." Her eyes widened so much I thought they would pop as the truth dawned on her. Honestly, it's almost as if she's psychic.

"Bloody 'ell, Kathy! Jimmy Quinn?"

I nodded as she went on.

"You actually shagged that bastard after all he's done to you? What planet are you on? I wouldn't touch him with a barge pole. I'd be scared of catching something!"

"Dee-Dee, stop it! Things are bad enough without you going on about it. I thought he wanted to get back with me. Just promise me you won't tell anyone, ever."

"Don't be stupid, of course I won't."

Jason came over to us and looked at me enquiringly. I nodded in confirmation.

"Well, that sorts out your conversation problems for the next eighteen years," he trilled, oblivious to the unfolding sub-plot. "Nappies, schools, babysitters, come on, let's celebrate; a glass of champers won't hurt." He opened a bottle and poured out three glasses. Taking a sip of his, he asked, "Does that taste corked to you?"

I forced a sip. "No, it's lovely." I lied.

He rolled his eyes at Dee-Dee who pretended to splutter over hers. "It's definitely off," she agreed.

Jason minced over to the till and rang in a void sale. Dee-Dee had, it seemed, found a soul mate. We clinked glasses and, as the yeasty bubbles hit my tongue, I suddenly felt okay about things. I could handle this; I was going to be a mummy. I held my stomach, almost expecting a conspiratorial kick from the tiny tadpole inside. *I'm going to look after you,* I silently promised. And if that means I have to marry Giles, then so be it.

It was almost dark when we got back to Grimley Manor and my upbeat mood faltered at the sight of Giles's old – sorry, vintage – car, parked by the main door.

"Now's your chance," said Dee-Dee. "Tell him you're preggers."

"I can't, not yet. . . "

Giles must have been looking out for me because, within seconds, he strode out the front door.

"Where have you been?" He said giving me a suffocating hug. "I've been so worried."

I backed away, took a deep breath, rooted in my pocket for the yellow form, and thrust it at him. He read it in confused silence. "I had no idea you even knew Barbara Cartland, she's one of Bertie's aunts. I'm surprised she wants children at her age."

I snatched the paper back and actually read it for the first time. It wasn't my name. It was somebody else's results! Oh thank goodness!

Dee-Dee was trying not to laugh. "You didn't expect me to give that slime ball your real name did you?"

I didn't have time to answer because for once Giles caught on. His eyes full of tears, he picked me up and kissed me. His breath was a disgusting cocktail of beer and smelly cheese.

"Kate, Kate, this is wonderful. We are going to be a proper little family. You've been so quiet recently that I thought you were having second thoughts about the wedding. But this is perfect."

And that was that, no questions, no blame – it was as if all his dreams had come true. I felt wretched, but if I told him the truth and called off the wedding I'd break his heart. And, of course, I needed to do the best thing for my baby.

He wanted to tell everyone straight away – the aristocracy are far less prudish than us when it comes to matters of procreation. But Dee-Dee and I persuaded him to keep quiet. As far as mother and the rest of the world were concerned, I was to have a premature, honeymoon baby.

When needs must

The day before I got married, 18 April 1974, should have been a happy time. Dee-Dee had planned a night on the town, but my morning sickness was lasting all day so I couldn't face a hen party.

I lay on the bed in the Grimley Manor Bridal Suite, which Mr B was letting us use as a changing room. Surrounding me was the paraphernalia of my great day: bridesmaids' dresses, flower baskets, and hymnbooks. I tried to summon the energy to try on my dress but felt terrified that it wouldn't fit. It wasn't that I'd put any weight on, but my boobs were enormous, swollen, and sore. They looked like they belonged to someone else.

Giles burst into the room. "Pumpkin, I've been speaking to the hospital."

Oh no, not again. Giles had taken it upon himself to project manage my entire pregnancy. I looked at him. "You shouldn't be in here; you're not allowed to see my dress. Mother'll go mad."

He didn't hear a word. "They strongly recommend you have an amnio-something test to make sure the offspring is one hundred percent – you know, given your family history."

"It's called amniocentesis and I'm not having it."

He looked at me, amazed. "But Pumpkin, it tests for mon . . . ehm, you know, Down's syndrome."

"It might make me have a miscarriage and, anyway, even if the baby wasn't" – I mimicked his plummy voice – "one-hundred percent, I'd never get rid of it. And don't tell me that's not what you're thinking." I felt myself shake, boiling with rage.

"Kate, Kate, that's your hormones speaking. Everyone knows a handicapped child means a handicapped family. It would be a life sentence."

"My brother is not a life sentence," I said in the strongest voice I could muster. "He's lovely and kind, and I can't imagine wishing he hadn't been born."

So there, in the bridal suite, twenty-four hours before the big day, we had our first argument. And as arguments go, this one reached World War proportions. The arrival of Dee-Dee, an unlikely ambassador for peace, heralded a ceasefire. She advised Giles to stop upsetting me and suggested he go for a walk to cool down. Well, her actual words were, "Leave her alone you fucking freak, and piss off out of here before she loses the bloody baby."

When he opened his mouth to argue, she practically threw him out.

I told her what had happened. I knew she'd be on my side because she'd seen me with Darren and knew how close we were.

"It's your baby," she said, "so tell him to shove it."

"I have but he seems so angry with me, I've never seen him like that."

"There must be something we can do." She was deep in thought, but I suspected all she really cared about was taking a lead role in tomorrow's wedding.

"Got it," she said. "Pretend to have the test and tell him it's clear. He's too thick – sorry, trusting – to think you're lying and, when the baby's born, it'll be too late to change anything."

I hated the thought of a marriage based on my lies but as mother always said, "Needs must . . ."

How to get on the property ladder

I was still furious the next day. It was my eighteenth birthday and my wedding day. Mr Purvis and I travelled from Grimley Manor to Havers Hall in Gile's big old Bentley. Dee-Dee looked stunning in her tight-fitting bridesmaid dress. Obviously, she didn't go along with the old 'don't outshine the bride' maxim. My three little bridesmaids, all daughters of Bertie, the best man, were waiting for me in the vestry: Clarissa, Claire, and little Charlotte, or the Clones, as Dee-Dee called them. They were wearing dresses in the same shade as Dee-Dee's but there the similarity ended. They looked for all the world like those little dolls mother made to preserve the modesty of our toilet rolls.

I ignored the niggling voices in my head and was deaf to the warnings rung out by the church bells. I needed a father for my unborn child and I wanted to be part of a proper family. Thankfully, there was Darren; I was so proud of him, all serious in his top hat and tails, showing last-minute arrivals to their pews. There no need for him to ask "bride or groom?" Anyone could work out which side of the church the guests belonged to. All Giles's friends and family looked virtually identical – slight with fine, sandy hair and skin so white it made alabaster look grubby. Most of them were called Rupert or Camilla, and in their shabby tweed and clashing accessories they oozed old money.

My lot, in comparison, had waged an assault on the High Street to ensure everything matched. Entire families were colour coordinated right down to the smallest toenail. Idiot that I am, I was still hoping my dad would show to give me away, even though he hadn't replied to the invitation. As usual, mother was right.

"Why would he turn up when he's not been near in years? Anyway, you're not his to give away – not after he abandoned us. Rees will walk you down the aisle."

"No way," I replied. "I'm not having him acting like he owns me." In the end, I chose Mr Purvis to be my surrogate father.

The organist, who I remembered as the sad-looking Christmas pianist, struck up *Here Comes the Bride* – played in the style of the Funeral March. Dee-Dee and the Clones took up positions behind me as Mr Purvis took my arm. Docile as the proverbial lamb, I allowed myself to be led down the aisle to my future husband who – oh no! – was wearing a kilt. In fact, he wore the whole ensemble: cummerbund, sporran, and socks held up with tiny tartan suspenders. I was mortified.

"Do you, Kathryn Mary, take this man, Giles Gilbert George, to be your lawful wedded husband?"

Baa . . . "I do".

I also promised to love, honour, and obey him for as long as we both should live. Surprisingly, the heavens didn't open, nor did lightening strike, but I did feel a bit hot under the veil. Maybe the hell fires were being stoked in readiness.

Then came the big moment as the vicar invited Giles to kiss his bride.

"What God has joined together, let no man put asunder."

So, I'd done it! Giles gave me the sunniest of smiles, tucked my arm into his, and walked me back up the aisle. (Thank God for that, I'd had visions of us dancing a bloody reel). I snuggled up to him, practicing my new wifely role. I was close enough to inhale his now familiar scent – Pears soap mingled with a subtle hint of gentlemen's cologne as far from *Brute, splash it all over* as you could get. The chapel air was filled with the smell of dusty old hymn books and the heady perfume of the orange blossom flowers chosen by mother because they symbolized purity!

We stopped in the old stone vestry, chilly despite the warm spring sun, to shake hands with the congregation as they exited the chapel. I recognized most of Giles's lot from his mother's funeral, but it was as if they were seeing me for the first time, my old waitress uniform having been an invisibility cloak.

We walked out into a shower of confetti and rice; and it was time for photographs. Giles was in a bit of a grump because he'd wanted some distant cousin to take the pictures, but mother had insisted on hiring a professional. So as Mr Flashman fussed around, posing us this way and that, Giles kept batting on about how old Lichfield would have done a much better job!

Mr. Flashman told us he believed in taking natural shots. It then took him two hours to capture Giles, Bertie, and the groomsmen spontaneously throwing their top hats into the air. He gave up trying for a portrait of me looking adoringly into my spouse's eyes. He was, after all a photographer, not a magician.

Eventually, we made our way down the freshly manicured path towards Havers Hall. Home: me with my brand new posh husband, and mother with her brand new posh accent. I noticed Dee-Dee arm-in-arm with the Vicar; they were having a deeply spiritual conversation.

"Do you think Mary was really a virgin, you know, when she had the baby? I'm only asking 'cos the exact same thing happened to Janice Eckersley in the fourth year and practically nobody believed her."

"Well my dear, people were sceptical about Mary to begin with."

"So you're saying that eventually people will come to worship Janice and little Starsky? Only, at the moment, she's on social."

He seemed enchanted by her innocence and had no idea she was winding him up. They were still debating the Immaculate Conception when we reached the huge purple marquee on the lawn by the lake. An army of waiters welcomed guests and served pre-dinner champagne. Giles was thrilled to see his old school chums and couldn't wait to introduce me.

"Pumpkin, Pumpkin do come and meet Biffo, Buster, and Morris Minor – at school they used to call us the Crazy Gang."

Of course they did. Putting salt in the sugar bowl and tying Matron's underwear to the flagpole – how wacky could you get?

Actually, they were quite nice in a blindly arrogant sort of way. Biffo thought my people were 'salt of the earth' – an epithet based entirely on their Yorkshire accents. All three agreed that Dee-Dee was top totty, and they wouldn't throw her out of the old sack for eating crisps. *Haw, haw, haw.* I couldn't wait to give her the good news.

The hilarity subsided as a tiny, angular woman dressed completely in black approached us flapping her way like an aggrieved bat.

"Master Giles, I'm surprised at you, your mother not yet cold in her grave."

Giles gave a delighted whoop. "Nanny, Nanny, you're really here." He picked her up and danced around the lawn. In his defence, he had drunk half a glass of champagne. They came to land beside me.

"Nanny, Kate, at last you meet."

Should I tell him? This woman was definitely an imposter. She bore absolutely no resemblance to the warm, loveable woman he'd drivelled on about for the last few months.

"Hello, pleased to meet you," I lied politely.

She made a harrumphing noise as she looked me up and down. "There's nothing to her," she sniffed. "It's a good job I'm back to look after you."

Giles was so overjoyed he could barely speak. Could my day get any worse? Well . . .

We were piped into the marquee for dinner, or tea as half of us called it. Everyone clapped, even Nanny, although I'm sure she was muttering a curse under her breath. Throughout the meal, mother alone did her best to bridge the inter-planetary chasm, flitting from table to table, dispensing wisdom and bonhomie. I heard her tell Lady Bosworth (who claimed to be twenty-fifth in line to the throne) that a bit of rouge would do wonders for her cheekbones and had she thought about streaking her hair? Mother added that she could show her how and, whilst she wasn't one to boast, she was a dab hand with the Hiltone!

Giles had chosen the menu. Foie gras, pigeon en croute, and profiteroles – or liver, chicken pie, and éclairs, as my granddad would have it. Whatever it was called, it turned to sawdust the moment it hit my taste buds.

As promised, after dinner, Bertie gave a hilarious speech, including an account of the stag night and how they'd debagged old Havers. *Haw haw haw!* Unfortunately, he kept slipping into Latin so my lot were more bewildered than ever. Then the band struck up as Bertie made an announcement.

"Ladies and Gentlemen, the bride and groom will take to the floor and lead the dancing."

Oops, that was me. Since the closest I'd ever got to ballroom dancing was shuffling round my handbag at the Penny Farthing while hoping my knickers didn't show, I was rather alarmed at being swirled and twirled round the marquee by an over-excited man in a skirt.

As if class was contagious, the guests stayed strictly in their own camps. In the blue-blooded corner, we had the Highland fling and the Gay Gordon, while the blue-collared section went for the Hokey Cokey and hand-jiving. Only Dee-Dee – who, according to my granddad, had "more front than 'arrods," – sashayed from group to group; from my past to my future, and turn, cha-cha-cha!

As was traditional, the bride and groom left the wedding party soon after the first dance. I'd wanted to stay much later but mother was having none of it. "Giles is your husband, and he'll want to. . ." her voice fell mysteriously, "get to know you better."

I couldn't really argue with that. So at nine o'clock I extracted myself from a semi-drunken conga line and went back to the house to change. Dee-Dee came with me. The sound of an inebriated rendition of *Rule Britannia* followed us up the stairs as we walked into my new bedroom.

"God," said Dee-Dee. "It's incredible."

"I know. Not exactly cosy though."

"No I mean you. You've only gone and promised to shag Giles, and only Giles, for the rest of your life. Mind you with a name like Giles Gilbert George at least he'll be an expert on G spots."

Put like that it was a bit daunting, but she didn't know how good he was in bed and I wasn't about to tell her, not with her track record. I struggled to zip up my new skirt – a birthday present from Giles. Dee-Dee had kicked off her stilettos and lay on the bed, glugging champagne from a massive bottle. I walked over to the jug on the dresser and poured myself a glass of tepid water. She looked at me in my smart brown shoes, new tweed skirt, and silk blouse. "Who are you going as, his mother?"

Trust her; I'd been worrying about what I would look like in my going away outfit. I bit my lip and brushed my hair, trying to ignore her as she went on. "Do you think they've twigged, you know, 'bout you being in the club?"

"I don't know; Giles's nanny kept giving me funny looks."

"That witch, who cares what she thinks? I know, let's find out what sex it is – give us your wedding ring."

"But I promised Giles I'd never take it off – ouch!" She'd pulled out some of my hair. Dee-Dee held out her hand and I obediently gave her the ring. She threaded it onto one of my long, blonde hairs, and told me to lie down on the bed while she dangled the ring over my tummy.

"If it goes from left to right it's a boy, but if it goes round and round, it's a girl."

We held our breath as the ring swung up and down from my head to my toes. What could that mean?

"It's gay," announced Dee-Dee. "You'll have to call it Jason." We burst out laughing. She confessed that she'd been messing about, so we tried it again. The ring started to move after a few seconds when in walked Nanny.

She didn't look pleased to see us; obviously she considered the bedroom to be Giles's territory.

"What are you girls up to?" she snapped.

I furtively slipped on my ring, hoping she hadn't seen what we were doing.

Dee-Dee put on her shoes, picked up the bottle, and swaggered out. "Please don't ground us, Matron."

Nanny glared at me. I ignored her and finished getting dressed. I was just about to leave when she came right up to me and pointed a bony finger in my face. "I've got your measure, Young Lady. If you go upsetting Master Giles, you'll have me to answer to."

Talk about melodramatic. I don't know where it came from but I put on a really haughty voice. "I would be grateful

if, in future, you knocked before entering my bed chamber."
(Hark at me! To the manor born or what?)

There was a driver waiting for us in the lobby. Bertie and Morris Minor had decorated the car with tin cans, shaving foam, and confetti. Everyone waved at us as we clattered down the drive on our way to the Cavendish Hotel in Baslow, probably the poshest hotel in the whole world.

Giles turned to me and squeezed my hand. "Pumpkin, you look so smart."

I looked down at my clothes doubtfully. "Are you sure it's not a bit, well, old for me?"

"But darling, you are my wife now."

He said it cheerfully enough, so why did it sound so much like an omen?

Learn about layettes, labour and lies

Mother was delighted when I announced I was pregnant. Despite her rant when I left home, I could tell she couldn't wait to be a grandma. It is amazing the difference a little gold ring can make.

Taking impending granny-hood seriously, she took up extreme knitting, arriving at Havers Hall with box after box of Day-Glo baby wear, shawls, bootees, and matinee jackets, all in lurid shades of yellow, orange, and green. It's a shame she hadn't been around to knit socks and balaclavas for the war effort; she could have single-handedly crocheted the enemy into submission.

If she wasn't creating the layette from hell, she was bombarding me with her superstitions. "Spit that strawberry out, our Kathryn, you'll be giving the bairn a birthmark, and don't reach up like that, you'll strangle the poor mite with its cord."

She even tried to stop me from bathing. (Don't ask!)

Meanwhile, Dee-Dee became fascinated with pregnancy and childbirth, and must have spent all her time researching the potential horrors. She would visit every few days to add to the list: stretch marks, varicose veins, hair falling out, weight gain, memory loss, piles, stitches – the tortures just kept coming. I should have turned to my husband for support, or even laughed about it, but Giles seemed to be under the impression that as my bump got bigger my brain got smaller. Luckily for me, Darren was around, so when it all got too much I would escape with him.

We spent hours walking through Grimley and its surrounds discussing names for the baby and Darren's upcoming role as Uncle Darren.

Despite mother's prophecies of doom – first labour's always the hardest, our Kathryn, I'd never known pain like it when I delivered Rees – and Dee-Dee's conviction that I'd never get my figure back – I was relieved when my contractions started. It was Bonfire Night, and there was a big party in the grounds of Grimley Manor. Fireworks along with all the trappings: mulled wine, roast chestnuts, and potatoes baked in the huge bonfire. It was a goodbye party for Mr B. He'd sold Grimley Manor to a hotel chain, and was retiring to the Pennines to run a small B&B. He told the staff their jobs at the Manor were safe, but Mr Purvis didn't look convinced.

Everyone was there so Dee-Dee, Rees, mother, and Darren all witnessed me clutching myself as my waters broke, soaking the cashmere jumper that Giles had thoughtfully provided as a cushion.

"It'll be the bangers, frightening the little thing out," said mother, (she could certainly give Doctor Spock a run for his money.)

I don't know if she had worked out the dates. Maths wasn't her strong subject, but if she was suspicious about the early arrival of her grandchild she, thankfully, kept it to herself.

It was a short labour and nothing like as horrific as mother had said it would be. Nevertheless, I was exhausted when I gave birth to a seven-pound baby boy just before midnight.

"Not a bad weight for one so premature," Dee-Dee said, keeping her face straight. "And doesn't he look like his dad?"

Giles wanted to call him Gilbert, but I was set on Guy, in celebration of Guy Fawkes and John, after my dad. In the end, we compromised and called him Sebastian. Giles added the inevitable Giles Gilbert George, but I didn't mind – nothing mattered. I was besotted with my son! He was beautiful with loads of black hair and big, blue eyes, which were to turn green, like mine.

Dee-Dee, consulting her baby booklet, said his hair would rub off. Mother agreed, adding he would be ginger like Giles (only she called it strawberry blonde). They were both wrong. He was, and always would be, my raven-haired cuckoo.

After giving birth you were held captive for at least a week. It gave the medical profession time to inflict further humiliation and ritual torture on mother and child. When finally released, I was naively thrilled to find Dee-Dee had taken time off work to "look after" me. It was lovely to have her around, but Florence Nightingale she was not.

Giles had wanted Nanny to slip back into her hallowed role of nursemaid and take charge of Sebastian. However, there was more chance of me stripping him bare and handing him over to the Spartans. So between us, Dee-Dee and I settled him into a routine of sorts – a round of crying, feeding, and changing followed by one of screaming, eating, and being sick. Very occasionally he would drop off to sleep for half an hour.

"Newborns tend to sleep for around eighteen hours a day," Dee-Dee read from *The Little Book of Lies* provided by the hospital.

I was exhausted but I didn't care because I'd fallen madly in love with my son.

When Sebastian was a couple of weeks old, Nanny's old friend, Mrs. Newsome, a health visitor, called on us in Nappy Valley. She was on an important mission – Sebastian had to be weighed. The first thing I saw of her was a pair of brown lace-up brogues and two very thick ankles encased in black wool tights. I'd been lying on the floor trying to squeeze into pre-Sebastian size eight jeans. Dee-Dee sat beside me painting her toenails voodoo purple. For once, Sebastian was sleeping like a baby, but not for long.

Mrs. Newsome strode into the room, clearly a woman on a mission. Tutting at the Addams' family-themed décor, she fashioned a baby sling out of a terrycloth nappy (this was the dark ages before disposables became *de rigueur*). She then whisked an angry Sebastian out of his crib, undressed him, and suspended him naked and screaming from the spring-weighing device. After much double-checking and referring to notes, Mrs. Newsome concluded that, as was normal, Sebastian had lost three ounces. Dee-Dee grabbed him and held him aloft as she delightedly pronounced him Weight Watcher of the week.

Ignoring her, Mrs. Newsome fixed me with a steady gaze. "How do you propose to feed your baby?"

"Well, I thought I'd feed him myself, at least for the first few months."

"And then we're going to wean him off milk and onto the cabbage soup diet," added Dee-Dee.

If Nanny and Gruesome Newsome had been given their way, Sebastian's name would have been placed at the very top of the 'at risk' register.

Despite spending all his time with Dee-Dee and me, the atmosphere of frivolity did not rub off onto Sebastian. He hated the trappings of babyhood. Not for him: lullabies, soft toys, and hanging mobiles. He loathed playing peek-a-boo and being tickled or cooed over. If a stranger dared look in his pram, to marvel at his shock of black hair or stroke his tiny fingers and toes, Sebastian would scowl demonically and yell. Dee-Dee adored him.

Mother didn't say anything, but I could tell that she was disappointed with Sebastian. All she'd ever dreamed of was one of those fat, pink, gurgling infants she could show off to the neighbours, and typically, I'd landed her with a grandson whose personality was pitched somewhere between manic depressive and psycho. How could she possibly win the Glamorous Granny competition when pictured with this sullen, glaring, bundle of sorrow?

Not one to give up easily, mother took to spending her weekends rooting around jumble sales on a quest to find that certain something that would bring a smile to my first-born's face: flower-shaped rattles, squealing monkeys, teethers, squeakers, a music box owl, and a singing telephone car. All these colourful tributes to her optimism sat, unused, on the nursery floor. Sebastian did at least look at her as he dismissed the latest offering, as though he derived pleasure from her disappointment. He seemed content enough to recognize the women in his life with a sort of half-smile, half-grimace but he staunchly refused to acknowledge Giles. It was clearly my husband's own fault – he would insist on calling Sebastian, "Gilbert old chap". I don't think he meant anything by it; he simply had no idea how to communicate with little people.

It was strange, given their uneasy relationship, that Giles couldn't wait for me to have more children. I wasn't sure I wanted another baby. We were such a perfect trio: Sebastian, Dee-Dee, and me. But, mad for his heir and spare – he actually said things like that – Giles went on an early mission to impregnate me.

"Oh no!" Dee-Dee said when I told her. "You must be on your guard at all times. Dawn raids cannot be ruled out; it'll be tally-ho and a quick chase to his orgasm, and next thing you'll be up the duff again."

I giggled. Sadly, loyalty to my husband was not a priority in those days.

Beware of truth serum

Before Sebastian was out of nappies, I was pregnant again – a horrible, nauseous time dogged by high blood pressure, swollen legs, and fatigue. The baby hardly moved in the last few weeks, so I wasn't completely surprised when my daughter arrived premature and still-born; a broken promise of undernourished flesh that, to my shame, I couldn't bear to look at, much less hold.

Mother had her own superstitious theories as to why she, (I never gave her a name) had been born dead, but I preferred to believe the doctors: placental insufficiency. See, I was so useless that I couldn't even feed my own baby.

Giles, somehow strengthened by my weakness, was splendid. He took me home, wrapped me in a giant duvet, and fed me soup and hot chocolate. He showered me, washed my hair when I hadn't the heart for it, and stayed awake, as if on guard, while I fitfully slept. He was always at his best when I was down.

Dee-Dee had taken Sebastian to stay with mother. I hadn't wanted him to go but inertia took over and I found myself listlessly agreeing with Giles that it was for the best. Dee-Dee stayed at mother's too, supposedly to help out but I suspected she was furthering her ongoing project: the seduction of Rees.

Giles loved having me to himself, but I missed Sebastian and wanted him home. Also another emotion was fighting my grief: boredom – extreme, torturous, boredom. But not to worry; Giles had a plan.

"We'll go away," he announced, "to the coast!"

I was not impressed, nor was the three-year-old child who had recently taken up residence inside my head and seemed to be doing most of the talking. "I don't want to go to the seaside."

"But Pumpkin, the sea air will do you good."

"I want Sebastian."

"It'll blow away those cobwebs. Please, say yes and then, when we get back, you'll be feeling much stronger and we can fetch Sebastian home."

That did it. I found myself gathering together flip-flops, sunhats, and two huge maternity smocks. Nothing else fitted me, despite the fact that no solid food had passed my lips for ten days. Somewhat optimistically, I did throw in a pair of skinny jeans. As I packed, I found myself remembering the family holidays we'd had when I was a little girl, long before Darren was born – paddling in rock pools with Rees and daddy, then scrambling into sandy shoes to go walking on the cliffs. I could almost hear the screeching of the seagulls as I remembered how we tucked into our traditional Cornish tea. I licked my lips, virtually tasting the buttery clotted cream and strawberry jam that would be spread thickly on freshly baked scones. I almost began to look forward to a trip away with Giles.

However, an hour into the journey and Giles casually ruined any hope I might have had of a good time. "Bertie and Lucinda are frightfully keen to see you."

Bertie and Lucinda! He'd kept that quiet. Didn't they live in a remote, windswept, tumble-down ruin in Scotland? Yes, they did. A long, long four hours later, we arrived at Bertie's castle. It was perched high on a cliff, overlooking the North Sea. Not a donkey in sight, no candyfloss, no sticks of rock. Not even a smutty postcard – just crashing waves, an unfulfilled promise of a ghost, and a very real threat of pneumonia.

To be fair to them, Bertie and Lucinda made me very welcome; they were solicitous about my health, tiptoeing around me, being careful not to use any words like pregnancy, baby, or milk. To save me any more heartache, they had even packed off their latest clone, one-year-old Charlie, to visit his grandmother. It was sweet of them but wholly unnecessary. It was my baby I wanted, not theirs.

"We thought we'd have a kitchen supper tonight," Lucinda informed me. "So no need to dress up."

Just as well really as I'd left my tiara at home. She shooed the boys – as she called our husbands – out of the castle and into the wild highland weather, having given them a list of projects to keep them busy until suppertime. Then she led me into the kitchen and sat me down by the huge, steaming Aga. She plonked a bottle of sloe gin on the table beside me and told me to tuck in while she cooked. It soon became apparent that multi-tasking wasn't her forte, but she wouldn't let me help so I passed the time by sampling her home brew. Alcohol had been a stranger for nine months and it was great to be reunited at last.

"Just help yourself; I made gallons this year," said Lucinda, cheerfully chopping the head off a long-dead pheasant. So I poured myself another, and another, and another. The smoky purple of the gin reminded me of Dee-Dee's favourite nail varnish and I wondered what she would be doing at home with Sebastian and Darren. Before long, in a muddle of gin-fuelled emotion, I found myself sobbing into Lucinda's pheasant-stained tea towel.

Lucinda, of stiff-upper-lip persuasion, was clearly at a loss. She blundered around picking feathers out of my hair, and dispensing tissues and clichés.

"Chin up Kate, dry those eyes now," she said. But I cried even more. She tried again. "Time to buck up, old thing, and count your blessings."

Eventually, she got the message. My sinews were not for stiffening. She slammed the casserole in the Aga and sat down beside me. In a valiant attempt at catching up in the drinking stakes, she poured herself a massive tumbler of gin, downed it, and turned to me. "Do you want to talk about it, I mean, her or . . ."

"I'm so sorry," I gulped. "It's my hormones, they're at war; I feel so empty. I feel like a big, fat, empty blob and I miss Sebastian and Dee-Dee, she's my best friend."

Too late, I remembered that Dee-Dee wasn't Lucinda's favourite person. Dee-Dee claimed it wasn't her fault. She said that she'd genuinely believed it was tradition for the chief bridesmaid to seduce the best man. Fortunately for Bertie, Lucinda was a sporting sort of a gal and turned a blind eye to their cavorting.

"But Kate," she continued, "you've got Giles to look after you now; you're so lucky."

"Lucky?" I said, "Lucky?" And then it was too late to stop, and I was too drunk to care. It all came gushing out of my mouth in an unstoppable flow: how I didn't love Giles, how I never had and never will; why I shouldn't have married him, even though he is rich and good in bed. Pretty much everything got an airing, whether she wanted to hear it or not.

"But," Lucinda eventually interrupted, "you don't have to love him! People get married for lots of reasons. Land, for example, or the joining together of two families." (Not round our way they don't). Lucinda was now throwing back the booze with the gusto of a parched Navvy. She continued, clearly on a roll. "He's a good provider and he clearly dotes on you. He even broke things off with Felicity for you," Her eyes went all dreamy. "I'd give anything for my Bertie to look at me the way Giles looks at you. But no, I'm just sensible, dependable old Lucinda."

"Who's Feli . . ."

Lucinda, she cut me off. "In fact, I think he's got a mistress."

"No!"

"Well tell me then, why did he suddenly start going away on business? Up to a few years ago, except for shooting and fishing trips, we never had a single night apart."

Bloody hell, sloe gin? Truth serum, more like. So as the rotting birds slowly cremated in the Aga, we opened another bottle and bonded in the way that only the truly inebriated can. You name it we covered it. By the time the boys came chortling back, we were as drunk as a couple of Paddies on Saint Patrick's Day. They had clearly downed one or two at the pub but were, sadly, way, way behind us in the Alcohol Olympics. It took Bertie, who seemed even dimmer than Giles, at least ten minutes to realize that not only was his dinner ruined but – heaven forbid – good old solid Lucinda was drunk and had clearly been infiltrated by the working class.

I'm not sure what happened next. I have a vague recollection of Giles force feeding me toast and putting me to bed. When I woke up during the night, there, waiting for me on the wobbly bedside table, was a pint of water and some painkillers. Reaching for them, I must have disturbed Giles because within seconds, he bounded round to my side of the bed.

"Are you all right, Pumpkin?"

I tried to nod, but it hurt too much.

"Here, take these tablets and try to drink up; you'll feel better in the morning."

I gulped them down then ran over to the little vanity unit to be sick. Giles held my hair back and made soothing noises until the vomiting subsided. Then he helped me clean my teeth before tucking me back in bed.

"That's better, old thing. You've been through a lot recently; don't think I don't know it. Now, you try to get some sleep." He kissed me gently on the cheek and stroked my forehead until I nodded off. It may have been the drink, but I went to sleep believing my husband was the loveliest man I'd ever met.

Bertie took Giles off shooting early next morning so we girls didn't surface until shortly before they returned. As I walked into the kitchen, Lucinda was extracting a bottle of vodka from a Wellington boot. She seemed a bit embarrassed but that didn't stop her from pouring herself a large tumbler of Bloody Mary.

"Hair of the dog?" She offered.

I shuddered a refusal and drank several gallons of water instead. Then, head in hands, I stayed in the recovery position waiting for the men folk to return. The planned meal in a posh restaurant was cancelled in favour of comfort food at the local pub, a short walk away. Once there, the men tucked into their pints of beer and game pies as if they hadn't eaten for days, while white-faced and valiant Lucinda toyed with the soup of the day and a glass of white wine. I drank lemonade. The men spent lunchtime banging on about the shoot, but I didn't mind; it was a relief not to have to speak. Bertie kept giving me strange looks, which I put down to the flowery maternity smock I was wearing. I'd considered squeezing into my jeans, but the effort of breathing in and pulling up a zip was beyond my hung-over state.

Lucinda made brave attempts at speech between sips of Chablis laced with Alka Seltzer. At first, I could only manage the occasional incline of my head, but eventually I pulled myself together and tried to laugh with her about the previous evening.

However, she was having none of it, and the meal limped to a close with Lucinda stoutly refusing to acknowledge that last night had ever happened. It was as if she and I had never opened up to each other, hadn't made fun of our husbands, or tightly hugged each other goodnight. Maybe she felt humiliated or ashamed but I longed to tell her that, where I came from, we'd had what was known as a cracking girls' night in.

Giles, as ever seeing only the best in me, thought the drunken bonhomie between Lucinda and me was genuine affection. He was delighted that I'd drawn good old Lucinda out of herself and was very excited that I'd found a little friend. He was keen that we plan family holidays together and invite them back to the Hall. As the day went on, and my hangover abated, I was able to ignore his over-enthusiastic ramblings, shroud myself in self-pity, and get back to the serious business of mourning my small evacuee.

How to ignore consequences

On Monday, we drove back to Havers Hall. I'd phoned mother from Bertie's to make sure Dee-Dee and Sebastian would be back that night. I couldn't wait to see them and was delighted when they arrived only a few minutes after us. As soon as I saw Dee-Dee, I could tell by her face she was hiding something.

"What's amusing you?"

"You'll see."

"Tell me."

"No."

I held Sebastian close and pulled off his baseball cap for a smell of his hair. I gasped. Clearly, a razor-wielding mad man had attacked my son's shiny black mop. He was practically bald but for a resilient little black tuft sprouting out over his forehead – a sort of joke fringe.

"What happened?" I gulped.

"Well," began Dee-Dee. "You won't believe this but he was abducted and held to ransom. Every day the kidnappers sent a lock of his hair in the post until Granny finally cracked and handed over her complete collection of commemorative plates."

I held Sebastian even closer.

Dee-Dee tutted and shook her head. "What do you think happened? Your mother got a bout of the old Vidal Sassoons. I tried to stop her, sorry."

She'd be at the receiving end of a Sweeney Todd when I got hold of her.

And there was more. Sebastian looked up at me and smiled. He actually smiled. "Rum weather, i'nt it?" He said.

Dee-Dee tried to stifle her laughter as it became apparent that the taciturn toddler I'd nurtured for the last two and a half years had, in just two weeks under mother's tutelage, morphed into an affable northern pensioner.

"Take yer coat off Dee-Dee, else you won't feel benefit," the child muttered.

Giles shook his head, horrified. I collapsed on the settee, laughing properly for the first time in weeks. Dee-Dee fell on top of me holding her stomach. Sebastian tried his best to scowl at us, but he couldn't fool me. He loved making us laugh.

"A star is born," proclaimed Dee-Dee.

"A black hole more like," mumbled Giles, and with that uncharacteristic flash of wit, he stalked out of the room.

Prompted by Giles, I sent a huge bouquet of yellow roses to Lucinda and Bertie to thank them for their hospitality. This was quickly followed by Lucinda ringing to say thank you for the flowers. I couldn't concentrate on what she said because Dee-Dee was trying to make me laugh; she seemed a little bit jealous of my friendship with Lucinda.

"Are you going to write to her to say thanks for phoning?" she asked in a stage whisper. I waved at her to shut up when, funny, I could have sworn I heard Lucinda say "Jimmy."

"Sorry, pardon I didn't catch that."

"I was just saying," she sounded desperately embarrassed, "that your secret is safe with us. We've discussed it at length and agreed, we'd never tell Giles."

"About?"

"About Jimmy, of course." She sounded puzzled. She wasn't to know I had absolutely no recollection of ever mentioning Jimmy's name.

I hurriedly brought the conversation to an end, put the phone down, and turned to face an astounded Dee-Dee.

"What the hell have you done, Kathy?" This was clearly rhetorical, as she had heard every word. "Why would you tell that old horse secrets that even I had to drag out of you?"

"I was drunk, and I don't need to tell you stuff; you already know everything there is to know about me."

"Only 'cos you're so bloody transparent."

I was too preoccupied to take offence. "Oh bugger, I must have told her all about Jimmy, and she's obviously told Bertie. So that's why he was funny with me in the pub. Anyway, she's not an old horse; she's really nice."

"You'd better hope so."

"It's Bertie I'm worried about."

"Well don't be. He's the least of your worries." Whatever could she mean?

How to handle Sundays (bloody Sundays)

Mother rang and Giles answered the phone. When I realized she was inviting us home for Sunday lunch I did a little pantomime of projectile vomiting and slashing of my throat. Giles looked alarmed and mouthed, "Are you alright, Pumpkin?"

Making a mental note never to partner him at charades, I staggered melodramatically over to him, removed his tie, wrapped it round my neck and pretended to hang myself. I was really getting into my death scene, making groaning noises and everything, when Giles said down the phone, "Lovely, Elisabeth, we will be with you at noon." And with that he hung up.

"Lovely!" I exclaimed. "Just remind me; which part of my mother doing her Lady Bountiful act answers to the description 'lovely'. The water logged cabbage perhaps? Or the fruit cocktail in heavy syrup served with the compulsory triangles of brown bread and butter? No I've got it – it's that glorious part of the afternoon when we get to sit in the front room, eating stale Ferrero Rochas and listening to mother warbling along to *Songs Of Praise.*"

"She's worried about you, and Darren's missing you," said Giles quietly. It was the only thing that would make me agree to a visit home. Giles manipulation skills were improving.

"My mother has never worried about me in her life, but it's okay, we'll go; just don't expect me to enjoy it." Usually, I'd have come up with a better retort than that but my display of method acting had rendered me exhausted.

Despite an assortment of delaying tactics – hiding the car keys, feigning illness, locking myself in the bathroom, and so on – we arrived at mother's just after twelve o'clock. She was in the front garden; she claimed that she'd just popped out to pick some mint from the patch of scrub she called a herb garden, but judging by her sub-zero body temperature when she pecked me on the cheek, she'd been keeping watch for hours.

"You're freezing; come on, let's go inside," I said, feeling a little bit sorry for her.

"Oh you know me," she answered with a girly giggle, directed at Giles. "I'm a hot-blooded woman." The slight feeling of sorrow I'd felt for her regressed into the usual intense irritation.

Darren was sitting on the bottom of the stairs, singing tunelessly to himself. When he saw me he rushed over, arms and legs flying all over the place, and greeted me with that big, soft smile of his and the usual snotty lick of a kiss.

"Kay-Kay," he said, almost shyly. I felt guilty for not spending more time with him recently – seeing him made pregnancy and depression seem like no excuse at all.

"Aye, aye, Captain," said Giles with a salute and a click of his heels. "How's tricks?"

"Ayes," said Darren, giving a sort of hop and a wave – his uncoordinated response to Giles's rather formal greeting.

Mother fussed around Sebastian, showering him with the latest load of offerings she'd bagged from a car-boot sale. A drum (would she never learn?), a football and a one-legged Action Man, clearly wounded in battle. Sebastian ignored everything except the drum, which he proceeded to bash for the rest of the day. Darren marched up and down with Action

Man strapped to his back, encouraged by mother's "A, hup, two, three, four . . ." The only relief we had from the incessant noise of her small but noisy platoon was when they surrendered arms to eat lunch.

Actually the food was better than usual: only one lump per forkful of mash, custard that actually moved around the bowl, and she'd even put a swirl of cream on top of the Heinz tomato soup! I soon found out why.

"This treacle tart is delightful, Elisabeth," simpered Giles

"It's one of Delia's," Mother smirked. "See, our Kathryn, Delia's a wonderful example of a self-made woman, and she got where she is without a single O' level."

The fact that mother had stopped me from going to university was an ongoing bone of contention, but now she had proof positive that she'd been right all along, in the shape of Delia and her lack of GCEs. I'm sure Mother would have gone on to extol the virtues of the good old days when eight-year-old children left school and worked in the cotton mills or got sent up chimneys, but she noticed that Darren was messing with his custard.

"Stop playing with your food, our Darren."

"I'm doing a picture," he replied.

"Not at the table you're not."

"Want to paint."

"No, it's too messy; finish your dinner and I'll get the crayons."

"No, I want to paint. Crayons are for babies; I'm not a baby." Then to prove his point, he burst into tears adding an extra touch of flavour to the Delia-inspired pudding.

"What's wrong?" I asked, taking his hand in mine, but he was sobbing too much to answer. I soothed him, gently stroking his forehead and whispering in his ear, just like I did when he was little. "Come on, tell me what's up. How can I help you if I don't know?"

He eventually calmed down enough to answer. "I said 'baby'."

"That's okay. It's not a swear word, you know."

"But Mum said I can't talk about babies, not now your baby's dead."

"But you can talk to me about anything," I said.

"My friend Luke went to heaven cos his heart stopped beating. He'll look after your baby." Darren said, cheering up.

Mother was beginning to look a bit stressed. Thankfully, Giles was on hand to create a diversion.

He tapped Darren on the shoulder. "Tell you what, Captain. How about coming to stay with us next weekend? We can make a studio in the barn and do some painting together. I'll pick you up from the centre on Friday."

"School." I shot at Giles.

"Bessy as well," said Darren.

"Who's Bessy?"

"His girlfriend," said mother wearily. "I'm worried to death. He's getting a bit, you know . . ." She nodded her head in the general direction of poor Darren's trousers.

"A bit what?" I asked, feigning innocence.

"You know," she lowered her voice. "Active in the downstairs area."

I covered my mouth with my hand and swallowed a massive giggle.

"Best not bring her, Old Chap," interrupted Giles, in his role of Patron Saint of Peacekeepers. "We're going to get down to some serious painting, so we don't want a load of women around the place distracting us." I loved the way Giles spoke to Darren, without any hint of talking down to him. I wasn't quite so sure about the sexist content though.

So we got into a routine of having Darren to stay every other weekend. After breakfast, he and Giles would disappear for hours on end taking with them their easels, brushes, and paints. Giles said Darren was a "smashing little artist," but I wasn't allowed to see his work. Apparently, it was top secret, but Giles was always keen to show me his own etchings. I'm no art critic but I can say with a degree of certainty that Picasso, he was not.

How to nurture your inner child

With the resilience of youth, I soon felt better and stronger after losing my baby and couldn't wait to get pregnant again. But I had to wait another three years for my daughter to arrive. In the meantime, my friendship with Dee-Dee grew stronger.

In winter, we went to the pictures or shopping, and in summer we spent long, sunny days in the beer garden of a nearby pub. We knew Giles wouldn't approve so we took the precaution of telling Sebastian it was the park so, in the unlikely event of Giles asking about his day, we would be in the clear. As Dee-Dee so often said, Giles had some very old-fashioned ideas about child rearing. I think at that time, Giles loathed Dee-Dee but, in a funny way, it was down to her that our marriage survived. She was fun and sparkle in contrast to my husband's earnest drabness. She could be insensitive to the point of cruelty, but she was such intoxicating company – if only Giles could see it.

I had a wonderfully serene pregnancy and was thrilled with the arrival of little Jessica. I couldn't wait to get her home, but on the day we were to leave hospital, Giles had a long-standing engagement with some clay pigeons. There was no doubt about it; he was a disappointed man. For some reason, he'd wanted me to have another son. Who knows, maybe he planned to spend some time with this one.

Dee-Dee took time off work to bring us home from hospital. In a startling career change, she was now the spa manager of the newly revamped Grimley Manor Spa and Fitness Centre. Her job entailed much tossing of hair and posing around in Lycra. She arrived at the maternity ward all skinny and sun-tanned, looking for all the world like an advert for shampoo.

"Gosh the lighting's awful in here," she said far too loudly. "Everyone looks shattered."

I ushered her out before the sleep-deprived mob had chance to turn on her. She had planned to take us home via the pub, but thankfully she decided that I smelled too strongly of yogurt so opted for home instead.

I wasn't sure how Sebastian would take to his little sister. When I'd asked what sort of baby he wanted he'd answered, "A baby gerbil."

Poor Jessica would have been guaranteed a warmer welcome from the men in her life if only she'd been born a male rodent. But I needn't have worried; Sebastian was delighted with his sister and very impressed with her seagull impersonations. I'd bought him a present – a toy garage with a lift, car wash, and four brightly coloured cars: yellow, blue, orange, and red. I told him it was from the baby and amazingly he loved it. From that moment on, in Sebastian's eyes, Jessica could do no wrong.

So in many ways, my life was ideal. I lived in a huge mansion with my two perfect children; I had a fantastic best friend, and a husband who adored me. But that was the problem. If only I could adore him back.

Dee-Dee had given me a load of women's magazines. Maybe I should follow the advice in *Cosmo* and "Rekindle the love?" Obviously a slight problem there, the clue being in the word rekindle! I flicked through a few more pages, searching for inspiration, when I came across an article entitled: *Nurture your inner child and the rest will follow*. It gave all sorts of advice about not stifling your child-like need to play and learning to frolic like a kid again. It said we should always look at the world in wonderment. I quite liked the idea of that and thought I'd be pretty good at it, but first I needed know what sort of child was living inside me. So I did the quiz, not just for myself but also for Dee-Dee and Giles.

According to my score, my inner child is sad, which is why I'm emotional and sensitive. I need to open my eyes to the beauty and majesty of nature. Dee-Dee came out as a free-spirited pixie with an elf living inside her (I would have said it was a demon). The article said she should throw herself a child's party and invite friends to bring their inner child to play children's games. I decided not to mention it to her as I couldn't really imagine her bobbing for apples or playing hide-and-seek, although I assumed she'd be up for kiss-catch. Giles didn't fall into any one category, so I repeated the quiz for him. But I still couldn't find his inner child. It wasn't coming out to play; it was hidden away, controlled and repressed.

Performing fellatio

Some dates stay with us forever, etched on our memory in indelible ink. For some, it's the death of an icon, say John Lennon. Others may remember major disasters such as Aberfan or the Munich air crash. After a couple of pints, my granddad is guaranteed to reminisce about the glorious day – Saturday, July 23, 1966 – when England won the World Cup. While mother bangs on interminably about the day Prince Charles was invested as the Prince of Wales. "Bless his little heart, all solemn and dignified in his brand new uniform."

Me, I will never forget Thursday, 19th June, 1984 – the day I fell under the spell of Rafael Margolis, a man every bit as glamorous as his name suggests.

It had started off as a pretty normal sort of day. As usual, I tripped on the threadbare stair carpet when I walked down the grand old Havers Hall staircase, and cursed Giles for his meanness in not replacing it. And, judging by the smell emanating from the kitchen, Nanny was still hell-bent on her one-woman campaign to raise the nation's cholesterol levels.

I picked up the post and sifted through it, throwing all the bills and circulars onto the hall desk. Did we want double-glazing? I doubted it; it was hardly in keeping with the Havers' family ethic and no, I did not want to join the RAC. But In amongst the drab and dross was something out of the ordinary – an invitation. I ripped it open.

Giles's accountant was retiring and his partners wanted us to join a celebration dinner. A party of accountants! Would the excitement never end?

The next letter was from Social Services, saying that as I hadn't attended the Mother and Baby Clinic for over a year, someone would be calling round on June 19th to assess Jessica's progress. Unnecessarily I looked at my watch. It didn't help: today's date was the still the 19th. Social workers terrified me; they made me feel entirely inadequate as a mother, and somehow Jessica picked up on this and played dumb in case she did the wrong thing and got whisked into care. I shoved the letter into my jeans pocket, wondering if I should go out for the day. I was about to pour coffee when the doorbell rang. To my relief, it was Bertie. He'd come to take Giles off to Scotland for a long weekend of fishing.

The night before I'd argued with Giles about the trip. I felt he should stay at home as Sebastian was having his first sleepover but, silly me, how could I have forgotten that parties were strictly women's work in the Havers' household? *Haw, haw, haw!*

I ushered Bertie into the morning room, where Giles was tucking into a huge fry up. There was much slapping of backs and hearty laughter as they realized they had both decided to wear kilts in honour of their trip.

Thankfully, Dee-Dee arrived. She was moving in to help with the children and keep me company for a few days. But of course, she had an alternative plan.

"There's a huge music festival going on, and I've got tickets," she whispered. "We'll go first thing in the morning."

"But I can't leave the children here with Nanny. Sebastian's invited half his class to stay." I felt really disappointed; Dee-Dee was so busy with work these days that we hardly saw each other at weekends. "And I've got Social Services coming round to check on Jessica's progress."

"Then immediate action is called for. You don't want them poking their noses in. We'll go today and take Jessica and Sebastian with us. Oh please say, yes; Sebastian would love it. Tell Nanny to ring round and cancel the party."

"But I haven't any spare money. I can't pay for a hotel. You know how tight Giles is."

She just gave me one of her mysterious looks and said it was all taken care of. I found myself agreeing to go, even though I knew I shouldn't be taking Sebastian out of school. I'd better make sure Giles didn't find out.

I had a feeling that Dee-Dee was up to something; she looked even more dazzling than usual. True, it wasn't obvious to the untrained eye because she was wearing hardly any makeup and was dressed in jeans and a little white t-shirt, but I wasn't fooled. I could tell that she'd put hours into that fresh, understated look.

"I'll just go and say hi to Giles. Is he through there?" she asked, pointing towards the kitchen. I nodded – I confess, I was confused. Usually, she did her best to ignore my husband.

We walked together into the morning room, and I watched her float around the table, all flirty and flighty, embarrassing poor Bertie who kept his eyes determinedly fixed on his plate of devilled kidneys. Dee-Dee doesn't like being ignored so she bent down toward Bertie and, thrusting out her cleavage, kissed him on the lips. He jerked away as if he'd been stung by an exotic, venomous creature and the coffee pot went crashing to the floor, splattering coffee over the rug and up the oak-panelled walls. Not like Bertie to be so clumsy. I tutted at him and half-heartedly dabbed at the mess with a starched napkin. Honestly, having Dee-Dee for a friend was like being twinned with an Exocet missile.

I looked at my watch. If our plan to go to Glastonbury was to work, we needed Giles and Bertie to leave before Sebastian's supposed school run. To aid them on their way, I gathered together food hampers, fishing tackle, and all the rest of their rigmarole. It was all going well until we realized that one of Giles's green wellies had gone astray.

"I know," Bertie said. "Let's have a search party. We'll go off in pairs. Giles and Jessica can look in the barn, and Sebastian and Kate, you search the Land Rover and Dee-Dee, you come with me."

Do public school boys ever grow up? I didn't dare look at Dee-Dee, who was bound to turn her nose up at this particular jolly caper, but to my surprise she looked perfectly happy.

Sebastian and I walked across the field to the garage. I opened the boot of the car and hallelujah, there was the orphaned Wellington boot. We strode victoriously back to the house, Sebastian waving the welly in the air. I remembered that I'd promised to put a road map in the car so I made my way to the study, Sebastian following a few steps behind so that I was able to protect him for just a few moments after I opened the study door. For there, sitting on my husband's desk, an expression of pure joy replacing the usual one of genteel bafflement, was Bertie. And, bobbing rhythmically underneath his kilt, was the head and shoulders of my very best friend! I was lost for words. Bertie was aghast, while Dee-Dee alone was happily oblivious to the scene, until my son piped up.

"Aunty Dee-Dee, are you playing hide and seek?"

"Yes, yes, she is," I cried, relieved. "It's your turn now so run, I'll start counting. One, two, three. . . " Sebastian sped off to hide. His innocence was enough to bring tears to my eyes as I quickly shut the door and waited for a red-faced Dee-Dee to emerge from her happy Highland hideaway.

I didn't say very much as we drove through the village. I was really mad with Dee-Dee for messing around with my husband's friend and was trying to work out what I'd just seen. Well, obviously I knew what I'd seen, but what did it mean? Bertie and Dee-Dee? Never!

Dee-Dee, of course, was acting as if nothing had happened. She just drove along, cigarette in one hand, steering wheel in the other, paying little or no heed to road traffic conventions while verbally abusing the good folk of Grimley.

"What is that woman wearing? Do you think that she actually got up this morning and chose to put that dress on? With those shoes? And what about him? Does he really believe that a polyester blazer is a good look?" She was just starting on an overly made-up middle-aged woman when curiosity overtook my silent disapproval.

"What was all that about?" I asked. "In the study?"

"All what?" As she turned to look at me the morning sun shone into the car, creating a misleadingly angelic halo of light around her face.

"You and Bertie, of course."

"Nothing!" She shrugged as if it was completely normal to have oral sex with other people's houseguests – not to mention other women's husbands. I thought of poor faded Lucinda in her worn-out brogues and cashmere twin-sets. What chance did she have against the fabulousness of Dee-Dee?

I continued with the cross-examination. "Nothing! What do you mean, nothing? You were . . ." Aware of my children playing in the back of the car, I lowered my voice to an accusing whisper. "You were performing fellatio on poor Bertie."

Dee-Dee burst out laughing. "Firstly 'poor Bertie' and his surprisingly ample, ginger willy were having the time of their sad little lives and secondly, 'performing fellatio'? Where did that come from? It makes me sound like a concert pianist or something." She carried on in a theatrical voice. "Tonight ladies and gentlemen for your delectation, accompanied by the gentlemen of the Grimley Church male voice choir, Dee-Dee Divine will be performing fellatio."

I burst out laughing and Dee-Dee joined in, confident that she had me back on her side. As if there was ever any doubt.

It was mid-afternoon by the time Dee-Dee swung her new, red MGB GT into the Cotswold Inn's car park. We must have looked a strange group as we spilled out of the car; I looked all mumsy because I hadn't prepared for the trip, while Dee-Dee looked half-nymph, half-porn star. The sun was so hot earlier that she had pulled in to a lay-by to take the top off her car, but she hadn't stopped at that – she had also removed her t-shirt and driven the rest of the way with her seat belt nestling between her Wonder Bra'd breasts, for once seemingly unconcerned about strap marks.

She abandoned rather than parked her car alongside a swanky set of Jaguars, Porsches, and Bentleys. She stretched her arms high above her head before squeezing back into her tee shirt. "Right you lot," she said, "give me a hand with the luggage."

"What are we doing here?" I asked. "I thought we were camping."

"Camping? Hell no! What gave you that idea?"

"You said it wouldn't cost much."

"Well, it won't. We're staying here. Come on, what're you waiting for?"

We followed her through the car park and into the inn's reception area, where a small dapper man with a phony sounding French accent greeted her.

"Miss Divine, so wonderful to see you again. I 'ave prepared for you and your friends our family suite." He lowered his voice. "As our guests, naturally."

How did she do it? Well, I had my suspicions of course, especially after the Bertie incident. But when I tackled her about it she just said, rather vaguely I thought, that they were old friends. So holding Sebastian's hand and carrying Jess, who somehow managed to cling on to her threadbare Piglet even in her sleep, I obediently followed Dee-Dee and the bellboy up the narrow stairs and along the oak-beamed corridors. The boy threw open the door to our suite.

It was so splendid that it made Grimley Manor look like a youth hostel. There were three inter-connecting rooms, all with low ceilings and elm beams. In one there was a huge four-poster bed, another had twin beds and a cot for Jess. Both rooms led into a vast sitting area. I looked around the room. Under the big picture window was a mini bar and beside that a long, mahogany table which was home to a bottle of local water, a tin of shortbread, a carafe of sherry, and four, tiny glasses.

I went over to get the children a drink and a biscuit. I was about to pour some sweet sherry for Dee-Dee and myself when I looked out over the car park.

And that's when I saw him.

I caught my breath and, for the first time in my life, I knew what they meant by love at first sight.

"Dee-Dee," I gasped, nodding at the window, "look."

She followed my gaze. "Nice, at least twenty grand's worth."

I nudged her to look again. "Not the car, the driver."

She wrinkled her nose. "Not really my type – a bit too smooth looking for me."

I knew this was nonsense. She didn't have a type; in fact, she always said that when it came to copping off her only stipulations were he must be male and over sixteen – although I suspected that in reality she wouldn't be too averse to an androgynous fifteen-year-old.

"Well, I think he's gorgeous," I said. "Just look at his body, those shoulders . . ."

"Kathryn Havers! I'm surprised at you – a married woman!"

"I can look, can't I?"

"You can do what you want, just don't give me a hard time about Bertie."

I was amazed at her audacity. "Admiring someone from afar is hardly the same as having casual sex with a married man."

"It wasn't casual."

"What do you mean, it wasn't casual?"

"He'd got his kilt on."

"That's not funny," I said although actually I thought it was. "Come on, tell – are you and Bertie having an affair?"

"God, Kathryn, just leave it will you?"

I shrugged my shoulders. "No, I want to know the truth."

"Okay. Who do you think bought me the car?"

"No!"

"Yes, and now you know, so shut up about it."

I saw the handsome stranger again later that night. Jessica hadn't lasted the course at dinner; she fell asleep face down in her sherry trifle, so I took her up to the bedroom. She hardly stirred as I changed her into her pyjamas and tucked her into the cot. I sat with her for a while, enjoying the sound of her breathing and the strange little animal noises she made. When I was confident she was in a deep sleep, I switched on the baby monitor and went to join Dee-Dee and Sebastian in the resident's bar. They were playing cards, Dee-Dee winning while Sebastian attempted a brave smile as he handed over the last few coins of his pocket money. There were times when Dee-Dee's competitive streak got a bit out of hand.

We were just about to order a bed-time Horlicks for Sebastian when *he* walked into the bar, strikingly handsome despite strange brown marks down his cheeks. He was carrying my daughter and Piglet in his arms, and the blatant hussy was smiling up at him with wide-eyed adoration. I stood up to retrieve her as he walked to our table.

"Does she belong to you by any chance?" he asked in a voice as deep and velvety brown as the chocolate streaks on his face.

Dee-Dee jumped up and pretended to check the label in Jess's sleep-suit. "Baby Chanel, yes, I do believe she's ours." She cracked out laughing, but the beautiful stranger locked eyes with me, apparently oblivious to Dee-Dee's chortling.

I forced myself to speak. "Where did you find her? She was asleep in her cot ten minutes ago." Banal words I know, but he looked at me as if I'd said I'd accidentally stumbled on the solution to world peace.

"She must have climbed out. Perhaps she's planning on being a mountaineer when she grows up. Although to be honest when I found her she was in the corridor helping herself to sweets from the maid's trolley, so maybe she's more suited to a life of crime."

I burst out laughing but when I looked at Dee-Dee to share the moment, all she managed was a sulky sneer.

I thanked him for rescuing Jess, and he introduced himself and asked if he could join us. I agreed at once, unlike Dee-Dee who weighed it up for a few minutes before saying, "Okay, but we only drink champagne."

This was clearly a lie as our table was littered with an empty bottle of the house white, a cork, and a couple of used glasses. But she had no shame.

The champagne arrived in an ice bucket, which inevitably Sebastian knocked over. Rafael – wet, chocolaty, but unperturbed – asked the waiter for another bottle and a foolhardy side order of Knickerbocker Glory for Sebastian. I wasn't sure why Dee-Dee was in a mood with me but the drink seemed to mellow her, and she was soon joking around with Rafael, saying that if it wasn't for do-gooders like him, we'd have one less child to drag around the countryside.

Sebastian began to tug at his hair, a sure sign he was exhausted, so reluctantly I left Dee-Dee and Rafael together while I put both children to bed. Thank God, Sebastian had grown out of bedtime stories and I could rush through the good night routine – I couldn't take the risk of leaving Dee-Dee and Rafael alone for long. On her current form, Dee-Dee would have shagged and bagged Rafael before I could say happily ever after.

But I'd misjudged her. When I rejoined them, she was innocently talking about the people she knew in Manchester. It transpired that Rafael lived and worked as a barrister across the Pennines, just a few miles away from Havers Hall. For once, I grasped the moment and said, "My husband would love to meet you. Maybe you could join us for dinner next week? Might be best not to mention Jessica's nocturnal wanderings though; Giles is of a nervous disposition."

He laughingly accepted the invitation and, as easily as that, Rafael was in my life. I had no idea where my new friendship was going or what I wanted to happen. I just knew that I had to see him again.

Dee-Dee and I had a massive argument when we got to the room; we were so loud that I was surprised the children slept. She turned all goody-goody and actually had the nerve to accuse me of coming on to Rafael.

"What the hell are you doing, Kathy? Out on the pull in front of your children, what were you thinking?"

"That's rich coming from you. What is this? The moral code according to Dee-Dee Divine – should be a refreshingly short read." Nasty I know but why should she be out to burst my bubble, just 'cos I got the attention for once?

Of course Dee-Dee retaliated viciously. "I may be a bit flirty from time to time, but at least when I have kids they'll know who their father is!"

"And what about Lucinda's children?"

"We're talking about you, not that old horse. Oh and by the way, Bertie says she thinks you're common and not nearly good enough for Giles. She says he should have stuck with Felicity."

"Who?"

"Bertie wouldn't tell me. His ex I expect."

I told her Lucinda would never talk about me like that but, even as I said it, I wondered if it were true. Either way, it took the sparkle out of the day.

I was so upset that I didn't think I'd be able to sleep but, to my surprise, I nodded off quite quickly and didn't stir until I felt Sebastian snuggle into me at around seven o'clock.

"Mummy," he whispered, "where's Aunty Dee-Dee?"

"Fast asleep, I expect."

"She isn't here, I've looked."

I felt suddenly alarmed. I wouldn't put it past her to storm off and leave us to make our own way home. I scrambled out of bed, padded over to the window and threw open the blind. Her car was still there! Relief was quickly followed by desolation as I realized that Rafael's shiny silver BMW had been replaced by a dirty, great big Tetley's delivery van. Bugger! Surely he hadn't left without saying goodbye or exchanging addresses.

I wasn't worried about Dee-Dee. I knew she was off on some frolic of her own, which probably involved French-kissing the not-so-French manager. In a way I was glad she'd gone because I was determined not to talk to her. But then there was a knock on the door and I knew it was Dee-Dee because, as always, she rapped out the beat to *Don't you want me baby.*

As I went to open it I saw something on the floor that made me want to laugh and sing and do cartwheels round the room. It was a letter from him. Luckily for me, my denim jacket was hanging on an ornate brass hook by the door so I quickly shoved the note into my pocket and opened the door to allow Dee-Dee to come dancing in.

I could see she was on a high and that last night's argument was nothing but a distant blip, so I gave up brooding about it. What was the point? The sun was shining, the children were happy, and I had met the man of my dreams.

Learn the power of the written word

I didn't read the note until I was home and the children were tucked up in bed.

> *19 Lowry Mansions*
> *Manchester*
> *22nd June 1984*
> *Dear Katy,*
>
> *So sorry I didn't get to say goodbye today but I'm afraid I had to leave unexpectedly early this morning. My mother called to say that I was needed urgently at home. Nothing to worry about – apart from missing you and breakfast.*
>
> *It was lovely to get to know you and your delightful children, and I am very much looking forward to seeing you on Saturday and, of course, meeting your husband.*
>
> *Please provide directions to your home, and confirm the time I should arrive.*
>
> *Kind regards,*
> *Rafael.*
>
> *P.S. Should I wear waterproofs or will the children be dining separately?*
>
> *Havers Hall*
> *Grimley*
> *Derbyshire*

A Young Woman's Guide to Carrying On

Dear Rafael,
We loved meeting you too, and I hope that everything was well at home. After you left, we went to Glastonbury where we had a great time and heard some fantastic music. To my eternal shame, Jessica liked Ian Drury and the Blockheads best. She spent the whole evening tottering around singing, "Hit me with your whythm stick" – I'm hoping that maybe the fumes from the hash and mash bar had something to do with her dubious taste!
I have enclosed a route map and we will expect you around seven o'clock.
Best wishes,
Katy.
P.S. Did I mention stopping the night? You are very welcome to - yes, bring bed-socks and thermals – the place is like an igloo, even in summer.
P.P.S. Dress is informal – waterproofs recommended for breakfast only!

I was pleased with my breezy reply. It was succinct and to the point, and nobody could have guessed I'd stayed awake for most of the night composing it. I didn't trust Nanny with my precious missive so I planned to take it down to the village Post Office after breakfast, which I should have missed altogether as it was hardly a relaxing experience. Sebastian fretted over unfinished homework, while Nanny force-fed poor Jessica with porridge and honey.

Giles was undoubtedly in a strop; funny how it didn't affect his appetite, but then nothing ever did. He kept rubbing his hands together in that irritating way of his as he tucked into eggs, bacon, sausage, tomatoes, fried bread, and black pudding. "Lovely Nanny, just the job." He almost swooned.

Strange how he managed to beam at Nanny and glare at me all at the same time.

Eventually, after he'd finished his breakfast, Giles spoke to me. Apparently, Sebastian's headmaster had telephoned to ask why Sebastian was absent from school last Friday. Nanny had taken the call and told Giles that it was a regular occurrence. So inevitably, Giles quizzed Sebastian about his weekend away. I have to say my son did brilliantly well under cross-examination, somehow making Glastonbury sound like a boy-scout parade.

I took complete advantage of any misunderstanding. "Oh sorry, Giles, did I say school camp? I meant his cub troop, of course. I'm sure I mentioned it and I must have sent a note to school – oh and that reminds me, I need some money for his outfit thing."

"You mean uniform," said Nanny with a scowl.

I gave her my sweetest smile. "It was so nice of you to look after Giles when he came home yesterday. As a thank-you, I insist you take next Saturday off. I'm having a guest over so I'll do the cooking, but could you arrive early on Sunday morning to clear up and serve breakfast?"

"But Pumpkin, I've already invited Bertie and his family over to stay next weekend."

It was Nanny's turn to bestow a triumphant smile on me. She knew I would struggle to look after all the children and cook dinner. Quick as a flash she said, "Thank you, a Saturday to myself would be very nice, if you're sure you can manage."

What could I say? I wasn't going to back down. It looked like I was in for a pretty busy weekend.

I left Jessica with Nanny and caught up with Dee-Dee for a lunchtime drink at Grimley Manor. She had a present for Sebastian, a signed Manchester United football shirt acquired, I'm sure, for the sole purpose of winding up Giles (soccer's very working class, don't you know?) She also had a gift for Jessica so she wouldn't feel left out.

She wasn't supposed to be in the bar while on duty at the spa but, of course, she got away with it. I told her that I'd landed myself with a load of extra work on Saturday and was looking forward to a good old moan about it, but she wasn't listening. She was making eye contact with a load of boisterous men at the next table, pouting, licking her lips and striking the oddest of poses.

To get her attention, I told her what I was going to cook. After men and clothes, food was her favourite subject. Somehow she got the impression that she was invited to join us for dinner on Saturday and started planning what to wear. I couldn't tell her she wasn't welcome, it would have been rude. But I wasn't sure it was a good idea, given her relationship with Bertie – and she was bound to flirt with Rafael. Still, at least she offered to come round early to give me a hand.

When I arrived back home, I realized that Gruesome Newsome was back on the scene. I heard her and Nanny in the kitchen having tea, cackling over their eye of newt and toe of frog.

"Oh she's a wrong 'un alright. Poor Master Giles has been taken for a proper ride. It's the poor kiddies I feel sorry for. She lets them run wild – no proper routine, bedtime whenever it suits her, and as much television as they want."

At one time, overhearing something like this would have made me want to cry and run away but, under Dee-Dee's mentoring scheme, I'd toughened up enough to confront them. I took a deep breath and waltzed into the kitchen.

"Afternoon, Ladies, not working too hard I hope?"

They glared at me in unison as Jessica scrambled off Nanny's knee and into my arms.

"Look what Mummy's got, Jessica," I said, swinging her up in the air. "It's a present for you; help me open it."

Together we ripped open the parcel to find a little box. We took the lid off and there, nestling between layers of silver tissue paper, was a pair of sparkly, candyfloss-pink, high-heeled shoes labelled: *For little ladies; just like Mummy's*.

I helped Jessica put them on, hoping that Monsieur Saint Laurent never got to hear of this cruel misrepresentation. Jessica giggled with delight as she teetered around the kitchen. I could see that Nanny was bursting to say something, but Mrs. Newsome beat her to it.

"You'd do better to get her some educational toys; she's very behind with her speech you know."

The heat rose up my neck, bringing a flush to my face. "She's just shy, she knows lots of words."

"Hit me with your wythem stick, das is good ich liebe dich," sang Jess obligingly.

"See, she's practically bilingual," I said as I scooped her into my arms and up to the nursery before she did any serious damage.

How to maintain lofty relations

I spent the rest of the week in a whirl of dieting, flossing, and twice-daily sessions on my sun-bed. I also had blonde highlights put through my hair and my nails painted a very vampy, shiny black. By the end of the week, with my light bits darkened and my dark bits lightened, I looked like a negative of my usual self.

And, as if we were under threat of rationing, I ordered enough food from Grimley Manor's finest suppliers to feed a small country.

By Friday afternoon, I had things under control with just a short list of tasks to be completed by bedtime. Thankfully, I had the night to myself. Giles was shooting at Bertie's and staying the night at the castle before they all descended on Saturday. I didn't tell Dee-Dee I was on my own. She'd make me go out for a night on the town and, while the idea of all that dancing and drinking was very tempting, I wanted to look fresh for the arrival of Rafael and I was determined to cook a fantastic meal to show Lucinda that I was a skilled hostess and not a common person unworthy of Giles.

I poured myself a glass of wine, and sat down to read my to-do list.

1. Choose wine from the cellar.
2. Make meringues for the gateaux – recipe says they will keep overnight in airproof container.
3. Make sauce for prawn/avocado starter.
4. Prepare stock from bones, and herbs for pork sauce – put in slow oven.

5. Wash and peel vegetables and slice thinly. Also, blanch chives to tie around veg to make into individual parcels. Leave in bowls of cold water.
6. Set table.

I decided to do the meringues first which is when I discovered whipping with just a fork is very hard and time consuming – not like in the Grimley Manor kitchen where you simply turn a knob on the big machine and, within seconds, mountains of cloudy, sugary dessert appears. I got a bit hot and bothered with all the wrist action so I poured myself another glass of wine, plopping in a couple of ice cubes to cool me down. Giles always banged on about how you shouldn't put ice in wine but he couldn't have been more wrong – it cools you down a treat.

Eventually, the meringues were standing up in stiffish peaks. The intention was to pipe them onto greaseproof paper, but I couldn't find the piping bag so I spooned it out into two big circles then put them to bake in the Aga. I was about to make a start on setting the table when there was a knock on the door.

Mr Purvis had arrived with the fruit and meat I'd ordered. I poured us both a small port – his favourite tipple. It felt like old times, sitting in a kitchen having a chat about this and that, except now he now called me "Madam". I told him not to, but he wouldn't listen. He said that he'd been to visit Mr B and rummaged through his pockets to produce a postcard. On the front was a picture of Mr B in chefs' whites standing outside his B&B wielding a big cleaver. He looked huge beside the little stone cottage – it was a wonder he could fit through the door.

On the back of the card he'd written: *I thought you and Dee-Dee were slap-dash workers, but tha's nowt compared to local lasses, so if yer ever fancy workin' in't middle of nowhere, tha' knows where to come. Keep laughin' x x.*

I smiled to myself and put the card in the kitchen drawer.

Mr. Purvis had to get back to Grimley Manor where a coach party was expected. Shaking his head, he told me about the changes made by the new management. Not only had they turned the lovely old restaurant into a pizzeria, they also made Mr Purvis wear a horrid green and gold uniform with a badge on the pocket saying "Bellboy".

As I showed him out, I decided to ask Giles to give him a job.

Alone again, I went to unpack the dinner party food. I was actually feeling a tiny bit tipsy as I poured another glass of wine – Dee-Dee always says that once you start drinking, it's best to keep the alcohol level topped up to avoid feeling hung-over before bedtime. I sorted out the meat first. There were eight fresh pork fillets, all pink and tender, some bones for stock, and lots of smoky-smelling bacon.

I wanted to try a new recipe I'd found in a magazine. First, you wrap the pork in spinach then bind the fillets together with homemade pate and encase the lot in streaky bacon. It sounded pretty easy and looked very elegant in the photograph. But when I sorted through the greengrocers order, I found a problem with my starter. The avocado pears weren't very ripe. I'd heard that if you put them in a brown bag with bananas, they'd ripen overnight. So I searched until I found one shrivelled-up banana in the bottom of Sebastian's lunch box. I mashed it up and spread a little bit on each pear; I couldn't find a bag so I put them on a brown plate and balanced the lot on top of a pile of towels in the airing cupboard.

Seeing all the linen reminded me that I'd forgotten to borrow a tablecloth from Grimley so I had a quick look through the piles of sheets and pillowcases. All I found was an awful flowery affair covered in scorch marks where some discerning soul had tried to burn off the pattern. It was possible that there was some heirloom linen hiding in the attic, but I wasn't sure I'd be brave enough to go up there on my own.

It was when I went downstairs to fetch a torch that I smelled burning. I snatched the meringues out of the oven. True, they were a little bit black on top and, when I broke into one it was soft and gooey, but that was okay, no-one would notice once I dredged them in icing sugar.

I put the torch in my pocket, picked up the bottle of wine, took a deep breath, and then, taking care not to look down in case it set off my vertigo, I tentatively made my way up the loft-ladder to the attic.

Among the spiders, Christmas decorations and ancient trunks were piles and piles of books, just the usual sort of loft clutter, except that these were probably valuable first editions. I nosed around for a bit, listening out for mice or bats, when I came across a huge wooden box full of old photographs. There was one of Giles at the opera with his parents, another at the ballet and a few showing restrained goodbyes on the quad outside his boarding school.

I picked up another handful of my husband's memories – Giles and his parents walking across some moor land. His father looked young and much more relaxed than he does in the stiff, formal portraits. Lady Havers, however, was much the same as I remembered. As I studied every photograph of her, searching for the bewitching beauty Giles talked of, all I could see was a bossy looking woman with too many chins.

Even when he was a baby, Giles looked exactly the same on every picture – more like a miniature adult than child. He was like a set of those Russian dolls that fit into each other, except instead of the glossy, black mane and the happy, painted-on smile, his ginger hair was combed flat into a side-parting and his expression was that of an anxious man. It's no wonder I'd struggled to locate his inner child.

A Young Woman's Guide to Carrying On

I was beginning to feel a bit squiffy, not to mention spidery, and was about to give up on my quest for linen in favour of a long soak in the bath when I noticed a tall, mahogany wardrobe in a dark corner of the loft. When I opened it, something overhead made little rocking noises. I looked up just as a huge vase fell off the top, spilling sand as it crashed to the floor. The gritty contents went everywhere. I rubbed the sand from my eyes wondering if it were something to do with Giles and his clay pigeons.

Pointing the torch towards the floor I saw that the pot had produced a messy sandpit strewn with cards, candle stubs, and dried flowers. It was then the unhappy truth hit me. Nervously looking over my shoulder for ghosts, I picked up the urn and all glimmer of doubt were removed as I read the inscription – *Mummy and Daddy Reunited Forever, February 1974.*

I shook my head and body violently but the ashes hung in my hair, off my eyelashes, and even in my mouth. For a moment I couldn't move but then, with a practical air, I swept up the couple's remains as best I could and popped them back into their final resting place. Forgetting all about my vertigo, I shot down the loft ladder with all the speed and dexterity of a fireman down his pole. Taking care not to swallow, I made straight for the bathroom cleaned my teeth and then braved the notoriously temperamental shower. It was of course freezing, but I didn't care. I scrubbed myself with a loofah until all particles of my parents-in-law had been removed. I still felt dirty and decided to have a bath. Whilst it was running, I dashed downstairs to the kitchen and put a load of vegetables and beef bones into a casserole dish with some herbs and a sachet of bouquet garni (later I realised it was a tea bag but nobody seemed to notice). I should have taken time to brown everything first, but I didn't want the bath to overflow and I was too traumatized for textbook cookery.

So I bunged the stockpot in a slow oven and ran back upstairs, pausing only to pour myself a brandy.

Fortunately, I was just in time to avoid a serious flood, and the lino was only hardly wet, just a few bubbly puddles really. I paddled round, getting undressed and applying moisturizer. Then I lit some relaxing, scented candles and got into the bath. Water dripped over the side of the tub but not enough to worry about. I soaked for ages and soon I began to see the funny side of my brush with death and planned how I to tell the tale to Dee-Dee.

It was lovely lying in the bubbles, sipping at my nightcap, and thinking how impressed Lucinda and Rafael were going to be with my hostess skills. I went to bed feeling that some of the jobs were out of the way and knowing that, if I made an early start tomorrow, everything would be organized by lunchtime. I made a mental note to check the guest room in case Rafael stayed the night. It was lovely to think of waking up next to him – just a shame that we'd be separated by a wall.

I fell into a deep sleep almost immediately and the next thing I knew, it was morning and Sebastian was waking me up from a very strange dream in which Rafael was a giant spider spinning a web around me. Round and round he went, mesmerizing me with his big, brown eyes. I thoroughly enjoyed being his captive until I saw, dancing around us in a very seductive manner, another spider who wore nothing but a pointy bra and four pairs of pink stilettos. It was Dee-Dee, of course.

I sat up in bed, my head pounding; I desperately needed fluids and painkillers. What time was it? I looked at the tiny clock on my bedside table. Gone half-past ten! Good job my children weren't morning people. I croaked a greeting to Sebastian.

"Darling, will you get me a Coke please?"

"Of course, Madame. Do you want vodka in it?"

"Very funny. Hurry please; it's an emergency."

As Sebastian scampered off on his mercy mission, I eased myself out of bed and into the bathroom to get some aspirin. I opened the door and saw chaos in the mirror – candle wax, smeared makeup, and severe water damage. Turning away, I realized that the bathroom was even worse!

I foraged in the cupboard below the sink to gather the tools of the trade – morning-after facemask, firming eye pads, and defrizzing shampoo. It took a good hour and all the wizardry of Estee Lauder to achieve the desired I-never-touched-a-drop-last-night-look-at-me-I'm-as-fresh-as-a-daisy effect. I sprayed myself with Innocence and made my way downstairs to face the day.

True to her word, Dee-Dee arrived mid-afternoon to give me a hand. She brought news that she'd cajoled Mr Purvis into being our butler for the night. She also brought masses of fresh flowers salvaged from an engagement party at Grimley Manor. While she busied herself making funky arrangements, she asked what I was cooking. As I'd suspected, she hadn't been listening last week in the spa. So I rattled off the menu again. Suddenly, she put her scissors down and looked a little alarmed.

"You do know that Rafael is Jewish?"

It wasn't like her to be racist. "Well, I didn't, but so what?"

"So if he's anything like the Jewish boys I know, he won't be eating your dinner." She gave me a withering look. "Prawns followed by pork – what're you trying to do, give his momma a heart attack?"

My fuddled brain was struggling to cope with such simple tasks as the peeling of potatoes and drinking tea, so the idea of having to plan, shop and cook a whole new dinner menu . . . I sat down at the big, old kitchen table, put my head in my hands, while reminding myself to breathe.

Thank God for Dee-Dee.

"Oh for goodness sake, don't be such a drama queen. Anyone would think you'd never worked in a kitchen!" She opened the fridge with a dramatic flourish and poked around for a few moments. Looking distinctly unimpressed, she went to the freezer and found a huge piece of meat, which she threw in a sink of water to thaw. Then back to the fridge where she ferreted out a crusty-looking wedge of Parmesan cheese and a lemon.

"Well, that's your alternative starter: venison Carpaccio. And I'll get Mr Purvis to nick something from work for mains – easy."

I thought, since she was on a roll, now was probably the best time to mention the disastrous dessert, and even that didn't faze her. "Easy. I'll just scrape off the burnt bits, chop up the rest and cover it with whipped cream and strawberries. We'll call it Havers Mess, to comply with the Trades Description Act."

GILES

I had a good trip with Bertie, although he is going through a tough time at present. Things are not going so well with Lucinda; she's taken to drinking rather a lot and then she becomes aggressive. She actually tried to strangle him other night. He intimated to me that they may separate but he told me to keep it under my hat. On which, of course, I gave him my word.

Arriving home from our fishing expedition, I was more than a little disappointed to see Dee-Dee's wretched red car parked directly in front of my garage. Obviously, the last thing I wanted was to block her in so I drove round to the stable block and parked in the shade of the big oak tree. I helped Lucinda and the children out of the car before removing the luggage from the boot, which I then closed with rather more force than I'd intended.

"Something wrong, Old Chap?" asked Bertie.

"No, of course not," I replied. I couldn't believe she was here. Surely Kate wouldn't have invited her to join us for dinner. I picked up Lucinda's trunk and marched the party over the lawn toward the kitchen door. Poor little Charlie, beguiled by a couple of peacocks, gave chase and somehow managed to stumble, crashing into the water fountain. He let out an almighty yell as he fell to the ground, holding his head. Naturally, Lucinda ran to him and clutched him to her in an effort to soothe him. Unfortunately, this had the opposite effect and the little chap yelled and yelled until he was blue in the face.

"Come on Charlie, be a brave soldier. You know that big boys don't cry. How about a smile for Daddy?" said Bertie. But the boo-hooing continued. I have to confess to a certain feeling of satisfaction as I reflected on the superiority of my son. Even as a toddler he would never have shown himself in such a cowardly light.

Inevitably, the three little girls joined in with their brother's screaming, and the cacophony alerted Kate to our arrival. She came rushing out and took control of things in that lovely, natural way of hers, mopping eyes and shushing cries with the promise of lemonade and cake.

Dee-Dee watched all this with what can only be described as a malicious expression on her face. "Welcome to Havers Hall," she drawled to Lucinda. "A haven of peace and tranquillity."

Lucinda must have been more worried about the little chap than I'd realized, for she didn't offer so much as a glance in Dee-Dee's direction, let alone reply to her.

We eventually went into the house where I was confident that Nanny would sort out the children, but I'd forgotten that Kate had given her the day off. Judging by the state of the kitchen I have to say that Kate was misguided in her generosity. Everywhere seemed rather chaotic. Flowers were stuffed haphazardly in vases alongside a bowlful of burnt cake crumbs and there were sides of meat thawing in the sink. I announced that we chaps would leave the women folk to it and repaired to the study. And that's where we remained, chewing the cud until the arrival of Kate's latest admirer.

The first I saw of him was his silver motorcar, a pretentious sporty design, and I watched from the study window as he unfolded himself from the driver's seat. He was tall and athletic-looking with a rugby player's shoulders and curly, black hair worn a little too long for a man of his age. He dressed, deliberately I suspect, in a tight, black vest that accentuated his concave stomach, and a pair of those denim trousers which, I believe, are commonly known as Levis.

I observed him as he removed a couple of bottles of champagne from the back of his car. He hadn't seen me and I was enjoying the temporary advantage I had over him. It was then that Kate ran out to greet him, her blonde hair shining in the sun and her face aglow with such pleasure that the blood drained from my face and my heart ached as if trampled by a thousand angry elephants.

I banged on the study window to get their attention and gave them the cheeriest wave that I could muster. Kate motioned that we should gather in the drawing room so I straightened my tie, flattened down my hair with the palms of my hands, and marched through the hall – the gloves were off!

"How do you do? Giles Havers." I introduced myself with a firm handshake and unwavering eye contact.

"Nice place you've got, Giles; pleased to meet you," he replied.

Ha! Round one to me. Only plebs and morons say, "Pleased to meet you." Everyone knows that the correct reply to "How do you do?" is "How do you do?"

I was smiling inwardly at his faux pas when little Jessica, all pink and giggly, flung herself into the room and ran towards me like an over-excited puppy heralding its master's homecoming. I felt a glow inside as I bent down to shake her hand but the treacherous little minx ignored me in favour of our glamorous guest.

"Waif, Waif, you came to my house."

I watched his easy grace as he picked up my daughter and swung her high above his head before setting her down on his shoulders.

"Waif, are you a giant?" she lisped.

Feeling rather bilious, I opened the cocktail cabinet and busied myself by pouring out extra large pre-dinner drinks. I'd expected Margolis to drink Bacardi and Coke or some such concoction but to my chagrin, not only did he drink single malt but he also seemed pretty knowledgeable about wine. Somewhat reluctantly, I invited him down to view my cellar.

Learn to entertain with style

Lucinda stepped into the drawing room, took one look at Dee-Dee flirting with Bertie and disappeared upstairs with Charlie leaving me to look after the rest of her brood. I launched a game of hangman; but middle clone, Claire, made it clear that they were too absolutely starving to play games or, as Clarissa put it, practically faint with hunger. I couldn't believe that in all my planning I'd forgotten that the children needed to eat. Of course, I had plenty of stuff for Sebastian and Jessica, but somehow the Clones didn't strike me as alphabetti spaghetti types.

I was even more wrong footed when Bertie followed us through to the kitchen. Thankfully, Dee-Dee was on hand to act as decoy – with her on the case, he wouldn't notice if I fed his offspring stir-fried cockroaches. I didn't; I gave them fish fingers, hoping, as I cooked them, that they wouldn't make my hair smell. I couldn't find any peas in the freezer so I served it with green salad, thereby completely alienating Jessica.

"Mummy, you know I don't like grass," she said, while an even surlier than normal Sebastian moaned about the lack of baked beans.

It was then that Mr Purvis, in full butler's attire, arrived at the kitchen door carrying trays of steaming hot quail. I was thrilled to see him and threw my arms around his neck. Unfortunately, Giles and Rafael chose that moment to emerge from the cellar so I was caught red handed – not just buying dinner, but also hugging the hired help. Although to be strictly accurate, I wasn't paying for either the food or the butlering!

Giles looked confused. "But Pumpkin, I thought you wanted to do the cooking."

I was lost for words.

Thankfully Dee-Dee, out of his sight in the pantry alcove, managed to remove her tongue from Bertie's ear just long enough to say, "Oh she's been slaving in the kitchen all day – these are just a few extras."

Giles beamed at Rafael. "My wife is an excellent cook, don't you know."

I was revelling in the praise when Clarissa held up her soggy fish-finger and said, "Aunt Kate, why are your goujons such a funny shape?"

By the time we sat down for dinner, I felt a bit more relaxed. Giles was being the perfect host, pouring wine and discussing vintages with Rafael, and Dee-Dee was helping Mr Purvis serve the starters from the sideboard.

She approached Lucinda first. "What can I tempt you with, prawns or venison?"

"Just a little venison please," Lucinda snuffled. "I don't have much of an appetite."

Dee-Dee's eyes gleamed as she piled Lucinda's plate high with raw meat and watched with gleeful malevolence as it bled into the Parmesan cheese. Lucinda looked decidedly queasy as she took the food; her pale blue eyes all watery and tinged with pink. She sniffed into a lace hankie, claiming she had hay fever, and gulped back her wine as if it were medicine. I think she'd argued with Bertie. I'm sure I heard raised voices coming from the guest room before dinner. Poor Lucinda, I couldn't help but feel sorry for her despite everything she said about me.

"Bertie, what would you like next?" Dee-Dee licked her lips.

He all but slapped her bottom. "What do you suggest, you saucy serving wench?" Clearly overdosing on the malt whisky had brought out his lascivious streak.

Amazingly, Dee-Dee resisted pouring the prawn cocktail over his head and settled for giving him an unattractive-looking mix of prawns and venison, saying, "Surf and turf for you."

She turned her attention to Rafael. "Carpaccio?"

He shook his head. "No, I'll have the prawns, thanks."

He then went on to eat pork for the main course and wolfed down his pudding with lots of extra cream. Obviously, Dee-Dee had it wrong for once – I guess ethnic dietary rules were never going to be her specialist subject. Either that or he wasn't really Jewish.

After dinner, Giles suggested that the women should retire to the drawing room whilst the men passed port around the table. Our guests couldn't have looked more taken aback if he'd suggested we should all strip naked and stand on our heads.

"I say, Old Chap, I'd rather stay with the girlies," Bertie said.

"I'm not much of a port drinker as it happens. I'll go with the ladies," said Rafael.

"For God's sake, Giles – welcome to the eighties," said Dee-Dee sharply.

Lucinda used the moment to make her longed-for escape. "I think I'd better go and lie down with Charlie for a while; he doesn't seem to be settling."

I felt, as hostess, I should ask her to stay for one more drink. To my surprise she agreed to a small brandy mixed with port, before retiring.

"That's right, old thing, a snifter will help you sleep," said Bertie, ruffling her hair with an unusual display of warmth. Dee-Dee glared at him and then with the sweetest smile imaginable – and with all the flourish of a conjurer pulling a rabbit out of a hat – she removed a letter from her pocket.

"Kathy, I forgot to tell you, I got a letter from that Aussie guy, the one we met at the fancy dress party." She addressed the table, but it was clear that her performance was for Bertie's benefit.

"I was dressed as a bunny girl, but he thought I was a kangaroo so he assumed I was Australian and came over to talk to me. When I told him I was a rabbit he said, 'That's an awfully long way to burrow. Can I get you a carrot juice or something?' " She giggled at the memory.

"Anyway, he's back home in Melbourne and wants me to visit. He runs a sky diving club, and I've always wanted to sky dive. If I go, he's promised to take me to the test match."

"You're not going are you?" Bertie sounded suddenly sober.

"Yes, I love cricket. I used to watch it on telly with my granddad."

"No, I mean to Australia. You're not going to Australia?"

"Of course I'm going to Australia. What's to keep me here? I only need money for the flight and I'll soon save that."

I felt a bit hurt by her reply but guessed it was directed at Bertie. Unfortunately for Bertie, so did Lucinda. She stopped sniffling and looked him in the eye.

"Why should that matter to you, Bertie?" she asked in a steely voice. "Or is the answer obvious?"

Bertie looked wildly around the room for assistance; obviously, he wasn't getting any help from Dee-Dee, or Giles; he was showing off his tin soldier collection to Rafael and was oblivious to any tension in the room. Luckily for Bertie, Mr Purvis was on hand to create a diversion.

"Excuse me, Madame, should I serve coffee in the drawing room?" I nodded as he continued speaking. "Miss Dee-Dee, I couldn't help overhearing your plans to travel. Can I be so bold as to make a suggestion? After all, we have been friends for a very long time."

Dee-Dee put her Bertie-baiting to one side and turned her attention to Mr Purvis.

"Some of my family moved to Australia in the sixties, and I'm sure they'd love to meet a charming young lady from the old country. Should I speak to them for you?" While Dee-Dee talked to Mr Purvis about her proposed trip, I ushered Giles, Rafael, and Bertie through to the drawing room. Lucinda made another escape bid and, this time, I let her run freely upstairs to the sanctity of the guest suite.

As the men spoke of manly things like shooting small birds and scaring foxes to death, I mulled over the evening's events. I knew I should be cross with Dee-Dee for behaving so badly towards Lucinda, but I was too upset at the prospect of her long trip to Australia to be genuinely annoyed. I comforted myself with the thought that she probably had no intention of going anywhere.

I couldn't help but wonder what Rafael was making of my guests. I'm sure he'd got Dee-Dee's measure because he kept exchanging knowing smiles with me as she cavorted round Bertie. And I noticed that, although he was polite when she turned her charm on him, he seemed completely immune to her allure.

I loved his relaxed and natural manner round the dinner table. One minute he'd be chatting to Bertie about his time in Oxford – they both attended the same college, although not at the same time – while the next minute he'd concentrate on being very sweet to Lucinda, appearing genuinely interested in the IQ, wit, and sheer brilliance of her children. And to my delight even Giles warmed to him, so much so, that he was actually proposing a trip to the opera together. Of course, I enthused about the idea, anything to see Rafael again. But I had to tread carefully because, ever eager to improve my mind, Giles had often invited me to accompany him to see *Madame Butterfly* and the like. But I'd always turned down these jaunts, being more of a *Jesus Christ Superstar* sort of girl myself.

Dee-Dee chose that that moment to burst into the room and the conversation. "Let's go and see *Cats*. It's supposed to be fantastic," she said.

Giles gave a little grimace, but he was too polite a host to argue. So, in no time at all, we'd all agreed to spend a weekend in London.

Always be punctilious

A letter arrived on the following Tuesday morning; of course, I recognized Rafael's extravagant handwriting immediately. I tried to look nonchalant as Giles read it out loud.

> *Dear Giles and Kathryn,*
>
> *Thank you very much for such a fantastic weekend. It was so nice to meet you, Giles, and to reacquaint myself with your delightful wife and adorable children. I was particularly impressed by your collection of tin soldiers. All painted by yourself! What a rewarding, if time-consuming, hobby.*
>
> *Being a bachelor it is hard for me to return hospitality in my modest flat. So I wondered if you and your family would do me the honour of joining me for a weekend in London? We could stay in my Chambers' apartment, and I will book theatre tickets for us to see Cats. Do let me know your thoughts.*
>
> *Kind regards,*
> *Rafael Margolis.*
>
> *P.S. I do hope Lucinda has recovered from her hay fever.*

I stifled a giggle at the tin soldier references, and asked Giles what he thought of the idea.

"Maybe we could go at half-term," I suggested.

"Out of the question; I'll deal with it." With an air of finality, he folded up the letter and put it in his pocket. I was determined that we would make the trip, but knew I would have to bide my time.

Later that day, I found Giles's reply to Rafael. It was on the hallstand waiting to be posted. I stuffed it in my pocket and locked myself in the bathroom. Then, taking care not to tear the envelope, I opened it.

Dear Rafael,

Thank you so much for coming to stay with us last weekend. You were the most perfect of houseguests; taking pains to entertain the gentlemen whilst effortlessly captivating our ladies and children. Indeed you were a great hit with my own dear daughter, Jessica; it is always rewarding to see one's own children successfully socially interacting in and out of their own class.

Thank you for your kind invitation. My family and I would of course be delighted to join you in London. Unfortunately, however, I have a very full diary at the moment and we are, as you must understand, unable to take Sebastian out of school. I do understand your difficulty in entertaining at your home so please think no more of it. You owe us nothing. We were paid in abundance by your wit and charisma.

In answer to your kind enquiry, Lucinda seems to be quite recovered from the atypical hay fever attack. I will make it my business to let her know that you asked after her. I'm sure she will be charmed.

Sincerely,
Lord G.G.G. Havers.

How could he be so dismissive of my friend? I was appalled by that rude comment about class and surprised at Giles. For all his faults, I didn't know he was capable of such snobbery. Before I had time to calm down and change my mind, I scribbled my own note to Rafael.

Dear Rafe,

It was lovely to see you again, and thanks for the letter. It really made me giggle. Giles took it upon himself to write the reply but as you can see I intercepted it. I think he may have been a little hasty in dismissing your fantastic invitation. The children and I would certainly love to come and visit over the autumn half-term holiday. Maybe if you invited Lucinda and Bertie, and they were to accept, then Giles might change his mind?

Probably best if you don't mention this letter to Giles, as he wouldn't approve of me reading something he'd addressed to someone else. He is very punctilious about these things, and we don't want him to have an apoplexy now, do we?

You were a great hit on Saturday but I wonder what you made of us all? It was such a pity you couldn't stay for the picnic on Sunday as we'd planned.

Love,

Katy

P.S. Don't you think punctilious is a great word? I heard it yesterday when I was listening to Radio Four (by mistake)!

P.P.S. Ditto apoplexy!

I put both letters in the envelope, resealed it and put it back on the hallstand Two days later, I got a call from Rafael asking if he could meet me on my own.

Watching paint dry is rarely fun

A few days before the big date, I popped in to see Dee-Dee and asked if she'd have the children.

"I don't know, why? Where are you going?" she asked.

"Manchester – why, what of it?"

"You're going to see him, aren't you?" She moodily picked at her nails.

"So what if I am?" I said.

"You're a mug Kathy. Surely you can see he only wants you for one thing."

"Since when did you become my mother?"

"Just don't trust him is all I'm saying. Don't forget what you stand to lose."

"So will you babysit or not?"

"Even Bertie thinks he's a fraud," she said, ignoring me. "He worked it out. The brilliant Mister Margolis never even went to Oxford, let alone get a blue there."

"I couldn't care less which university he went to or what shade of blue he did or didn't get. All I'm bothered about is whether you're going to babysit or not!"

Dee-Dee sighed and shrugged her shoulders. "Okay, yes of course I'll look after them; all I'm saying is take care, okay?"

Dee-Dee arrived in good time for me to get the train into Manchester and meet Rafael in the old Station Hotel. I was early and wandered round the shops. I looked in the sexy underwear department in Kendal Milnes and wondered if my own undies would stand up to scrutiny.

Behind me, a woman's voice called out, "What are you doing here?"

I jumped and turned around, wondering who had followed me all the way from Grimley, only to see that the woman was talking to someone else. Taking it as a sign that I was safe, I bought a new bra and pants set – black and pink, very sexy – and changed into them in the Ladies. I threw my old, functional garments in the incinerator, checked my makeup for the fiftieth time, and left the store. When I arrived at the hotel he was waiting in the foyer. He looked so thrilled and relieved to see me that I felt reassured that I was doing the right thing. He led me through to the lounge bar where we ordered drinks. Despite fancying Rafael like mad I felt unexpected misgivings about betraying Giles. I wondered if I should make an excuse and leave. But then he asked me if I was sure I wanted this.

He looked so handsome and appealing that, ignoring my belated attack of conscience and mother's warning voice twittering in my ear, I nodded. "Yes of course, more than anything!"

The King George Suite was grand only in title and had a seedy splendour associated with old cruise boats or music hall theatres; lots of dark wood, threadbare red velvet, and cracked plaster swirls on the ceiling. A smell of stale cigarette smoke made me wrinkle my nose, spoiling, I knew, the look of sex I'd cultivated. I tried to open the window to let in some fresh air, but the surrounds had been painted shut years before and wouldn't budge. Improvising, I sprayed the room with perfume to mask the stink. I guess I was stalling for time because I felt suddenly nervous and wasn't sure how to handle the moment. The occasion cried out for champagne on ice and romantic music, but the only thing on offer was tap water and the sound of a million niggling doubts buzzing around inside my head.

As Rafael took off his clothes and tossed them over the dressing table, I couldn't help but notice the way he sucked in his already flat stomach and squared his broad shoulders as he admired himself in the mirror. He posed around for a bit and then he turned his attention to me. Starting at my feet, he undressed me. First taking off my shoes and massaging my soles, then slowly unbuttoning my blouse and unzipping my jeans until I was in my underwear. Then with a flick of his hands, he expertly removed my bra and kissed me passionately as he carried me to the bed. His performance thus far was flawless and it occurred to me that he was no stranger to illicit afternoons of sex. As I checked out his erection, I felt fleetingly jealous of all the nameless women who'd gone – or should I say come – before me.

It wasn't the worst sex I'd ever had, but nor was it the best. In fact, as Rafael batted on trying to find my clitoris, I couldn't help but compare the prowess of my two men, an oddly ironic turn of events, to be fantasizing about sex with my husband whilst in bed with my lover.

But it was okay. He did a good deal of prancing around in the buff and made a great exhibition of foreplay. At one stage he actually said, "May I lick you?" What was I supposed to say? I didn't know, so said nothing, He changed position and resumed the cross examination from a different angle, asking me if I liked it soft or hard, fast or slow. I could hear Dee-Dee's voice saying, "For God's sake, are you going to shag her or not?"

There was a moment when I thought he was going to get on with it and actually try a little penetration, but no, he was still preparing to bestow on me the over-rated gift of oral sex – in my considered opinion the 'watching the paint dry' of the whole sticky business. I lay there while he licked and sucked and probed me and, just when I thought I might actually die of boredom, he got on top of me and we had a good old-fashioned shag. What can I say? It was very nice. He was very nice and it was a lovely way to spend the afternoon. He got my jokes, he listened to me and he was, without doubt, the most handsome man I'd ever seen.

I was sure we could work on his bedroom technique.

Beware of the pack at breakfast

I'd planned a secret breakfast picnic with Rafael, but Jessica was behaving like an insecure octopus that morning, and it had taken all my wit and guile to escape her tentacles. Giles barely noticed my leaving. He'd taken to getting up for an early breakfast before going out to plough the fields and scatter.

I wasn't used to him taking such an active part in the running of the estate and told him so when he professed himself too tired to read Jessica a bedtime story the night before. He said he'd had to get rid of a couple of farmhands and had taken over their duties himself.

"What do you mean you had to let them go? I thought they were two of your best workers." He shook his head wearily as if it was he, not them, who was out of work!

"Things are a bit tight, and it's a case of last in, first out, I'm afraid." It sounded reasonable enough – if it wasn't for the fact that the newcomers had been with him for the best part of twenty years.

"Will they get new jobs?"

"For goodness sake, Kate, I don't know if they'll get new jobs or not. I hope they will, I truly do, but at the moment they are the least of my worries."

"Well, if you don't care what happens to them I might as well save my voice," I said and scooped Jessica up onto my knee and read her the damn story myself!

So what with Jessica's clinginess and Giles's bad temper, I was glad to grab the yellow picnic blanket and my lovingly prepared hamper and escape to the secluded little hamlet of Unthank where I'd arranged to meet Rafael. As usual, he arrived late, which was a shame because I had to be back home by midday to make lunch and look after the children. Nanny was taking the afternoon off and, despite my rigorous coaching, Giles still hadn't managed to crack the mysteries of the microwave.

I tried not to look too sulky about my lover's tardy timekeeping as he unravelled himself from his car and strode towards me with a look of mock contrition on his face. A client had delayed him, he said and pointed out that, as he had no inherited wealth, the client was king even at the weekend.

He clearly wanted to get straight down to a bit of mid-morning nooky and began fumbling inside my blouse. I swatted him away, having decided he could wait until after breakfast as a penalty for his lack of punctuality. This was fortuitous for we were still fully clothed, thank God, and eating oysters and dipping chocolate-coated strawberries into Giles's vintage champagne, when we heard a far away rumbling noise – a noise that seemed to be getting closer and closer until a bugle call heralded the arrival of a scared looking baby fox. He put his head on one side, looked at us in astonishment for a few seconds, and then he scampered across our blanket catapulting scrambled eggs, smoked salmon, and bagels skyward. Less than a minute later we found ourselves surrounded by a hoard of red-jacketed, posh people on horseback.

One or two chaps doffed their hats and said, "Morning, Lady Havers." But in the main, they just sniggered and chased off to the local pub where, according to Dee-Dee's sources, I was the butt of many a joke.

It wasn't until they left that I realized Rafael was furious with me. It was almost as if he thought I'd planned the whole embarrassing scene. With no thought for my feelings he stormed off in a rage, leaving me to salvage what was left of the picnic and my pride. As I folded up the blanket, I couldn't help thinking that if Giles had been in Rafael's place, he wouldn't have been so nasty.

I drove off feeling wretched, but the ridiculous thing was that I was much more upset about Rafael stomping off in a rage than the prospect of Giles finding out about my little tryst.

To make my day worse, when I got back home Nanny was waiting in the hall wearing her Sunday best hat and coat along with a very imperious expression.

She fixed me with a glare and tapped her watch. "You're late. I've missed my bus, and my friend will be worrying. I don't like to be late."

I would have been frightened; except I was too amazed that she actually had a friend. "Isn't Giles here?" I asked, knowing he was because I could hear him pottering around in the study.

"Master Giles has enough to do without having to babysit."

"They are his children," I said. "You don't babysit your own children!"

"One day you'll get your comeuppance," she said. "Oh, and you'd better rinse out those thermos flasks before too long or else they'll go mouldy, and I haven't got time to clean them. Mrs. Newsome will be waiting for me."

How did she know about the flasks and did that mean she knew about the picnic? But she couldn't have seen me smuggle out the hamper this morning because she was upstairs. Maybe she really was a witch.

"I don't know what you mean," I lied.

"No, of course you don't," she said darkly. "And I'm the Queen of Sheeba!"

With that flourish of wit standing in for a formal goodbye, she flounced out of the house.

I went upstairs to swap my *femme fatale* wear for a tracksuit, and caught sight of myself in the mirror. It was a marvel – no Pinocchio nose or devils horns – still no trace of the harlot!

Wives should be lovers too

I lay sprawled on the sofa, watching though the window for Nanny to bring the children back from the park. I wished something would happen. I'd expected to hear from Rafael by now, but there had been no word, not even a phone call or a letter. I had an awful feeling that he was still cross about the disastrous picnic. I cheered myself up by wondering, if maybe, for some reason, he couldn't reach me – perhaps the phone lines were down! I hurriedly picked up the telephone, but the familiar burr told me we were still connected.

I walked across to our antiquated television and switched on the news, hoping to hear of postal workers around the country downing tools and refusing to deliver mail. But sadly our great nation was running like clockwork.

The big news on the screen concerned Prince Charles and Lady Diana. She had just given birth to her second son His Royal Highness Prince Henry Charles Albert David Mountbatten-Windsor – gosh it made Sebastian Giles Gilbert George Havers sound practically impoverished. The TV showed crowds gathering to wish Diana well. It seemed that Charles's fairy-tale princess had bewitched the whole nation; that is, apart from her husband. His three damning little words before their marriage still stuck in my mind: "Whatever love is." Unbelievable! If I had been Di, I'd have given him whatever love wasn't.

Soul-searching isn't really my thing, but I confess I was beginning to feel a bit guilty about Giles. He never went a day without telling me he loved me, while I never volunteered it back. Well, only during sex – which had settled into a strict three-times-a-week routine – and everyone knows that doesn't count. I wondered if maybe I should make more of an effort with him. It wouldn't take much to fuss round him when he got home at night, to pour him a drink, and ask about his day.

How did that song go? *Wives must always be lovers too, run to the door the moment he comes home to you.*

I was warming to my theme and even considered baking him a Victoria sponge cake when I was saved from transmogrifying into a fifties housewife by the arrival of Dee-Dee.

She'd been to Sheffield where The Spa paid for her to go to college on day-release. Her face was red and blotchy and she had that peculiar lavendery smell of an old lady's bathroom. I deepened my resolve not to let her try her latest skills on me.

She must have read my mind because she said, "Let me give you a skin peel. I've just had one."

I looked at the angry rash developing on her face and replied, "Hmm, now let me think about that. . . "

"Oh go on, it'll . . ." She put on the voice of a high-pitched cosmetics salesgirl. "Slough away those dead skin cells and reveal a whole new radiant you."

"I would, Dee-Dee, but I've got sensitive skin, remember?"

She paused weighing up how true that was. Deciding it was just about plausible she changed tack. "How about I practice on Jessica then?" I looked aghast. As if I'd let an exfoliator-wielding madwoman anywhere near my precious daughter's skin!

"Well it'll have to be you then."

She kept on at me to be her guinea pig, and I continued refusing. Honestly, I wasn't being mean or unsupportive, it's just that it took so long for my eyebrows to grow back the last time I let her near me, but then she played her trump card. "I spoke to Bertie today, and he told me that Giles has agreed to go to London with Rafael."

"How come? What did he say?"

She silently rapped her perfect nails against her toned, brown arm. Obviously, I wasn't going to get any information out of her until I'd agreed to be her guinea pig and persuaded Jessica and Sebastian to play at spas.

Between performing reflexology on Jessica – not very successfully, due to her extreme ticklishness – and massaging Sebastian's head, Dee-Dee told me that the plan to visit London in the school half-term holidays had been confirmed. Apparently, Bertie and Giles couldn't resist the VIP tickets for The Motor Show that Rafael had magically acquired. We were all going to see *Cats*, and then the women and children would spend the night at Rafael's flat while the Giles and Bertie bunked down in Bertie's club, which was convenient for the motor show the following day.

Dee-Dee took complete advantage of my elated mood and persuaded me to have a body scrub, "to get rid of all those toxins". It was an unpleasant and complicated procedure involving green, smelly, muddy stuff and roll upon roll of cellophane paper.

Unfortunately for my husband, at *the moment he came home to me*, I didn't run to the door to greet him because I was lying immobile on his priceless chaise lounge – film-wrapped and plastered with seaweed.

How to capitalise your opportunities

I'd reached the age of twenty-eight and had only been to London once before, and that was on a school trip.

Now it was really happening, and I was determined that the weekend was going to be fantastic. But we were an unlikely-looking bunch of revellers. Lucinda stayed home claiming a migraine and kept the younger Clones with her. Bertie and his daughter, Clarissa, and her little friend, Henrietta, joined us.

With two spare tickets for *Cats* free, I grabbed the opportunity to invite Darren. Unfortunately, that meant mother came too.

When we arrived in London, Rafael was still at work but he'd arranged for us to dump our bags in his sumptuous apartment – all black leather and cream shag pile.

Being such a mixed crowd, it was hard to decide what we should do with our free afternoon. I didn't care where we went as long as Darren had a good time, and we were back to meet Rafael at six o'clock. However, everyone else had a point of view. The two teenagers were dying to spend their birthday money – apparently they'd heard somewhere that the shopping in Knightsbridge was all right.

Mother said all she wanted was a nice cuppa. I couldn't think of anything worse but, to my relief, Giles said he would be honoured to escort her to afternoon tea.

Tempted by the lure of jam and cake, Jessica and Sebastian decided to go with them.

Bertie was clearly salivating at the prospect of spending some time alone with Dee-Dee, but he was aware that Clarissa was watching him. No doubt Lucinda had charged her daughter with the task of reporting his every move. Then Dee-Dee came up with an idea that suited everyone. We should go to Harrods where we could shop, browse or have tea all under one roof – the subtext being that she and Bertie would pair off, and he'd be able to spend lots of money on her.

So Harrods it was.

Bertie told Clarissa to organize transport and, to my astonishment, she readily agreed to the task. I was surprised because, although she'd been charm itself to the rest of us, she'd spent the better part of the day scowling at her father. But with a grin on her face and a skip in her step, she went into the study to use the phone.

Twenty minutes later, there was a ring on the intercom. It was our taxi. We filed down to the lobby to see a gorgeous young man – all floppy hair and biceps – in a chauffeur's uniform. He claimed to be an out-of-work actor and, judging by Clarissa's besotted smile, he need look no further for his leading lady. He led us outside where quite a crowd had gathered around a bright pink stretch limo. Bertie looked questioningly at his daughter who said, "Daddy, this is Roberto; he's our chauffeur for the weekend. Isn't it cool? It means we can all travel together."

Bertie was lost for words, but I saw a look of deep respect dawn on Dee-Dee's face as she congratulated Clarissa on the mode of transport.

Roberto ushered us into the limo. Darren climbed into the front passenger seat and the teenagers claimed the back row; Jessica scrambled up beside them.

"Do you take credit cards?" Bertie asked Roberto with a resigned smile.

"Of course, Sir, of course. Now, would you prefer vintage or non-vintage champagne?"

Say what you might about the motorized candy-floss-pink tribute to tackiness, we had a great time getting to Harrods. Darren was up-front, wearing Roberto's peaked cap and advising him on the route. The teenagers, their heads stuck out of the sunroof, spent the journey sipping Coke out of red cocktail glasses and planning what they should buy for their weekend wardrobes. Giles pointed out places of interest to our children.

"That's where the Queen lives. No, Jessica, they aren't her children, they are soldiers. They are there to protect her. Yes, I expect you could say it's a bit like having lots of Nannies."

In between sips of champagne, mother smiled graciously and waved out the window to the public, blissfully unaware that no one could see her through the blackened glass. Eventually, Roberto pulled up at the front of the famous London landmark and helped us out onto the busy street. As we said goodbye, he promised he'd be waiting for us, in the same spot, at five o'clock.

In the store we split into smaller groups. I was anxious to go shopping with Darren, but mother kept fussing, telling him not to wander off and to let me know when he needed the loo. Eventually, when she had irritated the hell out of me, Mother left arm-in-arm with Giles, the children in tow. Sebastian bent down to whisper in Jessica's ear, and as he did so a strand of his shiny black hair flopped over her golden curls and into her eyes. She giggled up at him, and it struck me afresh how they couldn't have looked less like brother and sister.

As mother teetered toward the lift in her Sunday-best shoes I heard her say to no one in particular, "This is my son-in-law; he's a Lord you know. We are about to partake of afternoon tea."

I wanted to see the famous Harrods' food department that Mr B had told me so much about. So with Darren's podgy little hand clasped in mine, I weaved my way through the jewellery stands, passed the leather goods, in and out of the cosmetics counters and into the grand hall with its beautiful aromas of meat, fish, cheese, chocolate and coffee.

It was no wonder Mr B loved it. The place was a gourmand's heaven, from the piles of shiny fresh fruits and exotic vegetables, to the jars of caviar and quails eggs stacked high on gleaming glass shelves.

Darren was transfixed by the confectionery on display: cakes in the shape of monsters, fairy-tale castles, and racing cars. There were bright plastic machines which, at the turn of a button, delivered a stream of coloured jellybeans. I was drawn to the Belgian fresh-cream chocolates and the man-made mountains of Turkish delight, coconut-ice and peanut brittle.

On the train to London, Giles had given Darren a little leather pouch full of coins. "There you go, Captain," he said as he handed it over. "A chap can't go to the city without a few bob in his pocket."

Darren gave him a happy, guppy grin and spent the rest of the journey putting the money into little piles and assessing his wealth – somewhere between £18.20 and £22.50.

An assistant, wearing a white cap and clear plastic gloves approached. "Can I help you, Sir?" she asked Darren. He gave her his goofy, shy smile and tried to hide behind me.

"Would you like to buy some sweets?" she asked.

"Can I have some Dib-dabs and flying saucers?"

"I'm afraid we don't stock those, Sir. Perhaps I might tempt you with some midget gems or a chocolate tool box?"

I'd heard it said that Londoners were a cold, unfriendly lot, but she was lovely and kind to my brother, and I was touched by the way she refused to be rushed by the impatient woman queuing behind us. Thirty minutes later, when Darren had finally completed his purchase of Parma Violets, Love Hearts, and sweet cigarettes, we moved on.

Darren doesn't like escalators, he feels too crowded on them, and I won't go in lifts. So we had to climb several flights of stairs to make our way to the toy department. Our every step was punctuated by the sound of Darren wheezing, sniffing and sucking sweets.

It was well worth the effort for the glittery, bright Aladdin's cave of board games, bicycles, tricycles, and dolls of all shapes, sizes, and nationalities. There were cricket bats, tennis rackets, bubble machines, and even a small trampoline. In the art section, I helped Darren choose oil paints for Giles and himself; they came in dark wooden boxes and looked like rows of tiny tubes of toothpaste. I could see that Darren was dying to squeeze them open and get his hands on all the lovely colours. When I said we had to wait, I expected him to cause a scene. But luckily Darren has a very short attention span and within seconds his eyes lit up at the sight of an assistant demonstrating magic tricks. He went over to the counter and offered him a Love Heart. The young man palmed the sweet and the next thing Darren knew it was dropping out of his nose. As the fledgling magician entertained my brother with his repertoire of tricks, I was able to relax and look forward to the evening ahead with Rafael – cherishing the prospect as a beautifully wrapped gift yet to be opened.

Later that day we met up with Rafael and treated the youngsters to an early meal in a restaurant just a short walk away from the Savoy theatre. It was all very Italian with the smell of tomatoes, garlic, and Parmesan cheese, red-checked tablecloths and empty Chianti bottles used as candlesticks. I noticed Dee-Dee, Clarissa, and Henrietta were checking out the waiters; even mother had a surreptitious peek at one particularly handsome Lothario. But our little group was getting a lot of attention from the other diners who were nudging each other and looking in our direction.

"If they don't stop staring at our Darren, I'll give 'em what for," said Mother. Darren looked at her in alarm, and I remembered what it was like when she was your protector in chief.

"But Mother, haven't you noticed Clarissa and Henrietta's new clothes? That's what everyone's looking at," I said. This had the dual effect of mollifying mother and delighting the girls.

In deference to the limo, Clarissa was a vision in luminous pink, toned down occasionally with a splash of orange. She wore a pink micro-mini skirt over Rod Stewart-influenced Lycra leggings, an orange sweatshirt ripped to expose a bare shoulder, and a pink bra strap. The addition of a huge, brass crucifix, fishnet gloves, and several rubber bracelets injected a touch of class. The outfit was finished off with an orange and pink Swatch watch, which, as she pointed out, cleverly brought the whole look together.

Henrietta wore a more subtle dance-inspired outfit of yellow leotard over blue tights, blue and yellow striped legwarmers, and a pair of red Converse trainers. She'd tied lots of little bows in her hair and wore a pair of turquoise sunglasses on her head, presumably to protect her scalp from the harsh theatre lights. Before we went out, Dee-Dee painted the girls' fingernails in silver with pink tips. They were thrilled, and I could see that Dee-Dee revelled in their obvious adulation.

God knows what Lucinda of shabby chic fame would make of her daughter's new image.

Cats was the best show ever – even Giles found it acceptable once he realized it was based on poetry. We sat on the revolving platform next to the stage and the actors slinked cat-like amongst us, licking their paws, purring and hissing. Jessica stroked Rumpleteazer and then squealed with delight when he licked her hand. Even Clarissa and Henrietta joined in the fun and giggled as Mungo-Jerry rubbed up against their legs.

On the way out, mother said they didn't make songs like they used to, but that didn't stop her from screeching "Memories" all the way back to the apartment. I guess being roped in for the church choir had gone to her head.

Dee-Dee left abruptly after the theatre, saying something vague about meeting up with a friend. Bertie looked as if he wanted to stop her but, in the end, he headed back to his club with Giles.

Back at Rafael's apartment, Darren put on his conjurer's cloak and insisted on staging a magic show. We played along cheering as he made playing cards disappear and gasping as the little red balls he was holding multiplied with a tap of his wand. The highlight of the performance was when he made Rafael's Filofax evaporate into thin air.

I looked at Rafael to share a secret smile, but he was flicking through the evening paper, oblivious to any magic between us or on stage. As Darren took his bow, Clarissa and Henrietta clapped him so enthusiastically that we had to sit through an encore that lasted almost as long as the original performance. Rafael stayed engrossed in the crossword.

For supper, I gave the children sandwich spread on toast and big mugs of hot cocoa with chocolate flakes and marshmallows floating on the top. And hallelujah! Rafael finally put down his newspaper and helped me dish it out.

"Does he take sugar?" he asked mother, nodding at Darren.

"Why don't you ask him?" she snapped. Oops, he'd only gone and committed the cardinal sin of treating Darren as if he were deaf.

"It's okay; I'll do it," I said, hurriedly smoothing over the moment.

Before long, Darren and Jessica were fast asleep in bed. Sebastian went into the study with the girls to watch television.

I was looking forward to spending some time with Rafael, but it was not to happen; not on mother's guard. She stayed up for the supper of cold poached salmon and salad, despite the fact that she'd eaten with the kids earlier and her conviction that, while she likes fish, fish does not like her. Then forgetting that cheese gives her nightmares, she ate a huge portion of Stilton washed down with "just a drop" of port.

Every time her back was turned, Rafael gestured for me get rid of her but I shrugged helplessly. He didn't know mother; it was almost as if she had a built-in radar that alerted her to my hopes and dreams – and an unstoppable determination to destroy them.

When she finally drained her glass of port, I was sure she would go to bed, but she turned to me and said, "You look washed out, our Kathryn, why don't you have an early night?" Washed out? I'd spent all week making sure I looked my very best. Is there any wonder that around her I had all the confidence of an aqua-phobic goldfish?

"No, I'm fine, why don't you turn in? We've got a busy day sight-seeing tomorrow."

Huh, no chance! She was determined to sit it out, regaling Rafael with awesome tales of the Mother's Union's trip to Scarborough, her latest knitting patterns, and her very individual take on the governance of Mrs Thatcher. Rafael eventually gave up, and we bade each other goodnight with chaste kisses.

I went to join Sebastian and Jessica in bed, but Mother grabbed me outside the bathroom door. "What do you think you're up to, our Kathryn?" She hissed.

"I've no idea what you're on about," I hissed back, aware that we sounded like extras from *Cats*.

"Leading Giles a merry dance, making eyes at your new boyfriend, I wasn't born yesterday you know."

I felt like saying, "That's obvious; I've only got to look at your wrinkles," but I decided that defending myself was more important than scoring points. "What makes you think he's my boyfriend?"

Mother gave a knowing snort. "Maybe he is, maybe he isn't – not yet – but you just watch yourself. And don't think Giles hasn't noticed 'cos he has, and I'll tell you this for nothing, he's worth twenty Mister Big-Shot Barristers any day."

"Why, because he's a lord?"

"No, our Kathryn, because he's a decent, lovely man and a wonderful father to those bairns. He thinks the sun shines out of you, and all you can do is play him for a fool."

"Have you finished?"

"I haven't even started but I don't see the point in carrying on. I might as well talk to myself."

Despite what she said, it looked as if she was going to continue with her tirade. Luckily for me a slightly tipsy Dee-

Dee chose that moment to arrive home arm-in-arm with Roberto. Mother took one look at them and flounced off to bed muttering something about alley cats. I was left to spend the night going over and over what she said, and all the smart replies I should have come up with.

The next morning, Dee-Dee was nowhere to be seen so we had breakfast without her. Rafael casually asked mother if she'd mind if he whisked me off to an art exhibition, adding, "And maybe we could grab a bit of lunch there."

She was having none of it; I think it was the word "art" that aroused her suspicions.

"No, it's a shame to split up," she said. "Let's all go together."

Quick as a flash, Rafael told her it was strictly for over-eighteens. But the lady was not for turning. "That's fine. Clarissa and Henrietta can take the little ones for an ice cream while we take our Darren to the art gallery."

Game, set, and match to mother!

In the end, we went on a riverboat up the Thames because Rafael was called in to work. He was very apologetic, but explained that an important client needed to talk to him on a matter of great urgency.

Whilst the others packed, I found Rafael in the box room, surrounded by a jumble of sports paraphernalia. "It's such a shame you have to go to work," I said. "Can't you catch up with us later? Our train isn't until late afternoon."

"I'd love nothing more, but it looks like I'll be stuck in the office all day." He cupped my face in his hands and gazed at me with those soulful eyes and then he kissed me, a slow lingering kiss, which left me a little bit breathless. "I need to see you," he said. "Soon, we need to talk."

I let out a long sigh, caught short by Darren shouting, "Kay-Kay, where are you? Dee-Dee's up." I had to go before they sent out a search party. Rafael promised that he'd phone in the next few days.

As we all said our goodbyes, mother was more than a little stiff. "You've been very kind putting up with us." Rafael's beautiful mouth rounded carefully to capture her Yorkshire accent. "It's been luverly to have you – you and your Kathryn."

I stifled a treacherous giggle but Dee-Dee flashed Rafael a very dirty look, then deliberately turned her back on him and helped mother into her jacket.

"It's fabulous, Mrs Dibbs, you're so clever; I wish I could sew," she cooed, stroking mother's sleeve.

"It's easy. I could teach you and our Kathryn – not that she's ever shown any interest."

"Come on let's go, Roberto's outside," I said. "And I'd move away from the jacket if I were you Dee-Dee; you don't want to be electrocuted by all that static."

As we were piling into the limo, Rafael drew up in his BMW. I walked over for another goodbye and noticed his squash racket and kit bag on the passenger seat; I gave him a deliberately puzzled look. He reminded me of Sebastian when he's been caught doing something naughty. And that's when I realized the blindingly obvious truth – that there was no urgent meeting. He was bailing out on us. I blamed mother.

"What is it?" I asked.

"I can't seem to find my Filofax. Can you ask your brother what he did with it?" I went back to the limo and asked Darren, but he couldn't remember where he'd put it. So I shrugged my shoulders in the direction of Rafael, who drove off with a tight-lipped nod.

We found the missing Filofax in Darren's rucksack on the way home. It was covered with the sticky remains of his sweets.

"I'll take charge of it," I said and slipped it into my case. I'd clean it up and send it to Rafael the very next day.

I hadn't the least intention of delving into it – absolutely not.

How to cope with ghosts

The next morning I wiped the sugary fingerprints off the Filofax and buffed up the leather cover with the wax Giles uses on his fishing jacket. I was just about to wrap it up and send it back to Rafael when it just sort of flipped open. I didn't want to be nosy, but my eyes were accidentally drawn to his personal details. The Manchester address he'd given – Lowry Mansions – was in fact his office address, but I was sure he'd said that he lived there. I wondered if he were married but, if that was the case, why not tell me? I was hardly free and single myself. I found myself looking through the rest of his book for clues but I could find no evidence of a Mrs. Margolis hiding in the shadows.

Giles had been at the accountants all morning and, when he got home, he stamped around for a bit before barricading himself in the study.

"Away from all the bloody noise," he said. Which was a bit of a cheek given that he was the one doing all the shouting. I wasn't sure why he was in such a grumpy mood. Maybe it was the state of his house which, I have to admit, was a tad untidy.

There were trails of Lego bricks, building blocks, and Barbie's accessories leading from the children's bedrooms, across the landing, down the stairs and into the sitting room. I'd spent the morning trying to develop their culinary skills, but clearly baking buns was a poor cousin to the exciting weekend we'd shared in London. The kitchen was a terrible mess of sticky fingerprints and hundreds-and-thousands scattered over the counters and flours, while white floury paw marks traced the cat's progress across the kitchen units and over the worktops. Jessica had decided to change Tabby's name to McCavity and, as part of the renaming ceremony, she'd anointed him with a generous sprinkling of holy icing-sugar. Try as I might to catch him and brush him down, McCavity remained as elusive as his namesake.

I knew that Nanny would be back soon and she wouldn't like what she saw. It would be best not to be here.

"Okay, go and put your shoes on and we'll go for a walk, some fresh air will do us good." They looked at me alarmed – who was this person pretending to be their mother?

Then it dawned on Sebastian. "Ah, you mean the pub!" he said, and scurried off to get his shoes.

I helped Jessica into her sandals as she practiced her new mantra: "Away from all the bloody noise . . ."

We ambled down the drive, across road and onto the heath. Sebastian held Jessica's hand and pulled her up the steep hill to Grimley. She leaned backward with all her might, just to make it more difficult for him. While going over the stream, he carried her and then pretended he was going to drop her in. She played along by screaming for him to stop. I was tempted to say something about the bloody noise myself.

It was one of those really hot and clammy summer days and, when we arrived at Grimley Manor, we were gasping for drinks. The play area was packed so I left the children queuing for the swings while I went into the bar to place an order. They'd just started stocking fancy new ice creams that came in hollowed-out fruits such as coconuts, oranges, and lemons. I couldn't decide which to choose so I ordered one of each; it was bound to cause a family argument but at least I got to taste them all.

I was walking out of the bar and into the garden, balancing a stacked tray of goodies, when I heard a voice that made my goose pimples jump to attention, despite the heat of the day.

"Long time no see, is one of those for me?"

Jimmy!

The heat prickled up my neck as I gave him the chilliest hello I could muster, which was not as cold as I'd have liked. I walked straight past him to a free table and set down my tray, hoping he'd leave me alone. He followed and plonked himself on the chair beside me, and that's when I noticed his smell. It wasn't just his signature smell of beer and stale cigarettes; it was a deeply ingrained dissolute odour. His face had taken on a loose, jowly quality, while his eyes were bloodshot and tired. He'd always been very particular about his appearance – vain really – so I couldn't help feeling shocked by his grubby tee shirt and dirty fingernails.

He mumbled something about missing me, lunged forward, and tried to kiss me. Drunk though he obviously was, he must have detected the fleeting look of revulsion on my face as I backed away.

"What's got into you, Miss High and Bleedin' Mighty? You were gagging for it last time."

I was praying the children would stay on the swings but I knew I only had a minute or two before they spotted the ice creams. So I forced myself to be pleasant in the hope of getting rid of him.

"I'm married now," I said. "To Giles Havers."

"So I heard. What's your title, Lady Gingernob?"

I ignored the dig, and turned the conversation to him. "What about you? Have you and Imogen settled down?"

He mumbled something about not wanting steak when he could go out for beef burgers. I was debating whether I should tell him he had the cliché wrong, when he stood and drained his pint. I was almost home and dry. Almost! Sebastian and Jessica came running up.

"Mummy, Mummy can I have the orange s'cream?" shrilled Jessica. She grabbed it and was tucking in before Sebastian could make a counter-claim.

Jimmy looked at my children as they squabbled. Something about his expression made me want to scoop them up in my arms and run to the safety of home. Thankfully, they were oblivious to any drama. Jimmy wavered from side to side – he was more drunk than I'd realized.

"What's their names?" he slurred, nodding to the children.

I told him.

"Why did'ya give him a poof's name?"

I didn't dignify that with an answer.

"She looks like you," he said, pointing a nicotine-stained finger at Jessica. I put a protective arm around her. "But the lad," he said. "Yer lad looks like Elvis."

Then, with a half-kiss, half-snarl, he leered his farewell, leaving the smell of long, sweaty nights in unchanged bed sheets behind him.

I had that strange hunch that something bad was about to happen and spent the rest of the afternoon worrying about Jimmy's reappearance. Seeing him had scared me but, I hoped he was so drunk that he wouldn't remember anything. But what if he did? And what if he thought more about Sebastian?

As it turned out, my sense of foreboding was justified, although it didn't involve Jimmy.

I'd just settled the children down to sleep with a bedtime story and was about to watch television when the phone rang. Giles took the call and when he came through to the sitting room, he looked even paler than usual. He sat down and took my hand.

"Pumpkin, that was your mother on the phone."

"No wonder you look so white." I said. But he didn't react in his usual mock-horrified way. In fact, he looked devastated.

"Darling, something terrible has happened."

I knew straight away – almost like a premonition of doom. "Not Darren?"

He nodded, and then he said the words that I'd been dreading since I'd first understood about Darren's condition. It was SCD – sudden cardiac death. He'd died of a heart attack.

I wasn't going to see my little brother again.

But I was wrong. I saw him all week. In the garden dipping his toes in the ornamental pond, then again late at night when a nightmare jolted me awake. He was there grinning at me from the foot of the bed. I even saw him swaying his body backwards and forwards, sitting in his favourite rocking chair. It was only the silent stillness of the rocker that persuaded me that he wasn't really there.

Mingled with my sadness was guilt. I shouldn't have taken him to London or walked him up all those stairs; he wasn't fit enough. It was all my fault. I could see that now, I'd crammed too much into the weekend and got him over-excited. I had let him down just as I had when I was seventeen and walked out the house leaving him with mother, even though he'd begged me to stay.

The doctor prescribed some little yellow pills to calm me down and dull the ache but, what he didn't realize, was that I needed the pain. Flushing my medication down the toilet bowl became part of my morning's routine.

I dreaded the funeral, which was to take place in our chapel. I couldn't even think about it without shaking all over, but Giles and mother used phrases like: "It'll be a celebration of his life," and "At least he's at peace now."

I wanted to slap them both.

Thank God for Dee-Dee. When she wasn't taking the children out, away from the depressing atmosphere and their clearly barking mother, she would sit holding my hand hour after hour. There were some days I didn't venture out of bed; I couldn't even bring myself to speak to Rafael when he rang, but Giles told him what had happened and the next day a lovely letter arrived.

Lowry Mansions
My Dearest Katy,

I am so sorry to hear your sad news. It's always awful to lose someone you love, and I know you were especially close to your brother. I am so glad I had the privilege of meeting him. He was a fine person and justifiably proud of his big sister.

Unfortunately, I am unable to attend the funeral but I send flowers and condolences to your family. To you, I send my love, my friendship, and the assurance that I will always be there for you. If there is anything you need at any time, please don't hesitate to count on me.

Rafael x

I carefully folded the letter and slipped it into his Filofax, which I had taken to keeping in my handbag. Several times a day I would take it out, re-read his kind words and wonder when I would see him again.

The night before the funeral Jessica came into my bedroom carrying Piglet. She kissed me goodnight and tucked Piglet in bed beside me saying he could stop with me until I felt better. A couple of hours later, Sebastian crept into bed with me saying, "Mum, please can you wash my hair? Nanny scratches."

But I felt too listless to move. "I'm not feeling very well, darling – ask Daddy."

"Will you play Monopoly then? I'll fetch the board."

"Not now."

He was on the verge of tears, but all I wanted was for him to go away.

"Where does it hurt, Mummy? When will you be better?"

"Go and play, Sebastian. Mummy's too tired to talk."

Later that night, Dee-Dee made me shower, wash my hair and then she persuaded me to have chicken soup that Mr Purvis had sent round. After I'd eaten, I felt a bit better, cleaner and fuller.

"Now you're up, why don't you go and say goodnight to Sebastian? He's awake."

"It's okay; I saw him earlier."

"I still think you should tuck him in. He's worried about you."

"I think I know my own son."

"Then you'll know that he's scared you're about to pop your clogs."

"Don't be daft. Why would he think that?"

"He asked me if you were going to die – like Darren."

That didn't alarm me, not as much as it should have. I told Dee-Dee that I wanted to reassure him but, somehow, I couldn't face it. I expected her to be sympathetic but I'd misjudged her mood.

"For God's sake Kathy, he's a frightened little boy who needs his mummy. You've got to pull yourself together."

"You don't understand . . ."

"What don't I understand?"

If I'd been more myself I would have picked up on her steely tone, and trodden carefully, but no, I blundered on and answered her question. "How awful it feels to have lost Darren."

She looked angry for a moment, and then she got to her feet. "Fucking hell, Kathy," she shouted, "you really haven't got a clue have you?"

I tried to say that she didn't know what she was on about but I couldn't find the words.

She sat down beside me. "No Kathy, it's you who doesn't understand."

"So explain then."

She hesitated for only a few seconds. "I'm going to tell you something now and I have to tell it in a certain order so don't interrupt me and I don't want any sympathy or bloody platitudes. Okay?"

I nodded – she can be pretty scary sometimes.

"It was Christmas Eve years and years ago, and Mum and Dad had gone to a party. I was invited along but I was nearly fifteen and a grown ups' party was my idea of hell. Grown ups! That's a laugh; they were barely thirty, my parents, and I was their fifteen-year-old reminder of the ultimate hazard of unprotected, under-age nooky."

"You never told me they had to get married," I said.

She rolled her eyes at me. "Welcome to the 20th century Kathy – ever heard of abortion? They didn't have to get married, they wanted to be together and they wanted me. Although I expect if she'd been fortunate to find a lord to palm me off on, she might have had a rethink!"

I felt the colour rush to my face, and tears filled my eyes. "Why do you have to be so mean?"

But she ignored me and continued her story.

"I swear they were the kings of cool those two. After much soul searching, Mum had ditched her beehive hair-do and had it cut short and spiky. When she came downstairs all done up in her little leather mini-skirt and knee-high boots, Dad told her she looked like a model, but she just punched him and told him not to be so soft."

I wanted to ask Dee-Dee if she looked like her mum and if she had any photos, but I reckoned one interruption was one too many so I kept quiet.

"She looked so happy prancing around the lounge to *Top of the Pops* that Dad put down his *New Musical Express* and joined in, grabbing me on the way. At first, I tried to act all aloof and pull away from him but soon the three of us were dancing and singing to The Beatles."

"So that's when you learnt to do the twist. . ."

She let me get away with that one.

"When the music finished, they walked out of the house arm in arm. I heard Dad say as he locked the door behind them, 'Don't know how you're going to get on the scooter in that excuse for a skirt.' He was a mod you see, my dad, with his Ben Sherman shirts and sharp suits, and his new red scooter was his pride and joy – shame about the L-plates. I laughed at my mum's reply, 'You'll just have to lift me onto it, won't you, Superman?' It was the very last thing I heard her say."

I wasn't sure that I'd properly understood what Dee-Dee was telling me. "You mean?" I started to speak but she shut me up with a shake of her head and I could see she was trying not to cry as she continued.

"The knock on the door came about three hours later; well, it was more of an insistent rapping really. I guess they needed to wake me up. It was too early for my parents to be back and anyway they had a key so I was a bit confused. When I got downstairs, I peeked through the window next to the door to see an unsmiling policeman and a woman dressed in ordinary clothes. I opened the door and he showed me his ID. I scrutinized it even though I hadn't a clue what it should look like. Then the woman said, 'Deidre?' and I nodded."

"Deidre?" I repeated, puzzled for a moment. "You mean your real name's Deidre?" Any other time I would have regarded this information as gold dust but I forced myself to say nothing else. I doubted she'd noticed her slip. I took her hand, half expecting her to shake me off, but I don't think she even knew I was there.

"The woman asked if I was alone and when I said I was, she asked, 'Is it alright if we come in?' So I stood back to let them in. She was small and pretty with auburn hair and I remember wondering what the hell she was doing here on Christmas Eve; she should have been out partying."

"Oh Dee-Dee, why have you never told me this?"

"I'm telling you now aren't I? If you'd just listen to me. Anyway, the policeman had wispy, black sideburns and dandruff on his collar, and he looked like he didn't know the meaning of the word fun. He was sweating despite the cold night and he kept dabbing at his forehead with a big, white hanky. He asked me if there was anybody he could call to be with me. When I said no, he explained there had been an accident."

Dee-Dee started sniffing and buried her face into the crook of her arm. Her shoulders were shaking but she made no sound. I wasn't sure what to do, so I put a tentative arm around her neck and hugged her to me. She clung on, snuffling into my neck like the scared teenager she once was.

It took her a few minutes to compose herself. "It turns out they'd come off the scooter. Dad had been drinking and somehow lost control and crashed into a wall. A witness said my mum was screaming with laughter as she somersaulted off the scooter and over a wall, but when she landed, she broke her neck. She died laughing." Dee-Dee shrugged her shoulders to signify the end of the story.

I reached out for her arm and was about to say how sorry I was, but she turned on me fiercely and shook me off. "No! Don't say anything; there's nothing to be said. Just don't ever tell me I don't know how it fucking feels."

Now I understood why she hated Christmas so much and why she wouldn't speak to her father. As she walked towards the door I said, "Thanks for telling me. I'll go and tuck in Sebastian."

She turned around, sat on the bed beside me and said, "Just one more thing.'

"Yes," I said, naively thinking I was about to be complimented on my listening skills.

Dee-Dee picked up Piglet and waved him in my face, saying in a passable imitation of Marlon Brando as Godfather, "If I ever catch you saying Deidre to anyone at any time, trust me – the Pig is bacon! Got it?"

GILES

I'm at my wit's end and I simply don't know where to turn, so I've decided to write everything down; maybe then I might see everything more clearly. Things have been rather frosty between Kate and myself recently. There have been good times naturally, but we certainly haven't developed the closeness I always longed for in my marriage. It hurts me to say this, but she seems rather resentful of me.

She is such a child and, of course, I knew that when I proposed to her – indeed it's her ingenuousness that I've always found so appealing. Yet there are times when I wish that everything wasn't so simple to Kate. Last month she even suggested that I should employ old Purvis as our butler! The problem is she sees the big house and family heirlooms and assumes I'm worth a fortune. I doubt she's even heard of death duties, etcetera. All she sees is my being miserly.

But this is all by the by. The real problem is that she's left, completely disappeared, and she's taken the children with her. I've no idea where she could have gone. I have racked my brains but to no avail. This morning I telephoned the police but they were most unhelpful. She left yesterday, the day of her brother's funeral, following a rather embarrassing scene at Grimley Manor. I would suspect Dee-Dee of hiding Kate's whereabouts from me had she not been involved in the argument.

The funeral went off without a hitch and, I must say, I was very proud of Kate; she successfully hid her grief and was most dignified throughout the proceedings. As I observed her bravery, and that of her mother, I couldn't help but reflect on the feelings I have for my own dear son, Sebastian, and the esteem in which I hold him. It may have been the solemnity of the occasion but I confess the thought of ever losing him brought a tear to my eye.

Despite the sadness of the occasion, Kate was clearly thrilled by the unexpected attendance of her father, John. I was most touched by the way that she couldn't wait to introduce me to him.

We found ourselves sitting together at the buffet – Dee-Dee, Kate, her mother and father. To be honest, I didn't take to the chap and nor did I expect to. After all, what sort of scoundrel takes off and leaves his wife and young family to fend for themselves? But of course, I was civil to him and told him what a fine fellow Darren was. And that's when it all went wrong.

John became very maudlin about the death of his son and, while I don't want to appear unsympathetic, I confess I found his sentimentality a trifle wearing. After all, he'd not been near the young chap for years. Kate is usually pretty sharp about these things but, to my surprise, she seemed to be charmed by his whimsy. Not so her mother; I could see she was getting rather aggrieved with her errant husband.

"Such a cruel blow, it can't be right for a man to bury his own son," he said as he shook his head and wiped his eyes in a most distasteful parody of grief.

Kate's mother, rather tartly I admit, said, "Bury him did you? I was under the impression that I'd sorted out the funeral and, even if you had gone to the trouble of choosing his coffin, can I remind you that it's the first and last thing you've ever done for him."

Kate was furious with her and shouted, "Don't speak to Daddy that way! He'd have done everything for us if you hadn't driven him away."

I felt really sorry to see them argue in this way, especially when I heard her mother's rather weary reply. "Oh grow up, Kathryn, love. Do you really think I wanted to be left alone to bring up three children? Drive him away? Don't make me laugh. He took one look at our Darren's flat little nose and slanty eyes and he couldn't wait to scarper."

The scene got nastier so I tried to intervene and calm things down. I told John what a wonderful job my mother-in-law had made of looking after Darren because, goodness knows it must have been hard for her looking after a disabled child in a man's body. I added that now he was at peace, she would be able to enjoy a well-deserved break. I fear I didn't choose my words very carefully. Kate somehow got the idea that I was saying it was a good thing that Darren had passed on. All hell was let loose; sides were taken and cruel words spoken, culminating in Kate rushing out of the room. That was yesterday afternoon and there has been no sign of her since.

I keep telling myself that they will be fine; Kate is a wonderful mother and would never endanger our children.

Learning when to let go

Funerals are never good, but this one was particularly awful. All through the meal Rees went on as if Darren had been a hindrance and mother was some kind of saint for looking after him. Then mother was appallingly rude to dad and to my amazement, Giles, who was usually so particular about manners, appeared to be taking her side! I couldn't listen to their nonsense a moment longer so I flung my cutlery down, grabbed the children, and stormed out.

I soon realized that, empowering though it felt to walk out mid-argument, I was left with the problem of where to go next. All my friends and family were at the wake in Grimley Manor and I had no intention of crawling back there. So I hovered around my car for a bit pretending to search through my bag for the car keys. I was convinced that someone would follow me out to fuss around and jolly me back inside. Surely, my dad wouldn't let me go off like this, not after I'd spent the day defending him? And didn't Giles always say that we shouldn't part in anger? I decided to give them a bit longer and, just in case anyone was looking, I made a show of checking the car's tyres, kicking at them as if I suspected a slow puncture.

Eventually, I had to make a move. It'd started to rain and Jessica was whimpering that she was cold, so I bundled her into the back of the car and tucked a blanket round her. As Sebastian jumped in and cuddled up beside her, I noticed that he looked a little bit worried so I forced a bright smile, put music on the radio, and drove off pretending that everything was just fine.

I had no idea where I was going but I was determined not to go home. I was trying to devise a plan when the fuel light came on. So I stopped the car and looked in my bag, hoping that I'd got my purse. Yes, there it was, under the letter from Rafael, but to my dismay it contained just a few pounds and a little bit of loose change. So I swung the car round and headed back to the local garage in Grimley village where Giles had a petrol account. It was a pain turning back but at least seeing Rafael's note had given me a plan for the rest of the day. I was going to drive to Manchester and return his Filofax.

It only took a few minutes to drive back to the bright lights of Grimley village and the promise of free petrol. I filled up the tank and bought a bag of Jelly Babies for the children and an A to Z of Greater Manchester. As I signed the chitty, I noticed that the proprietor seemed unusually surly and then, as he helped me into the car, he asked me to remind Giles that he hadn't yet settled last month's bill.

It was getting dark when I finally found Rafael's flat. I'd spent at least half an hour getting lost in the suburbs of Manchester. Rain was teeming down, and I could hardly see where I was going, so it was a huge relief when I spotted his car parked outside a modern development of shops and apartments. I put my car behind his, locked up, and dashed through the stormy weather into the flashy reception area. A security man took my name and asked me whom I was visiting before showing me into the lift.

"Fourth floor, number ten," he said as he pressed the button. "Is he expecting you?"

The elevator doors closed and spared me from lying.

We got out of the lift and dripped down the carpeted hallway towards his home, and it was then that I felt the first seed of doubt about the wisdom of my visit. All of a sudden I wanted to turn back, but I'd given my name to the man downstairs. Also it was clear from the way Jessica jigged up and down that she needed the loo. There was no option; I had to go through with it. By way of an alibi, I took the Filofax out of my bag in readiness to return it. We reached apartment number ten and I knocked on the door. Tentatively at first, and then louder until a glamorous woman who looked as if she'd been drafted in from an old Hollywood movie opened it. She proffered her hand and, even in my befuddled state, I couldn't help but admire her soft hands and long, red fingernails.

"Good evening," she said. "I'm Marsha Margolis. Do come in, the cloakroom is on the left if you would like to freshen up." She then turned her head and called out to Rafael, "Sweetheart, come through, more of your guests have arrived."

Marsha Margolis? The rat had kept that quiet. How could he be married to this beautiful specimen yet blatantly seduce me? Obviously, I was married too and therefore in no position to throw metaphorical stones, but somehow the irony of that escaped me as I shoved the Filofax into Mrs. Margolis's hands. I was about to muster some sort of a dignified exit when Jessica spotted Rafael coming toward us.

She ran to him shouting, "Waif, Waif, I want a wee-wee."

In a couple of deft movements, Rafael opened the cloakroom door for Jessica, switched on the light, and repossessed his Filofax. "Thank you so much for returning this," he said, holding the book aloft. "So lucky that you happened to be in the area."

God he was smooth! Ignoring him, I followed Jessica into the loo, and that's when I caught sight of my deranged face in the mirror. I needed a lot more than a freshen-up. I quickly brushed my hair, smudged on some lipstick, and did my best to cover the dark shadows under my eyes.

It wasn't until I went back out to the hall and looked through the glass door into the dining room that I realized there was a dinner party going on and that Sebastian seemed to have established himself as guest of honour.

Rafael beckoned me in; had he no shame? "Katy, Katy come and meet everyone, I'm so glad you could join us. Everyone, this is Lady Havers and her daughter Jessica, and going round the table let me introduce. . . " He rattled off a list of names that I hadn't a chance of remembering, finishing with, "and of course, you've already met my mother."

Seeing them side by side, it was blindingly obvious that they were related. It wasn't just that they had the same luxuriant black hair and slightly hooked nose or the shared imperious expression. It was something more mystical, a sort of magnetism that captivated everyone in their wake regardless of age or gender. Okay, everyone, that is with the exception of my own mother, who I admit was impervious to Rafael's allure.

"You're his mother?" I couldn't stop myself. "Not his wife?"

"Dear me, no," she said, shaking her head. "Thank you for the compliment." She gave a tinkling little laugh. "But I'm afraid he has no wife. I haven't managed to get rid of him yet."

The way she said it made it clear that getting rid of him was the last thing she wanted. I thought it very strange that a man well into his thirties was sharing a flat with his mother. However, it did explain the confusion over his address.

As Jessica scrambled onto Rafael's knee, everyone shuffled around to make a place for me at the table, each person urging me to sit beside them saying, "I insist that you should sit beside me, I have plenty of room." Or: "Come, come here, there's lots of space for a little one." In the end, I found myself squeezed into a chair between Sebastian and an elderly woman who everyone called Bubba.

Traumatized as I was by the day, I have a surprisingly clear memory of the meal. It was a Friday night and therefore, the beginning of the Jewish Sabbath, which explained why all the men wore yarmulkes tightly gripped to the back of their heads. Marsha lit candles and said a blessing, after which Rafael said a prayer over a silver goblet of wine before enthusiastically knocking it back. As far as I was concerned that was the first normal occurrence of the evening.

Bubba made a point of welcoming Sebastian and Jessica to the table, embracing each child in turn and holding their hands in hers as if she already loved them. Then she reached under her chair for her magnifying glass so she could take a closer look at their faces. Through the magnifier her milky brown eyes looked huge and tired; they were pink-rimmed and framed by hundreds of powdery wrinkles. I was scared that Jessica would say something inappropriate to her, but thankfully she seemed to be in total awe of the old lady. After an unrushed scrutiny of my children, Bubba put the magnifier down, then she took over the blessings, stumbling through the children's prayer that, she later told me, she'd once said on Shabbat for her daughter Marsha, then many years later for Rafael.

I didn't think I'd be able to eat anything, but the food was fantastic. We had nibbles of roll-mop herrings and chopped liver; then chicken soup, piping hot and comforting, followed by, roast chicken and latkes. Marsha kept referring to it as peasant food. Lucky peasants! I devoured every mouthful. I tried to catch Rafael's eyes for some sign that he was glad I was there, but he was too busy holding forth to his guests, telling anecdotes of his recent court appearances. I think that's when I began to realize that his light didn't glow quite so brightly when it wasn't shining on me.

As the meal drew to a close with a portion of delicious lockshen pudding, the weather got worse and soon an electric storm was crackling across the sky. Jessica, who had always been scared of thunder, began to cry. This heralded another outburst from the rest, similar to the great seating debate on our arrival.

"Hush, hush don't cry. Come, I'll tell you a story. . . "

"It's too late to drive home in this weather Katy, my dear. Why not stay with us? We live around the corner; our home is not much but you are welcome."

And craziest of all: "Don't worry Jessica, my little one – it's only the angels throwing a party."

Finally, in her role of matriarch, Bubba said to her daughter, "Marsha, you can't let little Jessica out in the storm, she'll catch her death. Come, you must put them up in the spare room."

So as the guests left, Marsha and Bubba made up the spare room, and Rafael showed us around the flat, telling us we must make ourselves at home, help ourselves to food from the fridge and all that. When we were out of earshot I whispered that I'd walked out on Giles and asked if it was okay for us to stay with him.

"Of course, you must stay for a couple of nights if you really have nowhere else to go." His voice was lukewarm, and I was too weary for a fight so I said my goodnights and went to bed with the children – the three of us snuggled up in one big bed. I knew Giles would be worried and that I should phone home. I was being selfish and unkind, but I just didn't know what to say to him, much less what my future held.

To my surprise, despite having told me that he wasn't in any way religious, Rafael spent a large part of the next day at the synagogue with his mother. I stayed in and watched television with Bubba and the kids. I was very eager to see Rafael again but when I finally caught up with him, he was nothing like the man I thought I was in love with. I rationalized it by telling myself that most people act differently around their mothers. And boy was she around!

She didn't leave us alone for more than a second and even took it upon herself to warn me off her beloved son, which she did with all the charm of a pre-menstrual rattlesnake.

"Oh, my Rafael isn't the type to settle down, that's why he always takes up with married women – oh sorry, dear, no offence, of course I don't mean you. Rafael has explained that you and he are mere acquaintances."

I was tempted to ask her if he usually shagged his acquaintances senseless but managed to bite my lip.

Marsha left in the evening to take Bubba home. As she swept out of the apartment she said, "So charmed to have met you. I do hope we see you again sometime."

So much for the famous Manchester hospitality.

I turned to Rafael and asked, "Why haven't you told her that we're staying?" He shuffled around a bit, playing for time, so I asked, "You do want me to stay don't you?"

He still didn't answer me, so I carried on.

"It's just that the other day you told me that you'd always be there for me which, forgive me if I'm being stupid here, I took to mean that you'd always be there for me!"

"But Katy, it's not that simple. My mother. . . "

"Your mother! You're thirty-six years old. Don't you think that maybe it's time to cut the cord?"

"But you're married."

"Which you've always known."

He sighed and then put on this pathetic, soulful expression as he knelt down beside me. "The thing is, Katy, I've thought about it long and hard. I've thought about nothing else. I'm not sure where you think we are going, but one thing I've realized is that I can't bring up another man's children. If you were to give custody of them to Giles, then maybe we might make a go of it here. Obviously, I'd need time for mother to get used to the idea. . . "

Did he really think that I'd desert Sebastian and Jesica? He clearly didn't know me at all. I didn't yell or argue and I certainly didn't put up a fight – after all, there was no way I would even consider moving in with him and that She Devil.

Clinging on to a small vestige of pride, I collected my children and our few possessions, and left without saying a word. I didn't even slam the door.

Finding your way

Driving back home, I took the advice mother was so fond of offering me: I had a long hard think. What was I to do if I'd permanently messed things up between Giles and me? With no real money of my own, they were pretty limited and – in the unlikely event of her offering – I could never go back to live with mother. The more I thought about it, the more I wanted to sort things out with Giles, and not just because Jessica and Sebastian needed a father and a roof over their heads.

It might sound contrived, but I couldn't help but think of Giles' true value. The imaginary Rafael was a great fantasy, but nothing compared to the loveable old duffer I'd married. Giles was a wonderful father and, even though he'd put his foot in it more than once about Darren, unlike Rafael, he'd always shown my little brother nothing but kindness. Added to which if our sex life had fallen into a bit of a rut, then I only had myself to blame. Yes, our marriage was worth fighting for. Maybe I could even learn to love him, if I tried hard enough.

I shook my head around for a bit trying to get rid of the madness. Clearly I wasn't thinking straight; it must be a reaction to Darren's death, or to my dealings with the treacherous Mr Margolis. I decided to blame the madness, the emotion of the day, and head for home – and Giles. Though, I decided not to tell Dee-Dee about my new plan to play happy families. She would only find it hilarious.

I took a deep breath, swallowed once or twice, and then opened the door to my home. The children ran into the hall, giggling and shouting as they chased each other around in a noisy game of tag. Giles must have heard the noise because he emerged from the study looking dreadful, as if he hadn't slept for days, and he smelled as though he'd been at a cigar-smoking contest in a brewery.

I'd half hoped he would take me in his arms and say it was all his fault, but it was quite clear from his expression that this was not going to happen.

"Sebastian," he said, "Would you take Jessica upstairs please? Mummy and I have things to discuss in my study."

"Gosh that sounds serious, headmaster's study? Please don't give me any lines."

I was only trying to make him smile, to lighten the moment, but he just grimaced and said, "Oh I think you have enough lines of your own, Kathryn." Kathryn! This was obviously worse than I thought.

I followed him into the study, sat down on the big leather Chesterfield and tried to look as innocent as possible. He didn't say anything for a while, as if he was choosing his words very carefully. When he finally began to speak he sounded so utterly heartbroken that I moved to hug him. But a dismissive wave of his hand told me this wasn't a good idea.

For a man reared in the big-boys-don't-cry-pull-yourself-together-now-you've-only-been-mauled-by-a-pack-of-rabid-Rottweiler's school of thought, he seemed dangerously close to tears. He started to speak. "Kathryn, firstly, I need to tell you how precious" – he choked and took a few short breaths before continuing – "how precious you and the children are to me." He turned away for a few seconds then abruptly left saying, "Please excuse me for a short while."

I sat at his desk making a chain out of paperclips as the minutes ticked by on the old grandfather clock, I decided to go and find him and walked out into the hall. I was about to go upstairs when he reappeared, a letter in one hand, a shabby old suitcase in the other. Oh my God! He was leaving me!

"I'm going to stay at Bertie's – give us both time to think," he said.

"You look so tired, maybe tomorrow. . . "

He shook his head. "I've written a note." He handed me an envelope addressed in his neat, tiny writing. "Read it when I've gone," he said and left quietly closing the door behind him.

Dear Kate,

Can I start by saying that I am so sorry I haven't been the husband you had hoped for and that clearly life with me has not met your expectations. I swear all I ever wanted was to make you comfortable and happy.

I spoke to a Mrs. Margolis this morning. She rang to assure me that you and the children were safe and well, and for that I was truly grateful, because I'd been going out of my mind with worry. She also hinted at your friendship with her son, a relationship she clearly disapproves of. Kate, I say this as your friend and the person who cares about you most. I have done some detective work on your behalf and I have to tell you that Margolis is not the man he appears; indeed he is a known cad, a cheat, and a womanizer. Dearest Kate, you deserve so much better and I beg you to think very carefully about continuing your relationship with him.

However, if you wish to make a life without me then I won't hold you back – indeed I wouldn't want you to stay with me out of pity or worse for pragmatic or financial considerations. Kate, I have loved you since that Valentine's night when you first took my hands in yours and have always hoped that one day you might love me too. That seems unlikely now so I want to tell you that you are free to go.

Unfortunately, money is a bit tight at the moment but I propose to reorganize my finances and, by the end of the month, I will be able to put funds into an account for you and the children. In the meantime, if you unlock the top drawer of my desk – the key is in the usual place – you will find I've left you an envelope containing a couple of hundred pounds.

Alternatively, if you feel we could make a go of our marriage then I beg of you, be here waiting for me when I return in a couple of days. We could talk things through and hopefully we could devise a way forward to a new happier future together. A life spent together without secrets or compromise.

Your husband, Giles.

He still loved me. I resolved he wouldn't regret it, not for a second; I would become the perfect wife. We'd be a proper family. I was still sitting on the stairs holding the note in my hands when I heard someone turning the front door handle. Hoping it was Giles, I ran to open it and found not Giles, but a very angry Dee-Dee.

"So you're back then. Have you any idea how you've upset everyone?"

"Not now Dee-Dee, I've just had a lecture from Giles. Don't look at me like that. I realize how stupid I've been, but everything is going to be alright; we are going to make a go of it."

I took hold of her arm, but she shook me off without saying anything. So I read out edited highlights from Giles's letter, but she wasn't listening. In fact, she was talking over me.

"The thing is Kathy, Jimmy has been hanging around looking for you and asking about Sebastian."

Jimmy! That shut me up. Shaking, I dropped the letter to the floor as she continued.

"I couldn't tell you before what with Darren's . . ."

"Tell me what?" I asked.

"I'm sorry Kathy, but he knows."

"You told him?"

"Of course I didn't tell him, he guessed. Apparently, Sebastian's the spit of his nephew. And it gets worse."

"How worse?"

"He wants to meet him."

"No way, he's not coming within a mile . . ."

"And he wants compensation for – as he put it – those lost precious years."

I felt sick, and as I looked down at Giles's letter, I realized I was crying. Great spurts of silent cartoon tears were turning the words on the page into an inky puddle of despair.

What could I do? My life had turned a full circle – the imperfect daughter had become an imperfect wife. My only option was to run away again, but where could I go? Obviously, the further away the better; London would be good. I could easily lose myself there, but how would we live and on what? I certainly wasn't going to ask any favours of Rafael.

In the end, I decided to go and see Mr B, hoping that maybe he could give me a job or at least a place to lie low for a while. That way, Giles could keep in contact with the children and surely I'd be safe from Jimmy.

I took the money from Giles's drawer and gave all but a few pounds of it to Dee-Dee saying, "See if you can get rid of Jimmy with this. I'm taking the children away. I'll let you know when we are settled."

SEBASTIAN

I sleep right at the top of the hotel in a place you wouldn't really call a bedroom; it's just a triangle of space made by the shape of the roof. It has two huge windows looking out to the sky. There aren't any curtains to close at night so when I turn off the light, I can lie in bed surrounded by stars like an astronaut. Last Friday, before I fell asleep, I saw Luke Skywalker – well, I think it was him.

And just like my bedroom's not really a bedroom, you couldn't really call where I live a hotel, which means the sign on the outside wall, *Welcome to Mr B's Bijou Hotel,* is a bit of an exaggeration if not a downright lie. The house I used to live in was at least three times as big as this whole building, including the little outhouse. And there were just four of us living there and one of those was Jessica, who's so tiny she hardly takes up any room at all. I'm not showing off or anything about my old house because when I lived there it didn't seem particularly grand; it was just, you know, home.

Then we came here, which is a bit of a mystery to me, but it seems that my mum and Gilbert-old-chap have split up even though they hardly ever argued or anything, well, only about stupid things. There was a massive row when he wanted to send me to boarding school. He said, "You've got to give him the best possible education, he's a very gifted boy, and we have a duty to nurture that gift." My mum got really mad, madder than I'd ever seen her before, and said, "Get used to it Giles; there is no way I'm letting you send him away from here. Children belong at home not holed up miles away with a load of strangers." So she brought me here instead. I think it's what grown-ups call irony.

It's probably a good thing that Gilbert-old-chap didn't come with us because I don't think he would like it very much. He certainly wouldn't approve of Mr B's swearing. He used to tell me that swearing was the result of an uneducated and lazy mind. I bet he wouldn't dare say that in front of Mr B's face though, because Mr B's so big and wide that he could flatten practically anybody with his right hand tied behind his back. I'm not saying that he would, just that he could.

When we arrived at this supposed hotel, Mr B opened the door and when he saw my mum standing there he picked her up and hugged her so tight that her face went all pink and, as he swung her around, he said, "Na then, I see, bad bleedin' penny's finally turned up." Then he looked at me and Jess and said, "Aye, and wi' a bit er loose change in tow."

As we walked in I noticed another smaller sign on the front door, this one said: *Vacancies. Hot and cold running water. No pets allowed.* And that's when my mum asked if we could rent a room for a while. Mr B told us to sit in reception while he looked in his big red book. He huffed and puffed so much he reminded me of the big bad wolf in Jessica's story book. In the end he said he had a twin-bedded room for Mum and Jess to share and we could stay as long as we wanted, "so long as young lad's alright in attic room."

I found it strange at first, the way Mr B didn't bother using some letters and sometimes he missed entire words out of his sentences, but I've had time to get used to it now. In fact, lots of boys and girls at my new school speak in the same way.

I thought we were just here for a holiday but it seems we've moved in forever – nobody tells me anything. In fact, it amazes me how secretive adults can be. They expect us to inform them of everything from where we're going, where we've been, what we had for school dinner, to have we cleaned our teeth? Done your homework? Got head lice? I didn't used to think like this about my mum, she is probably the coolest mum in the whole universe, but I do now.

Mum is what Gilbert-old-chap calls an ethereal beauty, which probably explains why he married a mere waitress instead of someone more suitable, like a duchess. In my old school, some boys bullied me because Gilbert-old-chap married beneath him but, as they flushed my head down the loo, I bet every one of them secretly wished that they'd got an ethereally beautiful mother. I don't think ten-year-old boys can be beautiful but, even if they can, I don't expect I am because I don't look like my mum. In fact, I don't look like anybody I know, which sometimes makes me wonder about the stuff Henrietta said. It makes me wish that I hadn't promised Clarissa not to tell.

It was when we were in London in the summer and I was supposed to be watching a video of *Star Wars*. I was really tired but Mum had somehow forgotten to send me to bed, and there was no way I was going to remind her. Clarissa and Henrietta were sitting by the open window, smoking cigarettes, and chewing bubble gum. They gave me a drink of their cider, straight out of the bottle, and two pieces of gum. Then they shared their cigarettes and tried to teach me how to blow smoke-filled bubbles, I was a bit scared of what Mum would say if she came in, but she didn't so that was alright. After a while, I began to feel a bit sick so I said, "I'm going to watch *Star Wars*." And I moved from the window to the sofa, feeling a bit wobbly as I walked.

"Don't say you'd rather watch a stupid film than hang out with us," said Clarissa, but not nastily – more like the way Aunty Dee-Dee says things, but that's when everything started to go wrong.

All I really wanted to do was go to bed, but then Henrietta came over to me and, as she sat down, she nearly fell off the sofa and she started laughing like it was the funniest thing in the world. Her face was red and she had bright pink lipstick all over her chin and she smelt horrid, like an ashtray. She snuggled down beside me putting her arm round me like I was her boyfriend or something. I pushed her away hoping that my sister will never drink cider or smoke cigarettes or embarrass boys.

And that's when Henrietta said, "Oh I get it, that's why you're so keen on stupid *Star Wars* – you think you're like Luke Skywalker, just 'cos neither of you know who your real father is."

Clarissa ran over to her and slapped her really hard and shouted, "Shut up, you stupid cow!" Then she said to me, "Ignore her, she's drunk."

I tried to make Clarissa tell me what Henrietta meant, but she wouldn't. She just made me swear on Jessica's life that I wouldn't say anything to anyone about it. I went to bed soon afterwards but I don't think I slept for more than a few hours and, when I woke up, I felt as if I was a different person.

Thinking about that night made me feel very confused, so I decided that since I'd been dragged here against my will, I deserved a few answers and, with this in mind, I went to find my Mum. It didn't take long because as usual, she was in the kitchen – she'd cleared up after supper and was busy baking, making those sponge things that they call fairy cakes, which if you ask me, is a very stupid name for a cream bun. She looked a bit tired but I didn't feel sorry for her, not like I usually would, so I didn't give her a hug. Instead, I sat down beside her at the kitchen table. She didn't say anything; it was almost as if she didn't know I was there. But when she had finished spooning the mixture into the little paper cases, she passed me the bowl so I could eat what was left.

It was her way of telling me we were still a team. When I was a little kid, whenever she baked, she always gave me the bowl to scrape out. It was our thing, and I knew she would never ever give it to anyone else, including Jess, not even if she threw a huge tantrum. I wanted to refuse it so my mum would realize I was in a sulk but, before I knew it, I was licking the raw cake mix off my fingers and smiling at her.

Then I remembered what I was there for and said, "When am I going to see Gilbert-old-chap?"

She sighed rather crossly and said, "What's with the Gilbert-old-chap?"

I made my face look innocent. "It's our middle name, he used to call me it when I was little, and now I call him it. It's a sort of a joke."

I said that even though I knew it wasn't what she meant. I thought she was going to go mad with me, but she just said, "Well, I don't like it. You should call him Dad. Or Father if you want to be more grown up."

"I don't see that it matters what I call him, if he's not around to be called it."

She told me not to be rude, which I didn't think I was being, but I realized I was getting nowhere with her so I went to my room and lay on my bed listening to my Walkman and waiting for the stars to appear. I must have gone to sleep because when I opened my eyes, I saw a supper tray on the floor beside my mattress. Mum must have crept in and left it for me. There was a glass of Coke with a straw, and she had made me my favourite egg and Marmite sandwiches on sliced white bread – which all goes to show that she was very sorry for something because she usually tries to make me eat Hovis and practically never allows me Coke at bedtime.

SEBASTIAN

I hadn't seen Aunty Dee-Dee for so long that I began to think I'd never see her again. But I knew that even if I didn't, I'd never forget her or the way she makes me feel all fuzzy inside. Last night I got tired of being an astronaut and instead of counting the stars in the sky, I lay on my bed thinking about my old life at Havers Hall and began to wonder if we'd ever go home.

Then I started thinking that of all the people in the world, Dee-Dee was the one most likely to know the truth about me because, as my Grandma used to say, Dee-Dee and Mum used to live in each other's pockets. I didn't get what she meant at the time but that's because I hadn't learnt about metaphors. I loved her sayings but I kept that to myself because I could see that they annoyed my Mum. For example, if I was going out to play, even on a warm day, Grandma would tut at Mum and say something like, "You're never going to let him go out like that, Kathryn? Put your balaclava on, our Sebastian, before you catch your death!"

I didn't even know what a balaclava was until Mum told me that it was a sort of knitted helmet they wore in the olden days. I was glad that Mum didn't make me wear one because I could just imagine what the waitress-haters would do to me if I showed up at school in a woolly helmet. It also made me a bit scared to imagine 'my death' basking outside in the sunshine waiting for the hatless me to turn up and catch it.

It was 5 November and everyone was coming to the Not Hotel for my birthday tea. We'd lived there for about ten weeks and I hadn't seen Dee-Dee, Grandma, or Gilbert-old-chap since we left home, although I had spoken to them on the phone. It was my idea to invite them over to celebrate my birthday and, because I suspected that Mum wouldn't be keen on the idea, I deliberately suggested it when Mr B was with us. I somehow knew that in front of him she would go along with my plan. She did, but judging by the look she gave me she obviously wasn't very pleased about it.

I hated my stupid new school in the village because I was bullied there just as much as before, but this time, it was not because Gilbert-old-chap had married beneath him but because I happened to mention that when he died, I'd become a lord. Not the best thing to boast about as I soon learned.

For my eleventh birthday, at lunchtime (except they called it dinner time), they gave me eleven bumps plus one for luck, which might sound like fun, but they did it really hard on purpose. Then after school, they followed me home throwing bits of mud at me; it didn't hurt much but it made me feel very sad and I resolved that I'd never make anybody unhappy on their birthday. When I got home and they saw where I lived, they laughed and jeered at me saying things like: "It's not a very big castle for a lord, is it?" And "Where do your servants sleep?"

I tiptoed in hoping to get changed out of my muddy blazer and trousers before anyone saw me. I sneaked upstairs wondering if I should take up judo or kung-fu to defend myself, as I wasn't getting much protection from the bullying by grovelling and begging. I'd almost made it to my room when Jessica spotted me. She flung herself at me screeching "Happy birthday to you!" People say she looks like an angel, but she definitely doesn't sound like one.

Mum came upstairs to tell us to be quiet and remind us that we're not supposed to make a noise in the public areas. When she saw the state I was in, she shook her head and told me to get washed and changed as quickly as I could. I scraped the mud off my blazer. The badge was the hardest to get clean but I scrubbed and scrubbed at it with a nail brush till the school motto – Dare to be Different – was legible again. I heard everyone arrive so I quickly wiped a flannel over my face and put on some clean jeans and a shirt. I felt a bit shy as I went down to say hello, which was a stupid thing to feel because they were mainly the people I'd known all my life.

I saw Dee-Dee first. She was standing in the little reception area wearing a bright pink coat that made her shoulders look twice as big as normal. I thought that she'd taken up weightlifting, but she told me that padded shoulders were the latest thing in fashion. I wasn't convinced and felt slightly worried that she was on steroids or something, but as soon as the man she was with helped her out of the coat, I saw her normal-sized body and I knew she was telling the truth. She introduced the man to all of us as her new boyfriend, Lawrence Penrose. I thought he looked too old to be anybody's boyfriend but, of course, I didn't say so. I also thought that if I was a woman, I'd hate it if my boyfriend, however old he was, thought I needed help to do something as simple as taking off my coat.

By the time Gilbert-old-chap arrived, we were all in the small sitting room – the one that Mr B calls the Hotel Lounge. From the moment I saw him, I was looking for clues: was he my real father? As soon as he walked in, he strode over and shook my hand, which you might think is not a very fatherly thing to do, but in fact, he shakes hands with everybody, even Jessica, and you only have to look at them to know that they are related.

The grown-ups were drinking wine, and Jess and I were sharing a bottle of Coke with two straws; she was blowing down her straw on purpose instead of sucking it and I got sprayed with drink – making this my messiest birthday ever. I cleaned myself up by wiping my face on my sleeve; I didn't want to leave the room because on the coffee table was a big pile of presents. I suspected everyone was feeling sorry for me and trying to make up for the fact that I was from a broken home.

I wanted to open my parcels but Mum said we had to eat first because after tea, she had to clear the table and reset it for the residents' suppers. When Mum said this, Grandma made a sniffing noise and pursed her lips, which seemed to make my mum cross. Then, as we all trouped through to the dining room, I heard Mum whisper to her crossly, "Don't start, Mother."

For tea, we had homemade cheeseburgers and chips, which just happens to be my very favourite meal in the whole world. Apart from Aunty Dee-Dee, all the grown-ups ate theirs with a knife and fork, which looked wrong, but somehow I couldn't imagine Grandma and the rest eating without cutlery. Jessica, Dee-Dee, and I and squirted ketchup over ours then picked them up with both hands and took huge bites, dripping cheese and sauce all over our fingers and chins. Mum was trying to be jolly but she looked a bit sad, and I wondered what she was thinking; perhaps she was worrying about being a single parent. But maybe she was just wishing that she was allowed to eat with her fingers in front of her mother.

For pudding, we had a big chocolate birthday cake covered in green icing. It was in the shape of a football pitch with little goalposts at each side and twenty-two tiny plastic football players. Half of them were painted in a red and black strip, the others in a blue one. I half expected Gilbert-old-chap to make some comment about rugger being the superior game, but he didn't. He just lit the candles with his silver lighter and sang *Happy Birthday* like everybody else.

Then I opened my presents; Mum gave me a new Walkman and the *Brothers in Arms* tape, which is an album by Dire Straits. On the front it's got a picture of a guitar sort of floating in the sky. My favourite track is *Money For Nothing*. I put the batteries in the Walkman and played it for Jessica; we had an earphone each and she screeched along with Dire Straits, virtually ruining it for me forever. When it came to the big line *Money for nothing and your chicks for free,* Jessica sang, "chips for tea" and everyone laughed like we were one big happy family.

Grandma said that it just goes to show how close Jessica and I are because most people wouldn't like the limelight being stolen from them by their little sister. Not on their birthday.

Aunty Dee-Dee gave me a Transformer Dinobot and showed me how to change it from a prehistoric monster into a robot by sort of turning it inside out. As usual, I got a W.H. Smith's voucher from Grandma; she always buys me one for Christmas and birthdays and that's because years ago she somehow got it into her head that I'm "a proper little bookworm". I kissed her thank you and didn't spoil her illusions by telling her I'd be spending the money in the music department. Jessica gave me a bag of sweets: Marathon bars, Opal fruits, and Chocodiles, which just happen to be her favourites!

Dee-Dee's boyfriend had to dash off but before, he left, gave me a box of Crayola crayons, the ones that look like lipsticks, which was nice of him but made me think that he probably doesn't know very much about eleven-year-old boys.

I was interested to see what Gilbert-old-chap had got for me, as I know for a fact that my mum used to be in charge of buying presents from him. First, I opened the card. I was expecting to see the usual sort of picture of someone fishing or a photograph of a foxhunt. To my surprise, there was a picture of a man and a boy walking on the beach – the man had his arm around the boy's shoulders and the boy was looking up at him and smiling. Written along the top of the card in gold lettering it said: *To a dear son on his birthday.*

This meant that either he actually was my father, or that he was lying to me. A third thought flitted through my mind – that he wasn't really my father but he believed that he was. But I didn't really consider that an option because surely he would know whether or not he'd made a baby with my mum.

I thanked him for the card and started to open the present. It was a long, thin box wrapped up in brown paper. I ripped off the paper and inside I found a black leather case. I tried to open it but it was locked. So I turned it over and found a tiny gold key taped to the bottom. I put it in the lock and, as I twisted the key, I wondered what could be so precious that it needed locking away. I was afraid that I might not like my present and that would be sad because I was sure Gilbert-old-thing would be able to tell because as everyone knows, I'm not very good at pretending.

I needn't have worried because Gilbert-old-chap had bought me a fantastic present – a telescope. "It's for your star gazing," he said. "If it's alright with Mum, perhaps we can watch the planets together at bedtime."

I looked at Mum who looked like she was going to say no, so I quickly changed the subject. "Maybe I could go home to Grimley one weekend, and do it there as well?"

Gilbert-old-chap gave me the happiest of smiles and said he was sure we would be able to work something out.

Suddenly, the sound of fireworks exploded into the room and the sky was filled with showers of light. "There's a bonfire at the recreation ground, can we all go?" I asked. But Mum said that she "needed to stay and talk to Daddy." Then Grandma said that she thought it best if she and Jessica watched through a bedroom window. I don't know whether Grandma was thinking of Jessica or herself but, in the end, it was me and Aunty Dee-Dee who put on our coats and gloves and scrambled out into the smoky night. I'd thought about taking my Walkman with me but I didn't because I realized I'd been given the perfect opportunity to interrogate my Aunty.

I didn't say much as we walked through the fields towards the bonfire. Instead, I wondered how I should phrase my questions. It wasn't easy. I couldn't just come out with, "Dee-Dee, do you know who my father is?" Or, "Actually, I've heard some rumours about my parents; can you tell me if they're true?" So in the end, I said, "Is Mum getting a divorce?" She didn't say anything at first and when she eventually did, she didn't give me a straight answer, which is not like Dee-Dee.

"They both love you, and that's the important thing."

"But are they?"

"I don't know; lots of people do get divorced if they are unhappy. Like my boyfriend, for example, he's in the middle of a divorce."

I felt the conversation was moving away from my parents and me, so I tried again. "Do you know who my father is?"

Now, if she didn't know anything, wouldn't she have said something like, "It's Giles, of course – what a funny question." But she didn't.

She stopped walking and turned to me looking a bit shocked. "What makes you ask?" Then she gave a little laugh that didn't sound real and said, "It's Giles, silly, who else could it be?"

But I didn't believe her, even though it's not like Aunty Dee-Dee to tell me lies. "That's what I'd like to know."

Dee-Dee didn't reply and that's when I realized that if I was to find out the truth, I'd have to be a bit cleverer than I'd been so far.

Finding dreams and deceptions

When Dee-Dee called me to tell me she was going away, I assumed she'd saved up enough money to go to Australia, but no, it was much more interesting than that.

"You've got to guess where I'm going and who with?" she said. I hate it when she does that but I knew she wouldn't tell me what was going on if I didn't play the game.

"Okay, you're going on holiday with your new bloke."

"No, don't be daft; I've dumped him."

"I thought you liked him!"

"He's alright. No, I'm moving to Scotland."

"Scotland!" I was sure she once told me she hated all things Scottish from tartan – a crime against fashion, apparently – to Rod Stewart who she once met in a London night club. I don't know what happened between them but she says he's a closet gay, so I can only assume he had the audacity not to fancy her.

"Why Scotland?" I asked.

"For the haggis, shortbread and whisky – not to mention the sporrans. Der! To be near Bertie of course. He's bought me a cottage about a mile from his castle. I'm going to be his next door neighbour." She giggled as if this was the funniest thing imaginable.

"But what about Lucinda?"

"Her idea – weird or what? It seems that I've been upgraded from being a bit-on-the-side."

God, those aristocrats are a funny bunch. Apparently, Lucinda found out about Dee-Dee and Bertie's affair ages ago. She hoped that if she ignored it, the whole thing would just fizzle out; but when it didn't, she had the maniacal brainwave of making the whole thing respectable and above-board by setting Dee-Dee up as his mistress.

"But it's in the middle of nowhere. No shops, bars, or anything. You'll hate it," I said. But she wasn't listening to me; she was already living the dream.

"He's going to let me do the cottage up and he'll give me a weekly allowance. Pin money, he called it. And he's just given me a load of cash to kit myself out for the frozen north."

She started laughing again, and I couldn't help but wonder if poor Bertie knew what he was letting himself in for.

"I've quit my job and I'll be going in a couple of weeks. See yah before I go. Bye." And with that, she put the phone down.

No matter how hard I tried, as I went about baking cakes and bottling fruit, I couldn't imagine my independent, free-spirited friend living in an isolated cottage devoid of shops and spas, dependant on a man.

A fortnight later, she came to stay at Mr B's, en-route to Scotland, her little red car crammed full of bags and cases containing all her possessions. As I went out to greet her, she opened a shoebox to show me her latest purchase: a pair of slinky, silver stilettos.

I gaped at them and said, "I thought Bertie had given you money to get some sensible shoes?"

She shrugged her shoulders, her face shining with innocence as she replied, "These are sensible. I bought them in the sale."

We fell into each other giggling and it was just like old times at Grimley Manor before all the complications, castles, dreams, and deceptions.

I had been butchering a small pig when she arrived so she joined me in the kitchen and painted her toenails a vivid orange while I hacked away at the poor beast. She looked as if she had something on her mind, and I wondered if she was having second thoughts about Scotland; it was so typical of her to jump in with both finely pedicured feet.

"Are you worried about something?" I asked.

"Yes," She said. "You!"

It wasn't the reply I'd expected.

"Why me?"

"Because Sebastian is asking questions about his real father. He mentioned it to me on his birthday and I shrugged it off. But when I went to say goodbye to your mum, she told me that he'd phoned her to ask her about your past; he said it was for a school project."

"Cunning little monster, what did he say?"

"He wanted to know if you'd had any other boyfriends before Giles."

Well, that was okay. I wasn't alarmed in the slightest. Mother knew nothing about Jimmy, or anybody else for that matter – luckily, mother and daughter chats had always been pretty low on our agenda. I felt relieved; hopefully the whole thing would just blow over.

"She told him that you might have met someone in France."

"But I've never been to France."

"Grape picking apparently."

"Grape picking! Bloody hell, don't tell me that's come back to bite me after all this time."

"He's decided that his real father is French, based on two important facts."

"Which are?"

"That he loves garlic and isn't keen on bathing."

"It's not funny," I said.

"It is a bit," she replied.

"Well that's as maybe, but I still don't know what to do."

"Do nothing and hope he gets bored with it all," Dee-Dee said. "And are you going to open that bottle of wine, or is it purely decorative?" So we had a glass or two of wine and spoke of other things, but always in my mind was the worry that my secret was very nearly out.

I still couldn't get my head around Dee-Dee moving to Scotland, but she was adamant she was doing the right thing.

"It's an adventure, imagine me in my own house, mistress of Bertie. It'll be like being in a film."

"But won't it seem odd living so close to Lucinda and the clones?"

"No, I get on right well with Clarissa, and Lucinda's usually too full of gin to care about what's going on. She's told Bertie that he can't let me mix with his children or her friends – well, that's no great hardship. No, don't worry about me. I'm gonna have the time of my life."

Before she left, she made me promise to visit her very soon, so she could prove it to me.

Dee-Dee had gone by the time Sebastian came home from school. I wanted to ask him what he thought he was doing, spying on me and my past, but I was afraid that if I did, he might start interrogating me. So I just smiled sweetly and said, "Have you had a good day?"

"Was alright," he replied.

"What did you do?"

"Oh you know – stuff."

"What sort of stuff?" He pulled a face by way of a reply and deftly changed the subject.

"I'll be late home on Wednesdays from now on. I'm going to do French after school."

"Why French? It's not like you to take on extra lessons."

"I've always wanted to learn French; in fact, I'm going to ask Gilbert-old-chap if he'll pay for me to go on the school trip to Paris." And with that, he picked up his schoolbag and went up to his bedroom quietly whistling the French national anthem.

SEBASTIAN

When Mum told me I had to go with her and Jessica to visit Aunty Dee-Dee, I told her I didn't want to go but she said, "You love Dee-Dee, of course you want to see her new house."

"Why is it that grown-ups always think they know what other people want?" I replied.

"Give me one good reason why you don't want to go," she said.

Well, of course, I couldn't say it was because I wanted to have a weekend with Gilbert-old-chap so I could get the truth out of him about my real father. So I told her the first lie that came into my head. "I don't want to go because it's a long way and I'll be travel sick."

"You can sit in the front and take a Kwell or something." It was obvious she didn't believe me, and she said that on purpose because she knows I hate taking tablets.

"Why can't I stay with Gilbert-old-chap?"

"Because he's away with Bertie on a fishing trip."

"Okay then, I'll go with you," I said. "But you'd better get me some barley sugars to suck on the journey." I wasn't going to let her have everything her own way."

It took us ages to drive all the way to Scotland and even longer to find Aunty Dee-Dee's cottage. What I hadn't realized, until we drove passed the castle, was that Dee-Dee lives really close to Lucinda and Bertie. I made up my mind that as soon as I could, I'd go off and find Clarissa and force her tell me the truth about everything. She might be bigger than me but I'm stronger.

Aunty Dee-Dee was really pleased to see us. She ran out to the car carrying a bottle of champagne and shouting, "Welcome to the outback. I hope you don't die of boredom!"

Before we'd even gone inside, or unpacked our stuff from the car, we sat on the garden wall to "watch the world go by." At least that is how Mum put it. Mum and Dee-Dee drank the champagne, and Jess and I drank Coke – we all ate crisps. People in cars and tractors tooted at us and waved or whistled as they drove by; it seemed as if Aunty Dee-Dee knew everybody in the whole of Scotland already.

I kept looking out for Clarissa but didn't see her, although I think I saw her mum go by on the other side of the road. I couldn't be sure for absolute certain that it was her because she was wearing a huge hat and big sunglasses that covered most of her face, and also because she didn't say hello. Jessica was sitting on the grass playing with her Piglet, telling it the story of the Big Bad Wolf. She was turning over the pages of her storybook but kept stopping to say things like, "It's all right Piglet, don't be scared; the pigs live happily ever after!" Dee-Dee said she looked so cute and went to get her camera to take a photograph. And as Jessica smiled into the lens, I thought how lucky she was to look exactly like Gilbert-old-chap; she would never have to go out searching for her real daddy.

Without thinking, I said to my mum, "If Gilbert-old-chap wasn't, you know, my actual father, would Jessica still be my sister?"

Mum didn't look at me, and I could tell she was trying to pretend she hadn't heard me, so I asked her again, louder, and in the end she said, "Just leave it, Sebastian."

I thought she wasn't being very fair. I bet she would want to know the truth if she was me. But I also knew it would be pointless to pester her because, as Grandma always says,

Mum can be as stubborn as I am; she says that's where I get it from.

What nobody ever tells me is where I got my black hair.

For supper, we went to what Dee-Dee called a child-friendly pub. I ate scampi and chips out of a basket followed by chocolate ice cream with a cherry on the top. After we'd eaten, I pretended I needed to go to the lavatory but really I walked through to the other bar. I went up to the lady who was serving drinks and said, "Excuse me, but I was wondering if my friend Clarissa ever comes in here? She's got red hair and freckles."

The man standing next to me laughed and said, "That describes most of the people in the village, son." And then the bar lady, who'd got a funny way of talking, said, "Anyway, you should nae be in here; the back room's for you kids!" Which didn't sound exactly child friendly to me!

But I wasn't going to give up that easily so I said, "She lives in a castle."

And the lady replied, "Then she'll be too hoity-toity to mix with the likes of us. Now scram!" I could see I was getting nowhere so I went back to Dee-Dee and Mum who were whispering to each other and giggling. I hate it when they do that, so I ignored them and played dominoes with Jessica, which was okay until she tipped the table over when she realized I was winning.

Aunty Dee-Dee's cottage was very old, and the ceilings were really low. The reason for this is that in the olden days, people were smaller than us because they didn't eat very good food. And even if they did grow tall, most of them got an illness called rickets, which made them all crooked and bent. I bet they would have given anything to eat scampi and chips in the basket and chocolate ice cream –

even in an unfriendly pub. Mum took Jessica and Piglet up to bed and I asked Dee-Dee if I could explore the cottage. She said, "Yes, but it's so small that even if you take your time, you'll be back in two minutes."

So I went up the funny little staircase, through the landing, and into my bedroom. When I looked out of my window, I could see the gate to Clarissa's castle, so I pulled my bag out from under the bed, took out my telescope and decided to spy on her and write down everything I saw. Nothing much happened so after about five minutes, I was beginning to feel a bit bored and I decided to wait till until morning. I went next door to Dee-Dee's bedroom.

It was the biggest room in the cottage and it had a huge bed that took up most of the space. It was covered in shiny, black material and had lots and lots of cushions – the sort that look as if they're made out of wild animals. I sat down on the edge of the bed and it was so squishy that I just had to have a bounce on it; I jumped and jumped, so high that I nearly banged my head on the mirror at the ceiling. When I stopped it took me ages to put the covers and cushions back exactly the way they were and, as I was doing it, I noticed on the table beside the bed there was a picture of Dee-Dee with Bertie. He had his arm around her and it looked like they were on holiday because Dee-Dee was wearing a tiny, black and red bikini and pointy high-heeled sandals. She looked really pretty, and I wished that it was me in the picture with her and not Bertie.

I didn't go in Mum's room because Jessica was in there talking to Piglet and, if she knew I was around, she'd make me read to her. Instead I tiptoed into the bathroom. I could hear Mum and Aunt Dee-Dee talking in the kitchen below. I quietly locked the bathroom door and lay down on the floor with my ear pressed firmly to the carpet. It was amazing; I could hear them speaking as clearly as if I was in the kitchen with them.

"Kathy, he's not going to give up. You've got to tell him the truth."

"I can't."

"Of course you can; he deserves to know. It's his right."

"But he's so young," my mum said.

Aunty Dee-Dee made a sort of snorting noise before she answered. "You didn't see the way he was checking me out earlier today; nothing little boyish about that I can tell you – the rascal."

I felt my face go hot and sweaty, and my willy went stiff.

"I know I should tell him but I just can't let him know the truth, ever!" Mum sounded upset, and I wanted to go to her, but I needed to hear more. Maybe my real father was a thief or a murderer or something and that's why it's such a big secret.

"If Giles found out he wouldn't forgive me, and he'd never take me back," she said. I was confused but glad; I didn't know she wanted him back.

They started talking about other stuff and I must have fallen asleep because the next thing I heard was the noise of Jessica banging on the bathroom door. The first thing I thought when I woke up was that Mum and Gilbert-old-chap must make friends, then we could all go home to Havers Hall.

Have A Highland Fling

It was my first morning at Dee-Dee's and I was wondering, as I looked out over the rolling hills to Bertie's castle, how she of all people coped with living such a quiet life.

Quiet! I should have known better – known that she'd never settle for an existence miles away from civilization with just pigs, cows, and the odd visit from Bertie for company. And so it was proved. As the sound of church bells beckoned the devout and pious to the local church, the less God-fearing amongst the villagers made a pilgrimage to partake of a boozy brunch with Dee-Dee at *Thistle Cottage* – or *The Highland Fling* as she'd recently re-named her love nest.

My fellow guests included Jay, a gay mechanic, and Ronald, his not-so-secret schoolteacher boyfriend, Miss Holden, the old lady who ran the corner shop, a poet called Jack, and a reclusive rock star who'd been driven to conquer his agoraphobia by the promise of eggs Benedict, Bloody Marys, and Dee-Dee.

I observed Sebastian smiling like a village idiot as he helped Dee-Dee by taking coats, handing round trays of nibbles, and pouring drinks. It was then I realized – call it mother's intuition – that he was up to something. He disappeared upstairs every few minutes and when I asked what he was doing up there, he didn't answer.

But Jessica piped up, "I know, I know; he's looking through his thing at the stars."

Sebastian made the most of the diversion and escaped further interrogation by retreating to his room. When we'd all finished feasting on the brunch and were settling down to some serious drinking, Sebastian came downstairs from his star-gazing and casually informed me that he was going for a walk. I told him to be careful not to get lost and off he went.

I decided it was time for Jessica to have a little nap mainly because I'd been informed that now was the time for spontaneous, group entertainment, and God only knew what that meant. As soon as Jessica was out of the way, Miss Holden rolled up a spliff, as the gay schoolteacher regaled us with his favourite passage from Oscar Wilde. Then Dave, the rock star, strummed on his guitar as Jack read his latest masterpiece, a long, uncomplicated poem focusing on the similarities between people and sheep. In his defence, I guess there wasn't much inspiration to be found around these parts.

Dee-Dee initiated a game of true or dare – which I for one dreaded. Thankfully, before we could get very far, she was interrupted by a loud knocking on the door.

"Must be the neighbours complaining about the noise or something," I joked, not realizing how near that was to the truth, as Sebastian rushed in, red faced and tearful, followed by Clarissa and a very angry looking Lucinda.

Lucinda squared her shoulders and glared at me. "Call yourself a mother? You should keep this young ruffian under control!" She held Sebastian by his shirt collar and shook him a bit. I felt tempted to kill her.

"Well yes, actually I do call myself a mother, Lucinda, and I would appreciate it if you would stop manhandling my son and treat him with a little respect," is what I wanted to say.

Unfortunately, it came out more like, "What's he done this time?"

"Nothing," said Sebastian and Clarissa in one voice.

"Nothing! I found you sitting on my daughter's head threatening to pull her eyelashes out one by one, and you call that nothing. Explain that to your mother if you can," bellowed Lucinda.

"He didn't mean to sit on me," said Clarissa, which made everybody, apart from Lucinda, scream with laughter.

"Same thing happened to me out of the blue, just last week," said Jay and was rewarded with a very disapproving look from his life-partner.

"What do you want, Lucinda?" asked Dee-Dee, "and why are you in my house?"

"Oh, it's your house is it?"

"Yes it is. Would you like me to show you the deeds?"

Lucinda paled, and Miss Holden let out a load guffaw sending clouds of cannabis fumes around the room.

Lucinda rounded on her. "And you should know better, smoking that disgusting stuff at your age!"

"Peace, Sister," came the reply.

"And don't call me 'sister'. You sound ridiculous."

"But we're practically related. Your great-grandfather set me up in the corner shop." She gave a suggestive smile. "One of my best customers, if you know what I mean." The mad, old hippy cackled as she dragged on the joint and lost herself in her memories.

"Mum, can we go now?" asked Clarissa.

"Not until we've sorted this out. I want an apology from that little thug." She pointed to Sebastian. "And I want to know what this is all about."

Dee-Dee decided to take the situation in hand. "Go home, Lucinda. I'll have a word with Sebastian and Clarissa and, when I get to the bottom of it, if he's done anything wrong, you'll get your apology."

"Oh, so having my husband isn't enough for you, now you want my daughter."

"You're beginning to get on my wick now." Dee-Dee sounded really angry, and I feared things were about to take a nasty turn so I told Sebastian to take Clarissa into the back garden. To my surprise, not only did they agree to leave the riveting scene, but they went off arm in arm like they were best buddies.

When they'd gone, I tried to calm Lucinda down but she was having none of it; in fact, I was the next victim of her wrath.

"And as for you Kate," she said, "I thought of you as my friend and all the time you were cavorting around with her." She gestured towards Dee-Dee. "Drinking champagne on my husband's wall, laughing at me for all the village to see."

"But I wasn't laughing at . . ."

"For the last bloody time, Lucinda, it's *my* wall, *my* cottage, and *my* front door, which I'm going to shove you through in a minute."

Lucinda decided to leave voluntarily, and as she slammed the door behind her, we heard her shout for Clarissa to join her. But her daughter, who had apparently developed a touch of deafness, stayed with Sebastian. So, peeking out of the cottage window, I watched as Bertie's wife, such a lonely figure, walked up the hill towards the castle, her home. Remembering Lucinda's kindness to me in the past, especially when I lost my baby, half of me wanted to follow her and comfort her, but my remorseless side couldn't forget that she'd once said to Dee-Dee that I wasn't good enough for Giles.

What is strange is that whilst I couldn't forgive her betrayal, a part of me agreed with her: yes, Giles was way out of my league, finer than me in every way.

I made a move to go and sort the children out in the garden but Dee-Dee said, "You're supposed to be on holiday Kathy, go and pour yourself a drink and I'll find out what's going on. Oh, and don't worry about that menopausal old trout; you and me were friends for years before she came along."

"Late middle-age and the menopause can be an enriching and rewarding time," said Miss Holden, belatedly joining in our conversation.

Much later that night when the children were asleep, I started clearing up the post-party mess, but Dee-Dee had a better idea. She phoned up one of the girls in the village and offered her a huge amount of money to clean up the cottage and baby-sit. We went out to the other village pub for dinner – the enlightened one that didn't allow children on the premises.

I sat at the bar, eating my prawn cocktail-flavour crisps and reflecting on the exhausting nature of a quiet day in the country with Dee-Dee, when she dropped another bombshell; it was beginning to feel like I'd landed in war-torn Lebanon.

"I got a letter last week from Jimmy Quinn," she said.

"I don't believe it. How did he find you? Did you give him your address?"

"Course not, stupid. The spa forwarded it on to me."

"Let me read it then."

"It's at home."

"What does he want?" I was dreading the answer.

"He's emigrating to Australia, which puts paid to any future plans I'd got to go there."

"And . . ."

"He wants to see Sebastian before he goes, that's all."

"That's all!" I rolled my eyes skyward. "Isn't that the one thing I've been avoiding all this time?"

She leaned into me and took hold of both my hands. "But don't you see, he's leaving for good. This is brilliant news."

"I don't want him anywhere near Sebastian." The thought of it made me shake. "He's trouble, and anyway, what would I say to Sebastian? Come with me son and meet this lowlife, oh and by the way, he's your father." I thought I'd scored the winning point, but no.

"He already knows."

"What?"

"He got it out of Clarissa this afternoon."

"What did Sebastian say to you?"

"That he wants to meet his dad."

"Bugger!"

"Trust me Kathy, I'll take him. Let me sort it all out."

"But what about Giles? Sebastian's bound to say something."

"No he won't; he'll keep quiet about it. He wants you two to get back together. Kathy, leave it to me and it'll all be okay."

GILES

This morning, Dee-Dee called me on the telephone and said she needed to speak to me on a matter of great urgency. She asked if I would I be prepared to meet her half-way between our two homes. I demurred at first because, as I told her, I'm very busy on the farm at the moment. But she used all her womanly guiles and powers of persuasion and, despite my busy schedule, I found myself agreeing to see her.

The truth is that I've never been able to resist the call of a damsel in distress, so when she said, "Come on Giles, it's important, so just chuck yer spade down and get on yer bike to Newcastle," I was putty in her hands.

We were to meet in a public house, but there was no sign of her when I got there. So I seated myself by the window and proceeded to read my newspaper. She was exactly five minutes late and, as she walked into the bar, everybody turned to look at her. This was unsurprising as she was dressed in a pair of those shiny slacks that look as if they have been sprayed on with model-soldier paint, and a cotton blouse that left little to the imagination. There was, I noticed, a frisson of interest when everyone saw that it was boring old me, in my conventional tweed jacket and corduroy trousers, who folded up my newspaper and stood up to greet her.

She flung herself into my arms and said, rather too loudly, "Gilesy baby, how are you doing? It's been too long!"

I wanted to know immediately what it was that she needed of me, but apparently she was spitting feathers and her stomach thought her throat had been cut, which I correctly deciphered to mean that she was in urgent need of some refreshment. It was clear that I was to be forced to wait a little longer for her revelation. So I placed an order at the bar and made small talk as we waited for it to be delivered to our table

I partook of a small glass of beer and a ploughman's lunch while Dee-Dee devoured a pint of lager and lime, and a beef burger. At one stage, she leaned over my plate, prodded her fork into my pickled onion and took an enormous bite leaving the remaining morsel of onion stained with her lipstick! To my horror, she waved it under my nose; presumably that was my cue to eat the rest. It was all I could do not to visibly shudder, especially when she said, "Sorry about nicking your pickle Gilesy, but I'm more than happy to divvy up mi burger."

To say I'd never get used to her mastery of the English language would be an understatement. In fact, a lesser man may tempted to rip out her tongue and fling it across the bar where no doubt the pub landlord could incorporate it into one of his ghastly burgers. I really don't know how Bertie can stand to listen to her for more than a few minutes at a time. Although the chap can be pretty hard to decode himself, especially when he gets together with his fellow countrymen for "a wee dram".

I was still wondering what on earth I doing there when Dee-Dee dipped her last French-fry into a puddle of tomato ketchup and ate it with just as much enthusiasm as she had devoured the first. However, she refused a pudding so I can only assume that her stomach was now in possession of the happy news that her throat had not, in fact, suffered any knife wounds.

"So what can I do for you Dee-Dee?" I asked, as a member of staff cleared away the remains of our luncheon.

"Truth be known Gilesy, it's more what I can do for you. Thing is I reckon that you're still in love with Kathy, and I can help you get her back.

"And what makes you think she would come back to me?"

"'Cos she's finally come to her senses and realizes she's in love with you – her words, not mine. She wants to be with you for evermore, but a few things need sorting first."

"What things?"

"Well, you see, the problem is I can't tell you that. But if you lend me fifteen hundred quid, I guarantee she'll be back home within the month."

"Fifteen hundred pounds? I'm not going to give you fifteen hundred pounds. What do you want it for? To stock up your clothing cupboards, I expect."

"Bloody'ell Giles, where do you think I shop, Paris or France or something?"

I was torn between telling her that she looked as if she shopped in one of those blacked-out, adult establishments or embarrassing her by giving her a geography lesson.

Then she said, "Joke! I do know where Paris is!" And it was I who was made to feel the fool.

"If you need money, why not ask Bertie for it?" I said.

"I have, he's bunging in two grand."

"Then he's got more money than sense."

"Listen Giles, the other thing is Kathy's doing dead well at Mr B's; she's doing mail-order hampers and everything. But she needs more room, a bigger kitchen, and one thing you have got at Havers Hall is lots of space."

"Of course she can use the kitchens. I'd do anything to get Kate and the children back. But with respect, I don't see what it has to do with either money or you."

"I've told you, I can't say. Maybe she'll tell you herself one day."

"Why can't she ask me herself?"

"She doesn't know I'm here."

"It's that scoundrel Margolis isn't it?"

"Not even warm. No, it's for something that happened way back, before she met that waste of space."

So Dee-Dee didn't like him either. I felt an unusual rush of warmth towards her. "Tell me, does Kate have any contact with Margolis these days?"

"None. She loathes him. Anyway, I told you – she wants you back. Just trust me and lend me the money."

"And how would you intend to repay me?"

"Kathy and I could go into partnership. I'm a brilliant chef and I could work from the cottage; God knows I've got plenty of time on my hands. I'd make Highland Hampers filled with whiskey-flavoured shortbread, haggis, and Scotch broth. I'd soon make enough to pay you back. Or if push came to shove, Bertie could bale me out."

"I need to be clear about this; you say the money isn't for the business, or for you?"

"It's not for either. Look, I'm not the sort of person to beg for money; I like to be independent . . ."

I was about to interrupt but she beat me to it. "And don't look at me like that – Bertie loves spending money on me. He says it's an honour for him to look after his bonnie lassie. Giles, I promise, I'm doing this for Kathy and you."

I had to admit she seemed sincere enough but I had another question for her. "I assume Bertie knows what the money's for, and he's comfortable with it?"

She nodded. "He'd give me more but Lucinda's been snooping around, looking at his bank statements. He said to tell you he'd guarantee any money you lend me."

Despite my misgivings I believed her, added to which Bertie is no fool, so I said, "You've persuaded me. I'll do it for a fifteen percent return on the loan." She threw her arms around me again and, as I untangled her limbs from mine, I added, "But I need a week or two to sort out my finances."

She looked surprised; I don't know why it is but people seem to think I'm made of money. As it was, I'd probably have to sell the chaise.

SEBASTIAN

Mum had finally allowed me to visit Gilbert-old-chap at Havers Hall for a whole weekend. At the same time, Aunty Dee-Dee booked to stay at Grimley Manor, supposedly to see her old friends. But we had a secret plan – she was taking me to meet my real father. I know his name now. It's Jimmy. Aunty Dee-Dee wouldn't say much about him, just that he was going to live abroad and he wanted to meet me before he left. I said it was a pity he was leaving the country, but it was okay because I could see him in the school holidays. She didn't say anything.

Of course we'd agreed not to tell Gilbert-old-chap what we were up to and, when she picked me up, Dee-Dee pretended that we were going to the cinema. I said afterwards that it sounded more like a lie than pretending. She said, "Oy, pint-size, I'm goin' out on a limb for you here, so less of the lip." Then she punched me, but in a friendly way and said, "Come on, Shrimp, let's get it over with."

Aunty Dee-Dee had come to Grimley by train so we had to take a bus into Sheffield, and then another one to a place called Crookes. I said to Dee-Dee that I thought that Crookes was a funny name for a place and she snorted and said, "Yet strangely apt in this case."

I said I didn't know what she meant, and she said, "Good."

When we arrived in Crookes, we went to the newsagent and asked for directions. Dee-Dee had arranged to meet my real dad at his brother's house. When we got there, it was a tiny house, even smaller than Grandma's. We rang the doorbell, and I began to feel a bit scared. After about a minute, the door was opened and I could hardly dare to look. But when I did, it wasn't my dad standing there.

It was a boy of around my age and the funny thing was that looking at him was like looking in a mirror. He said, "Who are you? Do I know you?"

As I opened my mouth to answer, a lady came to the door and said to Dee-Dee, "Hi, can I help?" And then she looked at me and said, "Crikey, who are you? You're the image of our Elvis."

"We're looking for Jimmy. Are you his wife?" asked Dee-Dee.

"Hell no! Wouldn't wish that on anyone." She wiped her hands on the back of her jeans and shook our hands. "I'm Mo, Jimmy's sister-in-law. I'm sorry; he's not here yet – always late. You must be Dee-Dee. I'm sorry; I didn't know you were bringing your son. Please come in and wait for him."

"He's not mine. Sebastian's the son of a friend of mine. Didn't Jimmy tell you anything?" asked Dee-Dee.

"Not really, only that he'd arranged to meet you here and that you owe him money. He's going away see so he needs all the cash he can get his hands on."

"Course he does," said Aunty Dee-Dee, who was beginning to look a bit cross.

After that, I wasn't really listening to Dee-Dee and Mo because I was trying to make friends with Elvis.

"Is Jimmy your dad?" I asked Elvis, but it was his mum who replied.

"Jimmy, a dad! What would he do with kids? He can't even look after himself. Anyway, who'd have him?"

"He's my uncle," added Elvis.

"That means you're my cousin," I said.

"No, I haven't got any cousins, have I, Mam?"

But I don't think she heard him. I was wondering what to say next. I felt a bit sad that Jimmy wasn't here on time to meet me. Gilbert-old-chap always says that "punctuality shows integrity". Gilbert-old-chap is never late.

Mo took us through to what she called the front room and we waited there for Jimmy to arrive. We sat down on their pretend-leather sofa and, while Mo went to get us a cup of tea, Dee-Dee read a magazine that she'd picked up from a sort of rack thing. Nobody was talking so, for something to say, I told Elvis that I like astronomy. He said he'd never heard of it. Then he showed me his set of Transformers; it was a much smaller collection than mine but I didn't say so. In fact, I was really polite about them, even GI Brawn and Huffer who happen to be my least favourite of all the Transformers.

All the time I was sitting there the backs of my legs were getting sweaty on the not-leather sofa that Mo called the settee. I was watching Elvis turning tanks into soldiers and robots into spaceships and all I could do was think, What should I say when he walks in? Should I call him Jimmy or Dad? Does he look like me? But what I wanted to know most was why he hadn't ever talked about me to Mo or Elvis.

Just when we were all getting bored of Transformers and magazines and cups of tea, we heard someone open the back door.

Mo said, "Wait here," and she left the room in a hurry. We could hear her talking to a man but I couldn't make out what they were saying.

Aunty Dee-Dee squeezed my arm and whispered, "You okay?" I nodded but I didn't look at her because I couldn't take my eyes off the door. It opened and, for a few seconds, I forgot how to breathe. There he was – my real father. I didn't run up to him and hug him, and I didn't say, "We meet at last," or "I've been looking for you," even though that's what I'd been practicing for weeks.

I just said, "Hi" and he said, "All right?" And we stood looking at each other for a bit. I remember thinking to myself, at least now I know where I got my black hair.

"Do you like horses?" he asked, which I thought was a funny way of starting a conversation, but I tried my hardest to give a good answer anyway.

"Yes I do like horses, but I prefer pigs. Gilbert-old-chap always says that you can't trust horses and that you should never turn your back on one. Gilbert says you know where you are with pigs." I knew I was babbling on, so I wasn't very surprised when he gave me a funny look, but I had sort of expected him to ask me who Gilbert was. He didn't; he just went over to switch the television on to watch racing from Doncaster.

"'Ave you brought it?" he mumbled to Dee-Dee.

"Delightful to see you too. And what do you make of your son?" Dee-Dee replied.

"Where's the dosh?"

"You're joking aren't you? You'll get it when I'm ready," she said. "Now, say hello to Sebastian."

I went over to shake his hand and say how do you do but he waved his arm around like I was an irritating insect or something and said, "Shh I've got twenty quid riding on this race." He sat down beside me, and I noticed that he smelt of beer and cigarettes. I'd got a list of questions to ask him but I thought I'd better wait till the race was over.

But Jimmy had money riding on all the races. He said it was called an accumulator or something and he wasn't really talking. I was beginning to wish I hadn't even bothered finding him. Dee-Dee must have felt the same because she marched over to the television and turned it off. Elvis left the room.

"Hey, Babe, I was watching that," Jimmy said.

"Firstly, I am not your babe and secondly, you said that you wanted to meet Sebastian and make up for lost time. So what are you waiting for? Now's your chance!"

Dee-Dee was shouting at him but what she was shouting made me happy. I didn't know that Jimmy had said that he wanted to see me!

With the television switched off, we talked for a bit and he asked the usual type of stuff that strangers ask: Where do I go to school? What football team do I support? And what do I want to be when I grow up? I hate talking about things like that so to change the subject, I took out my notebook and had a quick look at the list of questions I'd brought with me, just in case I forgot anything.

QUESTION 1: ASK ABOUT HIS FAMILY

"Have you got any other children?" I asked. Even though Mo had said he hadn't, I wanted to know for sure. I'd got my biro in my hand ready to write down his answer, which was, "None that I know of." He made a sniggering noise as he answered.

The next question I asked him was about his parents – my grandparents. And he told me his dad was dead but his mum was still alive. It felt funny to think I'd got another grandparent, one I'd never met.

"What's she like?" I was wondering if she liked knitting and had lots of funny old-fashioned sayings like my real grandma.

"She's alright. She's Italian, that's why I call her Mam – it's short for Mama, but me mates think I'm talking Sheffield." He sniggered again, and Mo rolled her eyes as if she'd heard the joke lots of times before. Then he looked at his watch.

"Do you want an ice cream or summat else from the shop?" he asked.

"Yes please," I said, so he shouted for Elvis to come down from his room.

"Take Sebastian t' corner shop," he said, then he looked at Mo. "Be a darlin' and lend us five quid will yer?" She tutted, but she gave him the money. Jimmy passed it on to Elvis saying, "Get us some fags while you're there."

So we went to the shop together, my cousin, and me. It didn't take long to get there and when we did, I was surprised when the shop assistant sold us the cigarettes. But he said, as he wrapped them up in a brown paper bag, "Tell Jimmy, in the future, he's got to fetch them himself. This is the last time I'm serving you booze or fags – you're under age!"

Then we chose our ice creams – I had a strawberry Mivvi and Elvis had a choc-ice – and we left the shop. We didn't talk very much on the way back. I don't think we're very much alike really, apart from the way we look. When we got in, Dee-Dee was waiting for me in the hall. Her neck was red and blotchy, and she looked really mad. I wondered what I'd done wrong.

"Come on Sebby; it's time we made a move." It was good that she called me Sebby; it meant she wasn't cross with me.

"But what about Jimmy?" I asked.

"He's gone, love. I'm sorry." So that was it. His horse had lost and he'd left without even saying goodbye.

I wasn't as upset as you might expect, so I said to Aunty Dee-Dee, "I never got to question two, but that's okay, it's time we went home. Dad will be wondering where I am."

She smiled at me, and we said goodbye to Mo and Elvis. Mo was really nice and said I was welcome to visit any time.

Jimmy was strange and nothing like what I'd hoped for or expected, but I was glad that I'd been there for two reasons: the first reason is that now I know that I'm not

French but that I am part Italian, and that's probably why I like pizza so much. And secondly, I'd met Jimmy at last, even though he'd made it pretty obvious that he doesn't like children very much. Maybe if I'd met him when I was bigger, he'd have liked me more.

I expected to feel different after I'd finally seen Jimmy but I didn't, not really. Only one thing changed and that was that I didn't call my proper dad, Gilbert-old-chap ever again.

Seeking Divine Retribution

I told Dee-Dee that I wouldn't believe Jimmy had actually gone to Australia unless I saw it for myself, which explains why I found myself in Manchester Airport, wearing a short, black wig and a rather fetching, orange trench-coat that was a good three sizes too big. Dee-Dee was dressed as a nun and, as we made our way through the concourse to arrivals, she paused repeatedly to bestow God's blessing on passing strangers.

We were walking past the duty-free shops when she decided it was her duty to stop and warn a cosmetics salesgirl about the perils of that little known eighth deadly sin – the wearing of too much bronzer. And that's when we spotted Jimmy standing by a bar, downing a pint of beer. I knew that in my disguise I was safe from recognition, but I was worried that with his penchant for deflowering virgins, he might see the nun's purity as a bit of a challenge. I was right.

He wandered unsteadily over to us and it was clear that he had been drinking even before he leered at Dee-Dee. "Alright darlin? Put a word in for me with your boss will you?"

"To be sure; God loves a sinner," Dee-Dee said in a fake Irish accent. "Except for fornicators and extortionists, of course. They'll burn forever in hell's fiery furnace with the devil and his dark angels."

I thought she was slightly overdoing it so I grabbed her arm. I wanted to get her away before Jimmy realized that he knew God's little messenger. But it was too late.

"Dee-Dee! What the fuck are you doin' here? Come to gi' me some more money?"

"No, just want to make sure you get on the plane."

"I'll be on it alright; can't wait to leave this fuckin' place for good."

"What do you mean more money?" I said, even though I'd already half-guessed the truth. I turned to Dee-Dee. "Did you give him money?"

"Yes. To get him out of your hair for good – yours and Sebastian's," she said.

Jimmy sneered at us nastily. "Don't worry; I signed the papers didn't I? Anyway, he seemed a right little poof to me."

I wanted to slap him, but Dee-Dee beat me to it. She grabbed his beer and poured it over his head, and then she kicked him between his legs.

"Come on ignore him, he's not worth it," she said. "Let's go."

People were gathering around us – one man used his new Polaroid camera to take a picture of Dee-Dee attacking Jimmy. The photo later appeared in the *Grimley Gazette* under the headline: *Local Man Attacked by Angry Nun*. There was quite a kerfuffle and some security men arrived. Dee-Dee blessed the crowd, issued Jimmy with fifty Hail Marys, and we fled the scene of the crime before we could get arrested.

Dee-Dee led me up to the viewing bridge where we waited for the bastard's plane to take off. In that time, she told me the whole sordid truth. In return for five thousand pounds Jimmy had signed a legal document and given up all rights to his son.

"Who knows about this?" I asked, praying that Sebastian would never find out what Jimmy had done.

"No one! Well, just Mo, and me; she witnessed his signature."

"But where did you get the money from?" I asked. "I only gave you a couple of hundred when I left home."

"I used my travel fund. Don't worry; there's no way I'm going to Oz now. I borrowed the rest."

"You are a fantastic friend; I'll never be able to thank you enough."

"Don't be daft, of course you will. You owe me big style now!"

"I'll pay you back."

"I've told you there's no rush. Anyway, with a bit of luck, Bertie'll forget his share."

I felt a bit uncomfortable about it all, but that was nothing compared to the joy I experienced at the knowledge that Jimmy had gone for good.

That's when I decided what I should do – I'd expand the catering business, maybe repay Dee-Dee by making her a partner, but when I suggested it, she was way ahead of me. She had already set up a meeting with Giles later that week to discuss a business venture and the chance of the children and me returning to Havers Hall. She had been busy.

I couldn't wait to see Giles again; I'd missed him so much and I dreamed of him most nights – erotic, tender dreams that made me want him back more and more. And with Jimmy far away on the other side of the world and Rafael nothing but an unhappy memory, I realized the life I wanted back – the life with my husband and children – was now within my grasp.

GILES

My darling Kate came to see me yesterday along with the children and Dee-Dee. And I have to say that for all her faults, Dee-Dee has been a good friend to both of us. We met for lunch at Grimley Manor, and I couldn't help but observe that my dear mother would turn in her grave to see what has become of the place.

Gone is the antique furniture and artwork in favour of teak benches and some rather bland abstract prints. In the public rooms, there is a plethora of one-armed bandits and cigarette machines, brashly inciting the clientele to gamble and smoke. Even worse, the combination of piped music and the jukebox ensures that there is a constant stream of popular music to assault the ears.

That said, we had a jolly lunch. Sebastian persuaded me to share a huge, deep-crust pizza with him. I'd never tried pizza before and it was actually rather good, especially as I washed it down with a glass or two of decidedly drinkable Barolo wine. However, the puddings were dire, inedible in fact, so Dee-Dee called over the manager to complain. She knew the chap from her days working at The Spa and I was impressed at how cleverly she charmed him, turning the situation to our advantage. She told him that we ran a catering business from Havers Hall and promised to call round with some samples of homemade bread, cakes, and puddings for him to try out, and we left having virtually bagged our first order.

We all went back home to Havers Hall in high spirits, although there was a sticky moment when Kate realized that I'd sold several family heirlooms.

"But you loved the chaise, how could you part with it?" she asked.

I bluffed and said something about wanting a more modern living space. Since this was so totally at odds with my recent rant about the changes at Grimley, she obviously didn't believe me. So I confessed that money was tight, and I'm glad that I did, because to make our marriage work, there must be no more secrets.

We talked about our plans to run a catering company with Dee-Dee working from Scotland during the week, and spending weekends at the headquarters, Havers Hall. And that's when Kathryn suggested that we turn Havers Hall into a small, country hotel. She said that we could easily accommodate up to six couples at a time and we could convert the old stable block into more bedrooms. She was convinced that it would be profitable and, as she discussed figures with me, I realized that this was a side of Kate I hadn't seen before – she was confident, enthusiastic, and quite determined that it would work. I felt very optimistic about the future.

The children were getting a little bored with all the grown-up chatter, so Dee-Dee took them into the kitchen to make a start on the baking samples for Grimley Manor. At last, I was alone with Kate. I put my hand into hers and it reminded me of the first time I held it all those years ago. She squeezed it and smiled warmly at me, and that's when I felt brave enough to say, "Please come home Kate, home to me, I mean, not just for the business, but as my wife." And it was the happiest moment of my life when she slowly nodded her head, and we embraced Then she shyly told me that she truly loved me.

There was a great deal to be done, of course, before we could put our plans into action. Quite rightly, Kate wouldn't leave Mr B's until his staff were properly trained to take over from her, and then there was the whole rigmarole of changing the children's schools. But the main thing was that I was getting my family back.

Much later in the day Dee-Dee left; she was meeting Bertie for a night out in Manchester before going back to Scotland. She said she would ask him to invest capital in our new venture. That would be such a simple solution to our cash flow problems. But if the answer was no, then I would speak to my bank manager about raising the funds.

However, I would think about that in due course. Tonight was a night for celebrations.

Making a clean start

I've never seen Giles leap into action the way he did over the next few weeks. We didn't know how much money we would be able to raise from Bertie and the bank, so we couldn't get on with major changes. But in the meantime, we were clearing out bedrooms, scrubbing them clean, and redecorating. I even turned my hand to curtain making and wished that I hadn't been so dismissive of mother's attempts to teach me the Joy of Stitch. Giles said Nanny was a wizard with the needle, so I'd hoped she would take over from me, but that wasn't to be.

It was a Monday morning when Nanny returned; she'd been away for a few weeks visiting her niece and family. Doubtless scaring them half to death with her proposed retirement plans to up sticks and go live with them. Giles had told me this sadly as if it was a bad thing and was most put out by my whoops of joy.

The family takeover bid had obviously not gone well judging by her sour expression as she bustled in and slammed her handbag on the kitchen table.

"Morning, Nanny, had a nice holiday?" I asked smiling sweetly.

"How many times do I have to tell you? It's Miss Simpson to you, young lady. I think you do it on purpose." I was about to reply that of course I did, when Giles intervened.

"Kate is only being friendly, Nanny; she would never dream of purposefully upsetting you." Evidence that, despite recent developments, he still didn't completely get me!

Giles excitedly told her of the plans to take in paying guests – a sort of upper class B & B – is how he'd taken to describing it. She nodded along showing more than a glimmer of enthusiasm as he listed the proposed activities. "I will hold watercolour classes, Nanny. I'm quite good with a paintbrush, and we can arrange creative writing weekends. And Kate is keen to organize gourmet food and wine-tasting events. . . ."

"Kate?" echoed Nanny in that thunderous voice that Giles mistakes for kindliness.

"Yes, Kate. My darling wife and I are back together, isn't it wonderful?"

She didn't answer, so Giles blundered on. "And Dee-Dee, whom I fear I have judged harshly in the past, will join us when she can. She's promised to help out with the catering at the weekend and to give the guests an option of in-room massage and so forth."

That did it. Miss Nancy Simpson snatched up her handbag and, with a chin quivering with rage, she said, "I refuse to have anything to do with your plans to turn this beautiful home into a house of ill-repute. Your dear mother must be turning in her grave."

"She was cremated," I said helpfully.

"Yes, and I rue the day. If Madam was still alive, you would never have got your claws into Master Giles."

"Nanny please, let's talk about this over a nice cup of tea," wheedled Giles, but she was having none of it and, as she stormed out of Havers Hall, I could practically hear the hairs on her chin bristling with indignation.

Over the next few weeks, the bloody mad woman did everything in her power to sabotage our project and turn the people of Grimley against us. She even set up a picket line with her sidekick and new landlady, Mrs Newsome. The two old biddies stood for hours on end at the gates of Havers Hall trying to stop trades people from entering the premises and waving anti-everything to do with the Havers' banners. We tried to reason with them, but even Giles's charm offensive did nothing to curb their antics.

Dee-Dee thought the whole thing was so hilarious that one morning she got up early – before the gruesome twosome arrived – and at the bottom of the drive she erected a banner proclaiming 'SOUP KITCHEN' and beside it she set up a trestle table laden with cans of Scotch broth, Oxtail and Mulligatawny, with a tin opener and a little primus stove.

I feared for her life!

Finding true love where you least expect it

"If I've got to make just one more vol-au-vent, I swear I'll kill myself," said Dee-Dee.

We were making yet another batch of puff pastry for the million canapés we would be serving at the opening party, which despite Nanny's best endeavours, was on schedule for the next weekend.

"That's okay; we're moving on to mini-kebabs next assuming, that is, that the chickens ever arrive!"

"Don't know why we can't just go and get 'em from Macro."

"Good idea, I'll leave it to you suggest it to Giles, shall I?"

Giles was insistent that we should always use local produce, which was fine in theory, but Nanny, who was still up to her tricks, regularly sabotaged our plans by phoning suppliers to change our orders or cancel them. Giles was very patient about it all and managed to convince himself that you really couldn't have too many tins of corned beef in the store cupboard.

"No, you tell him. He'll do owt for you. You tell him to jump and he says, 'how high?' "

"I know, that's the trouble; he's suffocating me. Always following me around, asking me if I love him. Yesterday he even missed a fishing trip. He said it was to work on the crèche but I'm sure it was really to be with me."

"Well, you know why, don't you?"

I didn't, but I was sure I was about to find out. "He's insecure – scared of losing you again."

"But he won't. I keep telling him, this time it's for keeps."

"I've got it," she interrupted, her eyes shining brightly and her legs were doing an excited little kick dance. I recognized the body language: she had a plan.

"Marry him again," she said.

"We never got divorced."

"Well, do it again anyway, now that you're back together. Oh, go on, it'd be so romantic. I'll be a bridesmaid like last time and so will Clarissa, and little Jessica can be the flower girl."

To be honest, I was warming to the idea; if we held it the day before the grand opening, everyone would be around anyway, and we'd have balloons and flowers decorating the hall and it would get Giles off my back – only metaphorically, of course.

"Okay, let's do it," I said. "As long as Giles likes the idea, I'll take him out for a romantic meal tonight and put it to him."

Which is why I found myself later that day, down on one knee, proposing to my rather baffled husband.

"But Pumpkin, we are married," he said, peering down at me.

"Yes, but I want to do it again."

"I don't see the point, not really."

"This time, I'll get you a wedding ring."

"I've got my father's ring," he said.

To be honest, I was beginning to feel a bit cross and rather stupid, added to which my knees were starting to ache. I shuffled round a bit and that's when I realized that being so close to the orange and blue swirls on the carpet was making me feel a bit queasy. But I wasn't about to give up, not without a struggle. Dee-Dee had set her mind on a party, and I didn't want to let her down.

"But this would be a ring chosen for you, by me, as a sign of my devotion and our rekindled love." I know, hardly in line with the doctrine of Germaine Greer – and I hang my head in shame at the memory of it – but I was desperate to put a few feet between me and the shag pile. Thankfully, it did the trick.

"I expect there's nothing to stop us renewing our vows," he said and I could see he was slowly coming round to it. Then, mainly I suspect because we were beginning to cause a bit of a stir in the restaurant, he said, "Yes, Pumpkin, I would be delighted to marry you again."

I got up off my knees and hugged him as everyone in the restaurant applauded us. Poor Giles went pink with embarrassment. Then, maybe a tad flamboyantly, I ordered champagne all round. Well, it's not every day that a girl proposes to the husband of her dreams.

We had plenty to do over the next few days so I concentrated on the grand opening of Havers Hall, while Dee-Dee, aided and abetted by Jessica, took on the role of wedding planner. I knew from the last time there was no point in asking my friend to keep it low key so I left her to it. I kept on telling myself it would all be okay. Surely, even Dee-Dee couldn't cause too much damage with less than a week to go.

Giles was busy on a project of his own, making the old library into a sort of crèche-cum-playroom for our younger guests. It was all very top secret and every time he left the room, he carefully locked the door behind him.

Dee-Dee was desperate to know what he was up to. "What you got in there, Gilesy – a couple of dead bodies?"

But he wouldn't tell her; he just tapped the side of his nose and said, "You'll just have to wait and see."

Sebastian was in on the secret, in the capacity of advisor-in-chief to Giles. I often heard them muttering about finger paints, play dough, and sand pits – all of which struck me as messy rather than mysterious. But despite Dee-Dee's subtle cross-examination (I'll give you a fiver for all you know) my son couldn't be persuaded to tell us what it was about. So we didn't find out until the night before the big day.

Giles and I were going to Grimley Manor for dinner, where I was being forced to spend the night, all because Dee-Dee insisted that Giles couldn't set eyes on me until the moment I walked into the chapel the next day. But I was so relieved that she hadn't planned a hen night that I happily agreed to spend the night alone. I was all packed and ready to go when I saw Dee-Dee emerging from Giles's study. She looked a bit frazzled so I asked her to join us for dinner but she said she was too busy, which I translated into, she'd got a hot date. I was going to quiz her about it when I realized I'd forgotten something.

"Oh no," I said, clamping my hand to my forehead. "I need a poem or something to read out tomorrow. I've been so busy. . . "

"Don't worry, I'll find something – now come with me, we've been summoned by Giles!"

Apparently, Giles was finally allowing us to see the new playroom and, as we made our way there with Jessica excitedly tugging at our hands, I couldn't help but worry that it was going to be something of an anti-climax.

Giles and Sebastian were waiting for us outside the room; everywhere looked clean and shiny and smelt of paint and new carpets. On the upper section of the playroom door there was a blue velvet curtain hanging from a brass pole. Giles handed out glasses of champagne and, pointing towards the door, he said, "Do the honours, Pumpkin, open the curtain."

I took a sip of champagne then pulled back the curtain to reveal an engraved metal plate with *Darren's Den* written on it. Underneath in smaller letters, it said: *In loving memory of Darren Dibbs, 1968–1985.*

Sebastian opened the door with a little flourish and gave us a tour of the room. Gone were the piles of books and the fusty old paintings. Some had been donated to the village library, and others sold to pay for the changes. The room was huge and bright with high ceilings and a massive floor space now that the bookshelves had gone. It had been cleverly sectioned off using different coloured carpet tiles. In the pink area were the girl's toys, dolls in prams, nurse's outfits, cuddly toys, and tea sets; whilst the blue carpet was home to boxing gloves, Meccano, and a miniature railway. Jessica put on the gloves and set about pummelling Sebastian.

"It's incredible, there's no trace of the musty old library," I said as we wandered into the orange section; the one with non-gender-specific toys such as Playdoh, jigsaws, and Lego. I picked up a pile of books and started looking through them, but my family seemed anxious to move me on. Jessica was pulling at my leg, Sebastian was jigging up and down, and even Giles appeared restless. I soon found out why. They'd saved the best to the last, for behind a bright purple lacquered screen was the art section with its easels, oil paints, charcoal, and crayons. There was so much to see I couldn't take it all in at first.

"We've done this bit in purple 'cos it was Darren's favourite colour," explained Sebastian. "And we've put his pictures on the wall."

For the first time ever I had a chance to see the works of art that Darren had done with Giles. There were six framed pictures grouped together: a bowl of fruit, apples, lemons, and purple oranges, all with smiley happy faces, a dog carrying a duck on his back, and a sheep – or was it a cloud – smoking a pipe. There were a few self-portraits entitled 'Me' where he'd depicted himself as much taller and slimmer than he was in real life. But the one that brought tears to my eyes was the likeness – and I use the term loosely – of me being hugged by a large, multi-coloured figure. I only recognized myself because scrawled across the top in Darren's childish, hesitant hand was *Me and Kay-Kay Dibbs – my big sister.*

Unable to speak, I reached out for Giles's hand and clung onto him tightly, finally realizing he was my lifeline.

Avoiding a Shotgun Wedding

When I woke up, it was to the sound of knocking on my hotel room door. Rubbing the sleep from my eyes, I padded across the room to see what possible disaster could have occurred that entitled someone to wake me up so early on my big day. It was the housekeeper; she carried a garment bag and a couple of small boxes.

"Sorry to disturb you, Madame, but your friend said I had to give you these first thing in case they need altering for the wedding."

I thanked her, feeling slightly bewildered as I already had my outfit – a nice little cream two-piece. But when I opened the bag, I found my old wedding dress inside. It had been seriously modified. The skirt was now short at the front but still long at the back and the scallops of lace had been replaced by hundreds of tiny pearls. To finish it off, the exquisitely made outfit had a silk suspender belt with seamed stockings and a pair of those old fashioned shoes with pointed toes and button fastenings. It goes without saying that I ditched my carefully chosen understated little number in favour of this flamboyant offering; I knew this was mother and Dee-Dee's work and knew better than to flout their combined force.

I'd arranged to meet Mr Purvis in the hotel lobby so he could escort me to the ceremony and I hardly recognized him when he walked over and said, "May I say how delightful you look today, Madame."

I knew he wouldn't be wearing the despised bellboy outfit and, if I'd thought about it, I would have imagined him wearing his shiny Sunday best suit for the occasion. But no, to my astonishment, he was dressed in a navy pinstripe suit with a pale blue silk shirt and matching tie and handkerchief set. And, as a finishing touch, tipped jauntily over one eye, was a fedora hat. Maybe he was going through some sort of late mid-life crisis, but it was all so out of character that I couldn't have been more stunned if he'd appeared naked.

I allowed myself to be led out the main door of the hotel and into the sunny car park, where a chauffeur-driven vintage Rolls Royce was waiting for us. As courteous as ever, Mr Purvis helped me in.

"Nice outfit," I lied.

"I wasn't sure you would think it was really me." There was a ghost of a smile on his face, almost as if he was laughing at me.

It didn't take long to drive the few miles to Havers Hall but, when we got there, instead of stopping at the chapel as I'd expected, the driver dropped us off around the back of the house where Clarissa, Dee-Dee, Jessica, and Sebastian were waiting to greet me. Sebastian wore a miniature version of Mr Purvis's suit, and the two girls had on dresses identical in style to mine. Dee-Dee, in her bright scarlet lipstick and little black dress, looked exactly like the old photos of Coco Chanel – she'd even had her hair cut in a chic little bob – and that's when I realized that a theme was emerging.

"We're flippers," said Jessica. "And Sebastian's a gangster, and Aunty Dee-Dee is Coco the clown."

"Flappers, silly," corrected Sebastian.

Jessica gave him a withering look and said, "And Daddy is Clyde."

I turned to Dee-Dee. "And I assume I'm Bonnie?"

"In one!"

They escorted me to the lawn where a marquee had been erected overnight. The guests were dressed as gangsters and molls. In fancy dress, the class differences that were so apparent at our real wedding seemed almost non-existent. My granddad, resplendent as Don Corleone, was entertaining Lady Bosworth and her chums by calling them "dirty rats" – he wouldn't have got away with that in his civvies.

Mother wore a layered, fringed, black, flapper dress, a red feather boa, and fishnet stockings (had she never heard of the mutton and lamb scenario?) and she smoked through a cigarette holder, blowing at Mr B in a most provocative manner. She had run up his Bugsy Malone outfit herself, a striped double-breasted suit over a red shirt and black tie; they looked worryingly together in their matching outfits and seemed as thick as the thieves they were impersonating.

Bertie came rushing over in blue suit, grey spats, and diamond-studded watch chain. He'd written *Al Capone* on his hat in case we'd missed the point.

"Are you going to accompany me to the Speakeasy?" he asked in his usual Scottish burr.

"I was wondering where Giles was?" I said.

"Come with me."

We all made our way to the entrance of the marquee where Giles was waiting, smoking a big, black cigar. I felt a shiver of excitement. He looked so handsome with his slicked hair, wing-tipped shoes and zoot suit, that I decided it was time I overhauled his country-gent-meets-local-tramp wardrobe. He caught my eye and gave me an appraising look and a lazy smile. Gosh, he was really getting into this role-play; it was going to be one hell of a second honeymoon.

"Did you bring the poem?" I whispered to Dee-Dee.

"No, I've written out something else – a passage from *I have a dream*."

I was impressed. "Are you sure Martin Luther King's words are suitable for. . ."

"Martin who? No I mean the Abba version." And she burst into song.

"I have a dream, a song to sing. . . "

I joined in, and we did a little jump dance. For a few seconds, we were teenagers again, getting ready for a big Saturday night out.

Sebastian and Jessica were calling us and, when we looked round, we saw them carrying a huge white cage covered with ribbons and flowers. As we went over, they took the lid off and two white doves flew out and circled around.

"It's you and Daddy!" yelled Jessica, jumping up and down. "Look, the birds are married like you and Daddy."

"All this must have cost a fortune," I muttered to Giles.

"Don't worry; the whole event is sponsored by Baron Bertie of Branrae. He insisted on paying for everything. He says it's his thank you for introducing him to Dee-Dee."

We were interrupted by the sound of Bertie banging his plastic machine gun on a table.

"Gangsters and Molls, please make your way into the Speakeasy to witness our very own Bonnie and Clyde retaking their vows. We will celebrate their union by partaking of hooch, moonshine, and gin. Before you are permitted entry, you must give your secret password to Sebby, the kid."

The guests filed into the marquee, pausing to whisper their passwords into Sebastian's ear. I stayed back with Mr Purvis and my bridesmaids, waiting for a sign from Bertie that we should follow. As I fiddled with my hair and straightened Sebastian's tie, I couldn't help but wonder what else today held in store.

We got the nod from Bertie and, as we made our way down, Jessica scattered flowers fashioned out of fake bank notes while a Frank Sinatra impersonator sang, *Love and Marriage*. Dee-Dee had not held back. There were big round tables decorated with feathers and orchids and given names such as Elliot Ness, Bugsy Malone, Lucky Luciano, and Pretty Boy Floyd. The top table was named Bonnie and Clyde, of course. It held a big, black cake in the shape of a machine gun. I wasn't close enough to read the icing inscription so I could only guess that it said: *Till Death Do Us Part.*

A casino lay ready for poker and blackjack on my left and a jazz band were setting up on the right. I turned round and whispered, "This has got to be the best party ever."

When I reached Giles, Sebastian handed him an eternity ring and took his sister's hand as they both sat down on cushions at our feet. Clarissa and Dee-Dee joined Bertie at Ma Baker's table. Giles slipped the ring on my finger and the band struck up *I've Got You Under My Skin.*

Giles began his prepared speech.

"My dearest Kate, I have loved you for . . ."

Behind us, noise rose up. I turned to see a strange woman wearing a nightdress and carrying a suitcase. Like everyone else, I assumed she was part of the entertainment; until she got closer and then, despite her deranged appearance and hacked off hair, I realized it was Lucinda!

As she let out a scream, the band effortlessly changed their song to *There May Be Trouble Ahead.* Of course, they didn't realize they were dealing with a mad woman.

Lucinda stalked unsteadily toward Bertie and emptied the suitcase over the table. Out poured Bertie's shirts, suits, and ties – all shredded to pieces – and mingling sadly amongst his ruined clothes were Lucinda's chopped ginger tresses and their torn-up wedding photos.

"I told you never to let that whore near my daughter. You promised!" She yelled.

"Hang on, old thing . . ."

"I've seen your bank statements. You've spent thousands on her."

The band stopped playing, and I felt cold and shivery despite the warm day. Clarissa whimpered into her feather boa, and Bertie did his best to calm things down.

But Dee-Dee had heard enough. "How dare you come here spoiling my friend's day you shrivelled-up old lush?"

Lucinda lunged at Dee-Dee, but Bertie caught hold of her arms and held her back; it didn't shut her up though.

"Spoil your friend's day? I'll do that all right. She's as common as you are." She turned to Giles. "I've always liked you, Giles, and I feel sorry for you. But it's time you knew the truth; your wife's a tart. Sebastian isn't even your real son, she told me so herself."

A loud gasp filled the marquee. My husband looked at me for a reaction. I gave a tiny, virtually imperceptible, nod.

Giles's shoulders sagged and he seemed to crumple into his suit. For a moment, I thought he was going to collapse, but then the old stiff-upper lip kicked in and he turned to Lucinda. "How dare you come uninvited into my home and insult my wife. Of course, he's my real son, you stupid woman."

But Lucinda hadn't finished. "You should have married Felicity, someone with class. She wouldn't have cheated on you."

Giles shouted. "The fact that he was spawned by another man is irrelevant. I brought him up; he's mine and I love him. Kate told me everything before we got married. Do you really think that my wife would keep such a massive secret from me?"

My God, he was splendid, but I was dreading the inevitable showdown. It looked like I'd reached the end of my marriage, and there was no one to blame but myself.

Lucinda, though, turned her attention back to Dee-Dee. "You're a slut, Dee-Dee. You have sex with my husband to get what you want."

"But sex with your husband is what I want," said Dee-Dee, smiling sweetly.

At that, Lucinda stormed out leaving her trail of debris behind. I felt stunned and wondered how we should carry on.

Giles didn't speak; he looked lost and lonely and seemed to have visibly aged.

Dee-Dee hugged me and apologized.

But then Lucinda reappeared toting Bertie's shotgun.

Giles leaned over and whispered to Sebastian. "Son, take your sister and hide under Grandma's table. Don't worry; I'll look after Mummy."

Lucinda's ranting started again. "You've ruined my life, and now I'm going to finish yours, you bitch!"

As she waved the gun in Dee-Dee's face, Clarissa ran over shouting, "Mummy please, no!" She flung herself at Lucinda, the gun went off, and the bullet hit, not Dee-Dee, but Clarissa who fell to the floor.

Lucinda dropped to her knees and held the unconscious Clarissa in her arms. Blood seeped into Lucinda's nightdress, turning it crimson. Nobody moved, until Mr B broke ranks. He sat down beside Lucinda, "Na then lass, there's been enough of a carry on for one day, give the gun to me."

She wavered for a moment then, to my horror, she turned the gun on herself and pulled the trigger.

EPILOGUE

LORD AND LADY HAVERS,
ARE INVITED TO JOIN BERTIE AND DEE-DEE AT
BRANRAE CASTLE
TO CELEBRATE THE LAST HOGMANY OF THE
MILLENIUM

I've never been a massive fan of New Year's Eve with all that forced *bon homie*, not to mention those 'auld' acquaintances I'd be more than happy to forget. But when I declined the invitation on the grounds that we'd be too busy working to attend, Bertie arranged for a helicopter to pick us up so we could join them for midnight. Which is how we found ourselves being piped into the grand banqueting hall at five minutes to twelve. The castle looked like something out of a fairy story. With the draughty old corridors and faded grandeur nothing but a distant memory, Dee-Dee had certainly made it her own after the shootout at Havers Hall.

Despite the rumours, nobody died that night, although Clarissa had to spend a few nights in hospital. Her mother, however, lost much more: her castle, her husband, and her mind. To this day, she languishes in a private clinic for the bewildered, visited only by Clarissa and her husband, Sebastian. Clarissa says that if they discover a stronger sedative, they'll take their baby, Darren junior, to meet his grandmother.

Bertie refuses to get divorced, but he won't go anywhere near his "bloody crazy wife" even though we've assured him that she won't try to strangle him again – not with her paralyzed left arm. So Dee-Dee carries on much as before despite having two clones of her own (twelve-year-old twins Coco and Chanel). As she points out, it's not as if she's married. Her new thing is toy-boys, of which there's a constant supply at the local spa.

The clock strikes midnight and we form a circle ready for the countdown. Rees joins us as Giles takes my hand in his, just as he did on that distant Valentine's night. His skin is much rougher now, and drier – the hands of my commis chef.

Only Jessica is missing from the crowd – out partying with her barrister friends. Rafael was right when he said she was suited to a life of crime!

As for Jimmy, he's never bothered us again. Mo told Dee-Dee that he owns a gay bar on Bondi Beach. It's called *Mama Mia*, and he runs it with his partner, Jason. Dee-Dee says she's seen a photo and swears it's the same Jason we met in the bar the day I found out I was pregnant. I don't know whether to believe her.

It's midnight – *HAPPY NEW YEAR!*

We exchange kisses and sing *Auld Lang Syne*.

As we sashay into the centre, I smile, as mother's voice rises above the crowd. "Watch out, our Kathryn, you'll break your neck in those heels."

THE END

ACKNOWLEDGEMENTS

Thank you to Yvonne Barlow for giving me this amazing opportunity - I still wake up in the middle of the night and pinch myself in disbelief.
Thanks also to all the book groups who participated in the competition for their invaluable feedback.
Thanks to Sheffield University Adult Learning, especially to Alison Ross for her help and encouragement in the early days.
To Sheffield Hallam University for the fantastic M.A Writing course and to J.F.N.G - now lifelong friends
To my son Oliver Shepherd, for believing in me and laughing at my writing only when he was supposed to.
To my daughter Francesca Shepherd, for all the giggles and for being a constant source of love and inspiration.
This novel is in loving memory of Sylvia Wosskow who, as she so accurately predicted, never did get to read it.

A Young Woman's Guide to Carrying On
By
Jilly Wosskow

Winner of the Hookline Novel Competition 2009

The Hookline Novel Competition is open only to students and graduates of MA writing courses.
It is judged by book groups from around the UK.

As a result, Hookline Books are truly reader endorsed fiction.

Lightning Source UK Ltd.
Milton Keynes UK
14 April 2010

152747UK00001B/2/P